DUKE OF ARROGANCE

Dukes of Distinction
Book 4

Alexa Aston

Dearest Reader;

Thank you for your support of a small press. At Dragonblade Publishing, we strive to bring you the highest quality Historical Romance from the some of the best authors in the business. Without your support, there is no 'us', so we sincerely hope you adore these stories and find some new favorite authors along the way.

Happy Reading!

CEO, Dragonblade Publishing

Additional Dragonblade books by Author Alexa Aston

Dukes of Distinction Series
Duke of Renown
Duke of Charm
Duke of Disrepute
Duke of Arrogance
Duke of Honor

The St. Clairs Series
Devoted to the Duke
Midnight with the Marquess
Embracing the Earl
Defending the Duke
Suddenly a St. Clair
Starlight Night

Soldiers & Soulmates Series
To Heal an Earl
To Tame a Rogue
To Trust a Duke
To Save a Love
To Win a Widow

The Lyon's Den Connected World
The Lyon's Lady Love

King's Cousins Series
The Pawn
The Heir
The Bastard

Medieval Runaway Wives
Song of the Heart
A Promise of Tomorrow
Destined for Love

Knights of Honor Series
Word of Honor
Marked by Honor
Code of Honor
Journey to Honor
Heart of Honor
Bold in Honor
Love and Honor
Gift of Honor
Path to Honor
Return to Honor

CHAPTER ONE

Blackstone Manor, Dorset—July 1802

JONATHAN SUTTON GAZED out the window as the carriage rolled through Dorchester. Once they traveled the length of the city, it would be another few miles until he would finally be home after his last miserable term at school. He shifted uncomfortably on the seat, his buttocks still aching from the caning delivered by Mr. Rochester, though it had been over a week since the incident occurred. The headmaster packed quite a wallop for a man in his sixties. He'd certainly had enough practice, especially when it came to Jon. He'd earned his fair share of punishments and then taken on more in place of Arch. Since they were identical twins, it had been easy for Jon to step in and accept the disciplinary penalty meant for his brother.

He often took the blame for Arch's actions.

Because he loved him. Everyone seemed to love Archibald Sutton, Marquess of Grafton and future Duke of Blackmore. Arch had a sunny nature and always aimed to please everyone he came in contact with, from the lowest servant to the highest peer. He also had a mischievous side to him, one which got him into frequent trouble. Most people didn't know that—because Jon always stepped up and claimed responsibility for whatever scheme Arch had gotten caught up in.

Most people didn't like Jon. They might have if they hadn't had his brother to compare him against. On his own, Jon was an accomplished rider and boxer and one of the smartest boys in his class. Next to Arch, though, he seemed sullen and moody. In truth, he was quite shy and covered it by acting as if he didn't care for the opinion of others. He actually liked following the rules which Arch broke all the time. Because Jon took the blame for his twin and suffered the consequences for his twin's actions, everyone expected the worst from him.

This last term of public school before he left for university had been the worst. While he had excelled in his classes with very little need to study, he'd gotten into constant trouble, this time of his own making since Arch wasn't around. His twin had been sent home early in the term with some mysterious illness. A rash had broken out across the palms of Arch's hands and the soles of his feet. It had spread to his trunk and down to his groin. He had run a slight fever, as well. The headmaster had declared for the other boys' safety that Arch should return home. Some coursework was sent with him but Jon didn't know if his brother would bother completing it. Arch only finished his assignments because he liked the competition between the two of them. Without Jon to spur him on, he was certain Arch had ignored the work. If he had, he might have to return to Harrow for another term to finish up.

It had been hard enough to be separated from Arch these last two months. They had never been parted, always sharing a room both at home and sleeping next to each other at school. Jon couldn't imagine himself at university and Arch still back at Harrow. The place was a hellhole. Despite the exorbitant fees, the accommodations had been atrocious, with the sleeping quarters cold and damp. Meals had been tasteless and meager, causing his belly to cramp more often than not. It was commonly thought if schoolboys could survive such abysmal conditions and adhere to the strict obedience imposed by those in authority, they would become the leaders society looked for them to be.

Jon only knew he was excited to reach Blackstone Manor and be reunited with his twin. Surely, by now, the village doctor would have seen to Arch and he'd be fit as a fiddle. Hopefully, they could go riding. Being confined in this coach had worn on Jon's nerves. Even though his rump was still raw, he'd rather be in the saddle and outdoors than cooped up inside. Especially if Mr. Rochester had written Father regarding Jon's latest brawl with the pretentious little sod who would be a viscount one day. The boy had said awful things about Arch, which had led to Jon thrashing him soundly. In turn, Mr. Rochester had caned Jon's buttocks so hard, it had caused them to bleed. The headmaster had told him he couldn't wait for the Sutton twins to leave Harrow. Since it was the end of term, he'd had to stand at the back of the room and lean over to write upon a desk since he wasn't able to sit. Both his history and Latin tutors had taken pity on him and allowed him to take his exams orally once the other students left.

If his father knew about this latest incident, though, it would be worse than a caning. The duke had little regard for his second son, who had missed being the heir apparent by seven minutes. All his life, his father had lavished praise upon Arch and condemned every action Jon took. His overt favor should have turned Jon against his brother. Instead, he loved Arch all the more for having to spend time with such a reprehensible man. All the Blackmore wealth, lands, and title would fall to Arch one day but Jon knew his brother would take care of him. That's what they did. Take care of one another.

The carriage turned and journeyed up the lane to Blackstone Manor, taking another fifteen minutes before arriving at the main house. It pulled up and the door opened. Standing in the doorway was Elizabeth, his little sister. Her face lit with a smile as she saw him and she began bouncing up and down in excitement.

"Jon! Jon! You're home!" She ran toward him, laughing.

He climbed from the carriage and swept her up in his arms, soundly smacking her cheek.

"I've missed you, Brat," he declared.

"I am not a brat," she retorted. "I am Lady Elizabeth Sutton."

"Well, I am glad Lady Elizabeth missed me for I certainly missed her."

"Will you take me riding?" she begged as he strode toward the house. "I'm just learning how but I know you would be a good person to teach me. Will you?"

"I will. If not today, then tomorrow. For now, I want to go see Arch."

The door opened and he greeted Roy, the footman who had been promoted to butler two years earlier.

"It is good to have you back, Lord Jonathan," the servant said.

"I can't tell you how good it is to be back, Roy. Tell Cook that I am starving. Have her send something up to our room." He kissed Elizabeth again and set her on the ground. "I'm anxious to see Arch, Sprite."

A shadow crossed the butler's face. Immediately, Jon asked, "What is it, Roy?"

"Lord Grafton is no longer in your shared chambers," Roy informed him. "He has been moved."

Puzzled, he asked, "Where is he?"

When the butler hesitated, Jon knelt and looked his little sister in the eye. "Elizabeth? Where is Arch?"

"The dower house," she said, her bottom lip trembling. "I can't see him. They won't let me." Tears welled in her eyes. "The doctor comes all the time. Father says Arch is very sick."

Jon stood. "I will go see him at once."

"Lord Jonathan, His Grace wishes you to—"

"His Grace can wait," he spat out. "I want to see my brother."

Hurrying from the main house, he set off at a quick pace and reached the dower house ten minutes later. A cart hitched to a horse stood outside it. As he approached the door, Dr. Broll ventured outside, his physician's satchel in hand.

"Lord Jonathan. You've come home from Harrow, I see."

"What is wrong with my brother?" he demanded. "When they sent him home from Harrow, he had a rash. Copper in color. It had spread. Has he gotten worse? Why would he be here, living in isolation?"

"Walk with me," Dr. Broll suggested, setting his case in the cart and then stepping away.

Jon fell into step with the man, apprehension filling him. His twin must have been much sicker than was first thought. The rash might be contagious, which is why he had been taken from the house. But it didn't make any sense. Father adored Arch. He doted upon him. If Arch were truly ill, his father never would have isolated him at the dower house. It didn't make any sense.

"What's wrong with my brother?" he asked quietly, apprehension filling him.

"Lord Grafton has contracted a disease," the physician began. "A very serious one. I should like to check you for it, as well, Lord Jonathan."

"I don't have a rash like the one Arch got on his hands and feet," he quickly said.

"What about ulcers?" Dr. Broll asked.

"I remember several months ago that Arch complained about ulcers inside his mouth. He also had one in the corner of his mouth which he said was quite painful. They healed, though. Have they returned? Is that what is making him so ill? I don't have any."

"They wouldn't necessarily be in your mouth. They could be on your genitals. Or your anus."

"No," he said quickly, covering his embarrassment. "I've experienced nothing like that. Has . . . Arch?"

Dr. Broll nodded. "His rash—the one he experienced at school—has spread rapidly. White patches cover the inside of his mouth. He's also suffering from other symptoms."

"What is wrong with him, Doctor? Surely, you can cure him."

The older man shook his head sadly. "Believe me when I say that I have tried to, my lord. I've even used mercury, as dangerous as it is."

"Why?" he demanded. "Tell me the truth and quit avoiding my questions."

The doctor placed a hand on Jon's shoulder. "Your brother has syphilis, Lord Jonathan. It is incurable. It will lead to severe problems as it spreads throughout his body, stage by stage. It can lead to problems with his heart. His brain. His nerves. It might paralyze him. Lead him to becoming blind or deaf. It will render him impotent. He may even go mad."

Disbelief flooded him. "No!" he shouted. "I don't believe you. Arch is only sixteen." He shucked off Broll's hand. "You're lying."

The doctor sighed. "I wish I were, Lord Jonathan. The syphilis will render your brother useless. He's already in a great deal of pain."

Anger now filled him. "Then why has Father sent him away? He needs to be with his loved ones, not stuck alone in the dower house."

Broll's expression grew pained. "His Grace is very unhappy. He blames himself for the circumstances Lord Grafton finds himself in."

"How? What did Father do to make Arch sick?"

Dr. Broll looked away. "I am not at liberty to discuss this with you, my lord."

His eyes narrowed. He glared at the physician. "How did my brother contract . . . what did you call it?"

"Syphilis."

"Syphilis. Where does it come from? Tell me," he urged. "Please."

Sadness filled Dr. Broll's eyes. "It is from sexual congress with an unclean woman who carries the disease."

Jon staggered back. Immediately, he thought of the visit Arch had made to a brothel, courtesy of their father. Jon hadn't been invited. It often was that way, with the duke taking his heir on various excursions, preparing him for his future role. Arch had allowed their father to believe it was his first time with a woman, despite the fact the twins had been sexually active since they were fourteen.

But to contract some horrid disease from a woman simply because you had sex with her? It was unthinkable. And now this man was telling him that Arch would slowly fall to pieces before their eyes.

"I want to see him," he said firmly. "Now."

"Your twin is in a great deal of pain. He might not want a visit from you."

He stared at the doctor. "Arch will want to see me."

Turning, he strode toward the dower house. Inside, he passed a maid, who looked startled to see anyone there.

"Where is he?" he barked.

"Upstairs. Third door on the left," she squeaked and hurried away.

Jon took the stairs two at a time and hurried down the hall, only to pause in front of the door. It was as if his feet wouldn't let him continue.

"This is Arch," he said under his breath. "He needs you. Go."

Steeling himself, he rapped lightly on the door. When Arch didn't call out, Jon let himself in and went toward the bed.

His twin was propped up with pillows behind him, a shadow of his former self. Jon forced his face to remain a mask, burying the shock of Arch's appearance deep within him. His brother had lost a good deal of weight and looked painfully thin. His face was flushed with fever. Much of his hair had fallen out.

"Jon," Arch rasped. "You're here."

"Of course, I am here," he said, lifting a chair and bringing it to the bed. "Do you think I would hang about school when I could be home with you?"

He sat and reached for his brother's hand. Arch pulled away.

"Don't touch me," he said, revealing a glimpse of white patches inside his mouth. He winced.

"Are you in much pain?"

"Every minute of every hour of every day," Arch said jokingly before he sobered. "Repulsive sores covering my genitals. Abscesses and ulcers decorate my body, a foul smell rising from them. My eyesight is fading fast. Though I haven't told Dr. Broll, I think he's guessed that's the case."

"You should tell him," Jon urged. "See if he can do anything for you."

"Oh, he tried, Brother. But this disease holds you hostage. It squeezes the very life out of you." He licked his dry, cracked lips. "Broll has been honest with me when no one else has been. I know I could be paralyzed. That my heart will weaken. The headaches are already blinding. He said it's a matter of time before I begin to lose control over what little muscles I have left." He closed his eyes.

"I am so sorry, Arch."

Jon sat in the chair, mute for minutes, watching his twin, each breath looking like a struggle.

"I should have worn a French letter," Arch muttered and opened his eyes again. "You always do. And I've made fun of you for it. Called you a coward. You were always the smarter of us, Jon. Now, you will be the duke one day."

Shock reverberated through him. "No!" he hissed. "You are meant to be Blackmore. Not me. Never me."

Arch managed a dry chuckle. "What beautiful revenge on Father, me dying and you becoming his heir apparent. He hasn't had a decent word to say to you in a good decade or more. Now, he will have to grovel while you'll have to learn to be someone you never wanted to be."

He leaned forward and placed his hand on his brother's. Arch gasped in pain and Jon withdrew it.

"Sorry," Arch apologized. "It hurts to be touched."

"Elizabeth said she's not allowed to come see you."

"No. I don't want her to think of me like this, Jon. She's only six. The memory would stay with her forever. Take care of her. You always have. I know she favors you."

He chuckled. "She's the only one who does."

Arch looked at him with tired eyes. "I know you have taken the brunt of my punishments. Gotten me out of many a scrape. Covered my tracks and made it look as if you were the guilty one too many times to count. At least your reward will be that you will be Blackmore. You'll be better at it than I ever could."

"Don't say that, Arch," he pleaded.

"It's true. Just don't be an ass to your second son like Father was to you. Love all your children. Not just your heir."

"I don't know if I want children."

"You'll have to provide an heir for the dukedom," Arch pointed out.

Jon smirked. "Perhaps that would be my greatest revenge on Father as he burns in Hell. Letting it pass to someone not of his immediate blood."

Arch closed his eyes again and they fell silent for some minutes. Finally, his twin opened his eyes again.

"I've waited for you to come home. I needed your help with one last thing."

"Anything. I swear it."

"It might cause you to join Father in Hell," Arch warned.

Jon never hesitated. "Whatever you need, I will do it."

"I am in a great deal of pain. Dr. Broll has left laudanum for me. It's in the amber bottle."

He turned and saw it. Standing, he retrieved it. "What do I do?"

Weariness blanketed Arch. "Broll has been putting a few drops in a cup of water."

He looked over and saw a pitcher sitting on the table, a pewter cup next to it. Retrieving it, he poured water into it and asked, "How many drops?"

"Dump the contents into the glass," Arch instructed.

Alarm filled him. "Arch, that would . . ." His voice trailed off as understanding filled him.

"Kill me."

"Kill you." Jon looked at his brother, the person who was a part of him, the one he loved more than anyone in the world. "Kill you," he repeated.

"Please." Arch's eyes pleaded with him. "Please, Jon."

He saw how much pain his twin was in and how he was the only one who could end Arch's misery.

"Dr. Broll is certain you won't improve?" he asked, wanting to be certain before he acted.

"Syphilis is a death sentence, Brother. Some can live with the symptoms for years but they never improve. Some go downhill rapidly, as I have. I cannot take the pain anymore, Jon. My sight is going. I fear my mind will be next. Already, things are fuzzy to me when I try to recall them. The headaches are excruciating. The sores throb and ache constantly. I lie here in my own urine and wish I was dead.

"Help me. Only you can."

Indecision might render him useless. Jon thrust it aside, thinking of how much he loved

Arch. He opened the bottle of laudanum and turned it upside down, emptying the contents into the cup. With a heavy heart, he handed it to his twin. Arch couldn't hold it steady, even using both hands. Jon placed his hands around his brother's and brought the drink of death to Arch's mouth.

"Are you certain?"

"More than you could ever know."

With a nod, Jon tilted the glass and Arch drank the entire contents. Jon pulled a handkerchief from his pocket and dabbed his brother's lips.

"Fill the bottle with some water," Arch said. "It won't fool Dr. Broll but he won't say anything."

"You told him I would help you?"

His brother nodded. "I told him you were my other half. That we share in everything."

Jon sat on the bed, taking Arch's hand. "You will always be with me. You know that."

"I do. Go make something decent of yourself, Jon. I won't be around to drag you down. Find good friends. Live an interesting life. Marry a woman who will challenge you. Have children."

"No one could be a better friend than you, Arch. And if I do have a son, I will name him after you." He smiled sadly. "That way an Archibald Sutton could one day become the Duke of Blackmore."

He didn't know if his brother heard his last words. His eyes closed and his breathing ceased. Jon waited a few minutes and then kissed the top of his brother's head.

"Farewell, Archibald Sutton, Marquess of Grafton."

Bringing the bedclothes up, he covered his twin and left the dower house. He would see what his father wanted. More importantly, he would never let the duke belittle him again. He would stand up and hold his ground.

Because now he stood for two. Himself and Arch. Forever and always.

CHAPTER TWO

J ON WENT TO the basin in the room and thoroughly washed his hands, not knowing if briefly touching Arch had spread the wicked disease to him. He doubted it but thought he should take the precaution nonetheless. Returning to the house, he found Elizabeth waiting for him in the foyer.

"Did you get to see Arch?" she asked anxiously.

He didn't want to tell her that her brother was dead but knew it was better hearing it from him than anyone else.

Seeking privacy, he took her hand and said, "Let's walk down to the stables. You can show me the pony you've been riding."

He let her chatter on as they crossed the lawn and headed toward the stables. She told him about learning to read and that she could already add sums in double digits. She seemed to like her new governess but what she really wanted to do was learn to ride.

They entered the stables and he greeted the head groom. "Good afternoon, Mallory. I hear my sister is learning to ride. Who is teaching her?"

"It's good to see you back, Lord Jonathan. And Lady Elizabeth has only had the one riding lesson with me."

"Might I step in and help with those lessons?"

"Of course, my lord." Mallory winked at Elizabeth. "You'd like that, wouldn't you, my lady? Your brother is a fine horseman. I'm happy to put you in his capable hands."

Elizabeth's eyes lit up and she stared at him in adoration. "You'll really teach me yourself, Jon?"

"I will. You are the perfect age to start."

"I already love horses."

"She does, my lord," Mallory seconded. "Lady Elizabeth comes to the stables every day and talks to every horse in its stall. She also likes to help me brush the gentler ones."

"I hope Father doesn't know about that."

Mallory shrugged, a twinkle in his eyes. "We know not to bother His Grace with small matters."

Unsaid was that the duke would have put a stop to Elizabeth's visits. The thought of his daughter doing manual labor would have thoroughly disgusted him.

"I'll take over the lessons for now," he told his sister, "but if I'm not available, Mallory is an excellent teacher. He taught both Arch and me." A lump formed in his throat at speaking his twin's name.

"Come see my pony," Elizabeth urged, taking his hand and dragging him along.

They visited the horse and several others before he said it was time to head back to the house. As they walked together, he knew he couldn't put off the bad news any longer.

"Elizabeth, there is something I must tell you. About Arch."

She stopped and gazed up at him. "He's dead, isn't he?"

Jon nodded. "He was very, very sick."

Her mouth set in a hard line. Suddenly, she looked years older. "I should have been able to see him. To tell him goodbye."

"You should have," he agreed. "But Arch didn't want you to remember him that way."

"He didn't?" she questioned. "He said so?"

"We talked about you. He missed seeing you and loved you very much. But he's gone now."

She blinked several times, her eyes bright with tears, and then clasped him. "You won't die, will you, Jon? If you did, I couldn't stand it."

He lifted her in his arms. "I am far too mean to die, little sister."

"You aren't mean," she chided. "Arch could be mean sometimes. Not to me. But sometimes to others."

"I know. But we still loved him, didn't we? And we'll go on loving him. He will always be a part of us." He tapped his chest. "Here. Inside our hearts."

He carried her back the rest of the way, her cheek against his chest. When they arrived at the house, he set her down.

"Go find your governess. I need to speak to Father."

Elizabeth shuddered. "He'll be angry."

"I suppose he will. He loved Arch and now he is gone."

"You'll be the duke now, won't you, Jon?"

"I will when Father is gone."

"I hate him," she said vehemently, surprising him.

"Why?"

"Because he doesn't like you or me. He only liked Arch. He never wants to see me. He said I was a silly girl and he didn't have time for girls."

Jon smoothed her hair. "Fathers can be many things. Sometimes he is mean. Sometimes he is nice. We just happened to see more of the mean side of him."

"You won't be a mean father, will you?"

He laughed. "I may not be a father at all."

Her eyes widened. "You have to. If you're

the duke, you have to have a boy so he can be the duke after you."

It surprised him that at six, Elizabeth had already grasped the politics of the family.

"Well, I am only sixteen now though I'll be seventeen shortly. I still must go to university and then I have years before I need to wed and have children."

"I will be a good mother when I have children," she proclaimed. "Even though my mother died, I think I can be a good one."

He kissed the top of her head. "You will be a wonderful mother, Elizabeth. Off you go. I must speak to Father."

He opened the door and watched as she skipped across the foyer and scampered up the steps. It saddened him that their father had cast her aside. He thought, in part, it might be because Elizabeth favored their mother so. She'd died giving birth to her daughter. Knowing the duke, he held Elizabeth responsible for her mother's death. Jon vowed to keep a close eye on his sister and make sure she had both attention and affection from him since she lacked receiving either from her only parent.

Turning to the footman in the foyer, he asked, "Do you know where His Grace is?"

"He was in the library the last I knew, Lord Jonathan."

"Would you send for Dr. Broll? I need to see

him at once. It's most urgent."

"Of course, my lord."

Jon nodded and proceeded upstairs. He entered the library and saw his father seated in a chair, gazing out the window. Slowly, the duke turned his gaze upon his son.

"You were to come to me when you arrived home." His wintry tone could have frozen the lake at Blackstone Manor.

"I needed to see Arch first."

His father's features softened for a moment before they twisted. He glared at his son, his ire obvious.

"You are to obey me, Jonathan. In everything. Without question."

"You are not a general. I am not your foot soldier. I spent far too long being afraid of you. I was fearful of the beatings you dispensed and yet still longing to impress you. Hoping for a single look or a kind word. When I stopped caring what you thought or said, it was quite liberating."

"You insolent, ignorant—"

"I'd wait on listing so many derogatory adjectives. Especially when you describe your heir."

His words were like a slap in the face. His father went from stunned to grief-stricken in a matter of seconds. For a moment, Jon wanted to comfort him. He held his ground, though, knowing the duke would recover. As expected, he did, and turned his venom on his only remaining son.

"You are worthless as an heir," Blackmore lashed out. "You look like Archibald and, yet, you are nothing like him. My son is good and kind and smart and wonderful."

Jon kept silent. There was no need to blacken his twin's name. Even if he told his father what Arch could be like, the duke never would have believed him. He'd favored his heir from the very beginning.

"The tutors at Harrow would tell you that I am intelligent," he pointed out. "Athletic, as well. I may not be the duke that Arch could have been but I sure as hell will be better at it than you. I can't help it that you took my brother to a place where a whore gave him syphilis. I cannot change the fact that he was in agony until he took his last breath. And yes, I got to speak to him before he died. I might have missed that opportunity if I had come to see you first."

His father leaped from his chair and slapped Jon. The sting his face felt was nothing compared to the curses that sprang from the duke's lips. He berated Jon, calling him vile and useless, telling him he would disown him if he could.

Finally, Blackmore collapsed into a nearby chair. "I loved Archibald. I gave everything I had to him. He was my heir. My hope for the future. You are a worthless nothing. I hate you. I never want to . . ."

Jon had already turned to leave, not wanting to listen to the continuing tirade. He spun around, however, and saw his father sputtering. His eyes went wild. His left hand clutched the right arm and shook it. Then he slid from the chair and hit the floor. Jon returned and knelt as his father tried to speak—and couldn't.

Calmly, he said, "You have suffered at attack of apoplexy, Father. I had a friend at school whose uncle suffered one. He was bedridden for years, one side of his body paralyzed. That could be you. Or you might go quickly. Knowing you, you will want to be with Arch."

He rose. "I'd already sent for Dr. Broll so he could confirm Arch was gone. I will see that he tends to you, as well."

Leaving the library, he met up with Roy and said, "His Grace has fallen ill. He will need several footmen to carry him to his chambers. Dr. Broll should already be on his way back to Blackstone Manor. We lost my brother today."

The butler's face betrayed no emotion. "I'll see to His Grace at once, my lord."

Dr. Broll arrived an hour later. By then, the duke had been taken to his bedchamber, unable to speak and only moving his left hand. His mouth drooped to one side, drool dribbling down his chin.

Jon rose from his chair by the bedside and greeted the physician.

"I believe my father has suffered a sudden attack which may be apoplexy. And during my visit with my brother, he passed on."

A look of understanding passed between the two men and the physician said, "It was not unexpected. Lord Grafton was very ill. I know he was comforted in getting to see his brother a final time before he moved on."

"We had a good conversation," Jon confirmed. "He was at peace when he went."

"Let me examine His Grace."

Dr. Broll went to the bed as Jon crossed the room and stood next to the window. He gazed out on the rolling green lawn as he heard the doctor ask several questions. His father could only grunt a response. Despite the horrible treatment he had received over the years from the duke, inwardly, Jon flinched. It didn't take a doctor to tell him that the once larger than life Duke of Blackmore had been reduced to nothing in a matter of seconds—and that he would never recovery his robust health again.

After several minutes, the physician called to him and Jon returned, coming to his father's bedside, Broll facing him on the opposite side.

"His Grace's condition is very serious, Lord Grafton."

Jon tried not to react, hearing himself referred to by his brother's title for the first time. A title that was now his. It seemed surreal to think he was now Lord Grafton, a peer with a title. A man who was heir to a dukedom.

"What can be done for him?" he asked, looking to the bed and seeing his father's gaze fixed upon him, his eyes full of hostility even now as he lay helplessly in the bed. For his part, Jon could only ignore it. He'd grown rather good at ignoring his father the past few years.

He turned back and saw Dr. Broll had witnessed the silent exchange between father and son. Pity filled the physician's eyes, making Jon angry. He tamped down his ire, knowing to express it would serve no purpose.

"His Grace can be kept comfortable," the physician said. "Eating will be a challenge since I doubt he can chew. Many peers who find themselves in this position have their valets act as a nurse to them. If His Grace chooses not to do so, I can recommend—"

The doctor's words were interrupted by wild grunts from the duke. Seeing he had their attention, he tried to speak. Only garbled noise came out, frustrating him further. He attempted to shake his head.

"How long does he have, Doctor?" Jon asked.

"It's hard to say, my lord. I have seen men live for years in this state."

A whimper came from the bed. He forced himself to look upon his father, now defeated, and saw him go limp, as if he'd given up. His eyes closed. It looked as if his breathing halted.

The physician grabbed for his stethoscope and placed it to the duke's chest, listening for several seconds. He finally lifted it and placed two fingers against the duke's throat and shook his head.

Dr. Broll looked to Jon. "Your father is dead, Your Grace."

In the midst of a single hour, Jon had gone from being a sixteen-year-old with no title or fortune to becoming one of the most powerful figures in all of England.

CHAPTER THREE

Oxford—November 1813

ARABELLA JENNINGS FINISHED pinning up her hair and made her way to breakfast. She hoped her father, an Oxford don, would be in better spirits today. Yesterday, he had received a letter from the widow of one of his brothers, informing him that her clergyman husband had passed away from a heart attack. Arabella didn't know this brother, who was a dozen years older than her father and the third son of the Earl of Barrington. In fact, she had never met Reverend Jennings or the eldest two brothers. Her father told her the second son, fifteen years his senior, had gone into the army, as was expected of second sons. The current earl, the eldest of the four boys and the one who had inherited the title, was eighteen years older than her father.

In part because of the age discrepancy, Arabella's father had never been close to his brothers, who were all away at school when he was born. She came to understand that these three men blamed her father for killing their mother, since the countess had died giving birth to Reginald, a very unexpected arrival. It led to an estrangement that had never healed. Her father had no social connections, being a fourth son, and he had told Arabella that the way Polite Society worked, his brothers hadn't needed him because he could do nothing for them.

From the moment she had learned of this hostility and how her father's position in the birth order caused the family to practically disown him, she'd had no tolerance for the ways of the *ton*. Fortunately, she would never experience moving through society. She didn't need it and it certainly would have had nothing to do with her.

It didn't matter. She liked her life as it was, other than Mama harping on occasion for Arabella to wed. She didn't have time to be married and have babies. Her life was much too exciting, being her father's assistant. As an Oxford don, he lectured and regularly met with his students. Over the years, she had spent much of her time sitting in the back of his class, soaking up all the knowledge he bestowed upon his rapt pupils, and even attending the seminars of small groups which her father led in various discussions. After all this time, Arabella had come to write most of her father's lectures, researching in various libraries and adding to his already full notes.

Her favorite times were when they ate supper with the young men he taught. Many of the dons regularly dined at night with their pupils throughout the various colleges. Since her mother ate like a bird and never wanted anything at the evening meal, Arabella and her father had taken to having their final meal of the day with his students. The lively discussions—some turning to arguments and occasionally heated blows—were always intriguing and entertaining. At first, students new to university would question her presence but she proved herself time and time again as being an intellectual equal. They then forgot she was a woman and often sought out her opinion on a variety of topics. It warmed her that by the time a young man left Oxford, she would have won him over. She only wished that women could become tutors but she knew that was only wishful thinking on her part.

The Michaelmas term was about to end, however, which would bring weeks of quiet to their household until the new year, when Hilary term would begin in January and run through March. Arabella found herself becoming bored during these breaks and flung herself into further research to occupy her time.

She found her mother already sitting at the

breakfast table. Her father hadn't yet arrived.

"I've made toast for you," her mother said. "There's some new marmalade, as well. The tea is ready. Pour out for you and me if you would."

"Of course, Mama. Thank you for making breakfast."

As she readied the tea, she felt a pang of sympathy for her mother, who had been a doctor's daughter. Mama had always wanted to be a part of Polite Society and had thought marrying the son of an earl, who was an Oxford don, would change things for the better. Instead, she quickly realized that her husband had no standing in society. Her mother wore her disappointment in her lot in life as a blanket, her dour expression rarely changing. At least Papa earned enough for them to have a maid and cook come in twice a week. The maid did all the heavy cleaning that Mama didn't want to do, including their laundry, while the cook prepared a few hearty meals they could eat from for a few days. That was why Arabella enjoyed going to eat with her father's students because the fare at the places they dined stuck to her ribs. She enjoyed eating and was fortunate that she never seemed to put on weight despite her healthy appetite.

Her father came and sat, a pensive look on his face. She wondered if he still thought about his dead brother—and if it caused him to think about his own mortality even though he was years younger than his three siblings.

"Tea, Papa?" she asked.

He nodded and she prepared a cup for him as her mother filled his plate from a chafing dish. She placed eggs and ham in front of her husband but he seemed lost in thought, pushing the food around on the plate.

When Arabella had finished her tea and toast, she saw he wasn't going to eat and said, "Papa, I would like to go over your upcoming lecture with you. I found a few fascinating facts that I'd like you to include."

"Hmm. What?" he asked, his distraction plain.

"Papa, the term is almost over. You only have two more lectures to give. I wish to talk about them with you. Why don't we go to your study?"

"Of course, Arabella." He rose and smiled fondly at her. "I look forward to seeing what you have discovered." His eyes twinkled at her. "Sometimes, I think you are more the scholar than I am."

Relief filled her. He suddenly seemed like his old self again. "Good. Come along then. I have a tidbit or two that will surprise you."

It didn't take but a moment to reach his study. Their house was small, consisting of a parlor that doubled as their dining space, along with a tiny kitchen, the study, and two small bedchambers. Once when she was much younger and her mother had told her she was the granddaughter of an earl, she had asked Papa about the house he'd grown up in and he had told her all he could remember. It shocked her that he'd had no idea how many rooms it contained. The more he spoke, the more she realized how far down in the world he'd come. While he might be a distinguished university don, their entire home would most likely have fit inside his childhood home's drawing room.

They entered the cramped room, where they had their two desks pushed together, facing each other, and each took a seat opposite the other. Arabella began telling her father what she had discovered and told him the exact place he could weave the new facts into his lecture.

"Oh, my!" he exclaimed. "This is enlightening. A bit controversial." His eyes lit with mischief. "And it will make for an excellent discussion topic at supper tomorrow night after my pupils have heard it."

"I thought so, too," she agreed quickly. "Lord Smithson will totally embrace it. Mr. Johnson will merely fight him tooth and nail."

"Because Mr. Johnson enjoys verbal sparring," Papa said, laughing. "More than most young men his age."

"I would also add Lord—"

The door swung open, her mother bursting

into the room. Immediately, Arabella knew something of importance had occurred because Mama never interrupted them when they were at work.

"You must come quickly, Mr. Jennings," she said, out of breath, the color high on her cheeks. "A solicitor from London has arrived. He says he has news of the utmost importance. Oh, I wonder if I should have offered him tea," she fretted.

Both Arabella and her father rose and he said, "Let's see what he has to say first, my dear. To see if he is worthy of tea."

Mama gave him a bewildered look. "Of course, he's worthy, Mr. Jennings. He's from London! I will go now and put on the kettle." She quickly turned and left them alone.

"Shall we go see what this so-called important visitor has to share with us, Daughter?"

"Perhaps it has something to do with your brother's passing," she ventured.

He frowned. "I don't see why it would. The living was near Barrington Hall, where I grew up. It will go to someone new, of course. It wouldn't have anything to do with a London solicitor."

"Let's not keep him waiting, Papa," she urged, taking his arm and guiding him to the parlor.

When they reached the doorway, she looked at the small parlor through different eyes, wondering what the well-dressed visitor who sat there thought about the place. He was a small man, his pate bald and his clothing immaculate. His dark eyes cast about the room. Something in his expression told her he found things lacking.

"Good day. I am Reginald Jennings," her father announced as they entered the room. "This is my daughter, Arabella. My wife said you wished to see me. How may I be of help?"

The man rose. "I am Malcolm Price." He glanced to Arabella and then back to her father and said, "I have a grave matter to discuss with you."

Her mother rushed in. "The kettle's on, Mr. Price. We'll have tea in no time," she said brightly.

The solicitor nodded curtly. "Thank you. As to the matter at hand, I believe we should speak in private," he said, directing the statement to her father. "Perhaps we might go somewhere else."

Papa chuckled. "There is nowhere else to go, Mr. Price, unless you want to speak in my bedchamber while seated upon the bed." He held out a hand. "Please, have a seat again. We will stay here and talk."

"Then I would ask that the ladies—"

"My daughter will stay," Papa said flatly, brokering no nonsense. "I value her opinion and would have her hear what you've come to say to me."

"What about me, Husband?" her mother

asked.

"Of course, you will also stay, my dear." He smiled benignly at her and then took a seat, indicating for Arabella and her mother to also sit in the remaining chairs. "Go ahead, Mr. Price. Share your news."

The solicitor took a deep breath and exhaled it slowly. She tensed, worried what he might say. Already, her father was upset over the death of his brother and she didn't want something to be added to the burden he carried.

"I have come with several pieces of news," Mr. Price began. "The first is that your brother, Reverend Jennings, passed away a week ago."

"Yes, I know of it," Papa said brusquely, his voice tight, making Arabella realize he was fighting back tears. "My brother's widow wrote to me. I received the letter only yesterday."

"My impression was that you were not in touch with anyone within the family," Mr. Price said, surprise evident in his voice.

"We weren't," Papa assured him. "I have not spoken to or written my brothers in decades. The letter came as quite a surprise."

"Well, there are more to come," the solicitor said cryptically.

His words irritated Arabella and she said, "Speak plainly, Mr. Price. My father is a busy man, preparing for his final lectures of the term to be delivered later this week."

His brows knit together in what she decided was anger because she'd spoken up but, for some unknown reason, the solicitor held his tongue. Disapproval still shone in his eyes as he continued.

"Your second brother died three weeks ago from war wounds previously received."

Papa started. "Oh, my."

"Yes. Lieutenant General Jennings was hit by a stray bullet almost two months ago. The doctors thought they'd gotten out all the lead but must have been mistaken."

"A lieutenant general, you say. He would have been happy to achieve such a high rank," Papa murmured, his eyes filling with tears.

Arabella took his hand in hers and squeezed. "I am sorry you have lost not one but two of your brothers, Papa. Perhaps now would be a good time to reach out to the earl and share your sorrow. I know you are estranged but you might be able to offer him some comfort."

"That won't be possible, Miss Jennings," their visitor continued. "You see, I am also here to deliver the news that Lord Barrington passed away four days ago. He had been ill for quite some time. The earl only had one son, who predeceased him in death many years ago. His other two children were girls." The solicitor paused. "I know this comes as a shock but, Mr. Jennings, *you* are now the Earl of Barrington."

CHAPTER FOUR

London—Opening Night of the Season—1815

JON DESCENDED THE stairs and found Elizabeth tapping her foot.

"You're going to make us late to the first ball of the Season," she told him.

"Being late is fashionable," he drawled. "And you were so popular during your come-out last Season, I'm sure no event would have the audacity to start until you make an appearance. Or at least nothing of interest will occur until Lady Elizabeth Sutton has arrived."

She slugged his arm affectionately—but it packed a punch all the same. It pleased him to know how fond she was of him and how she'd taken his lessons to heart. He'd sat Elizabeth down before her debut last year and stressed the rules of Polite Society. He didn't want to see her ruined and wed to an unsuitable man. He'd taught her a few defensive moves to use in case she ever found herself in a situation not to her liking.

Taking her arm, he said, "Come. The carriage awaits." Then he led her outside.

Once they were on their way, she said, "Jon, I want you to be *you* this Season."

He frowned. "I am always me, Elizabeth." Something told him they were about to have a heart-to-heart and he'd wind up on the short end. As usual.

She returned his frown. "You are deliberately misunderstanding me. I know of your moniker. The Duke of Arrogance."

His frown deepened. Jon knew it was impossible to stop Elizabeth from hearing gossip but it troubled him all the same. He wondered what else she'd heard about him since her come-out.

"I know that isn't truly you. You are neither offensive nor overbearing toward me. I also know that you quit being the scoundrel the *ton* knows last Season because you were trying to be on your best behavior for me. To improve my chances of making a decent match."

He started to protest but she waved him away.

"No, let me finish. I know of your women. You have never been terribly discreet as far as that goes. Because of it, society has talked about you to no end. Then last Season, you weren't outrageous. You didn't flaunt any of your liaisons. You behaved in a manner most unlike you. All because you wanted me to wed." She grinned. "As you can see, it didn't make a whit of difference."

"Why didn't you wed?" he asked, curious about a topic they'd never spoken about until now. "You were one of the acknowledged beauties of the year. I had to chase suitors from the house at all hours."

Elizabeth laughed. "Because I was having fun. Going to parties and balls and the theatre and concerts. Being fussed over. Oh, Jon, you have been not only brother but father to me. Somewhere deep inside, I fear there's still that little insecure girl who longed for her father's attention and never received it. I know, you have lavished me with attention in the years since his death. You have taught me to be confidant and strong. I must admit that it felt good getting noticed last year by so many men. It helped me become more assured and feel as if I were worthy."

"You're my sister. Of course, you are worthy," he insisted, though he understood her underlying insecurity since he felt it, too, even all these years later.

She took his hand. "Thank you. But being the daughter of one duke and the sister of another— not to mention my fabulous dowry—I will always have men pursuing me. I merely used last Season to enjoy myself and scope the lay of the land, much as an army scout might. This Season, I promise to become more serious in finding a husband. But I want you to feel free to do and say as you please. Your actions will not reflect upon me."

He snorted. "I am glad to hear you think that."

She sniffed. "Dukes are forgiven practically everything simply because they are dukes. I simply am saying that you should behave normally." She gave him a wry smile. "Even arrogantly, if you must. It won't interfere as I look for love."

He grew still. "You want love? Elizabeth, I can tell you that you are chasing a fantasy."

"Am I?" Her direct gaze seemed to pierce his soul. "Two of your closest friends, the Dukes of Windham and Colebourne, have both wed for love and are quite happy. You also know that the Duke of Treadwell has let us know he is determined to wed Lady Ruthersby by this Season's end."

Jon laughed. "I think Treadwell is in lust. Who wouldn't be? Lady Ruthersby is most beautiful."

Elizabeth shook her head. "I quite disagree. I have seen the smoldering looks he's given her. There's more than lust in them. There is passion.

Desire. And, yes, I believe even love."

"What do you know about passion?" he demanded, thinking this a most inappropriate topic for him to be discussing with his little sister.

She laughed. "I may not have felt it yet but I will know it when it happens. I've already kissed several men and—"

"You've kissed men! Elizabeth, you must—"

"Don't you Elizabeth me, Jon. Of course, I have kissed a few men. I've been out a whole year now."

"Who? When?" he demanded.

She grinned. "I must be pretty good at it since you haven't heard. Of course, I'm sure no one would ever tell you or you'd soundly box their ears."

"I'd do more than that," he muttered.

"Rest assured that it's only been a few men and only ones I was interested in."

"How was it?"

She shrugged. "Boring for the most part. A few times it was pleasant. I know I am on the right path, though. I will know it when it occurs."

"Love? Know love?"

"Yes," she said dreamily.

Realizing it would be hard to convince her otherwise, he said, "You do understand that most of Polite Society never considers love when they enter a marriage. Marriage is for strengthening coffers and social ties among families."

"I know." Her mouth set in stubbornness, a true mark of a Sutton.

"I will admit that love does come sometimes to couples. Most likely, though, after they have been wed a while. I would ask that you not think you must have stars in your eyes to wed. Find a man who is suitable. One who is intelligent. Kind. One you can respect. If you are compatible, then love may grow." He paused. "A love that can deepen with the passage of time."

"When did you become so mature about love? You sound so wise."

He chuckled. "Well, I am to be thirty soon. Hopefully, something sensible has invaded me."

"All right," she said. "I will look for a congenial man. One that I get along with remarkably well. One who would make for a good husband and father—and is also a good kisser. I understand your point about love growing. I will keep an open mind."

"Good."

His own thoughts regarding love were convoluted. He hadn't believed in it at all. Then he had seen the changes in Andrew and George. And now Weston. The trio, whom he had nicknamed the Eton Three, had become fast friends with him at Cambridge, along with Sebastian, who still was fighting on the Continent. When Jon began at university, boys whom he'd known at Harrow all of a sudden fell over themselves, trying to be his friend since with his father's death he'd become a duke. Some were the very ones who had spread ugly gossip about him, the ones who had thought him to be horrible—so he'd lived up to their expectations. He refused to have anything to do with anyone from his Harrow days.

That's why the bonds of friendship had become so firm between him and his small group of friends. He trusted them more than any men of his acquaintance. Even during the last decade in society he hadn't made any more friends. True, men still groveled at his feet, while women flung themselves at him. He was close to none of them. He was a duke and could ignore whomever he chose.

Jon understood what Elizabeth mentioned earlier because an insecure boy still lurked deep within him. That boy who'd been alternately ignored and berated by his father. When he had suddenly found himself wealthy and titled, he'd wanted to rub it into the faces of everyone who'd maligned him over the years. He also knew he had a lot of living to do, both for himself and Arch. So he'd taken the freedom being a duke gave him and acted fully entitled to everyone other than his small circle of friends. And Elizabeth, of course.

It almost seemed an act now and had grown stale. He was tired of bedding countless women, many he didn't even recall their names minutes after the act.

Could he find love as the Eton Three had? Did it truly exist?

It must. While Andrew had always been the honorable one among them, George—and Weston, in particular—had grown quite cynical after both suffered broken engagements. They raced through years being two of the biggest scoundrels in Polite Society. Yet Andrew was now wed and Phoebe expected their first child any day now. George and Samantha, who'd been childhood friends, were also wed and downright giddy with happiness. Weston, the biggest cynic of all, had declared his intentions toward Lady Ruthersby and what Weston wanted, he always got. Jon wasn't as sure as Elizabeth thinking Weston loved Elise but it wouldn't surprise him if that turned out to be the case.

Suddenly, he felt very alone. Isolated. Would his friends now leave him behind, marrying and having children? A deep yearning grew within him, wanting what they had. Women who challenged them all the while loving them. Children to play with. Long ago, with Arch in his last minutes on earth, they had discussed the need for Jon to provide an heir for the dukedom.

He decided that time had finally come.

He may not find love, as his friends had, but he could take his own advice which he'd dispensed to his sister. He could look for a suitable woman. One of elegance and grace. Beauty and charm. One who would make for an excellent duchess and mother. She had to be among the *ton* somewhere. Someone he could care for, if not love. Someone he could enjoy spending time with. A woman he could admire.

Determination filled him. As the carriage slowed, Jon said, "While you look for your future mate this Season, I believe it is time for me to do the same."

Elizabeth's eyes widened and then she threw her arms about him.

"Oh, that would be lovely, Jon. Why, we could even have a double wedding!" she declared.

He laughed. "I wouldn't go that far. All I am saying is that as I approach thirty, perhaps it is time to settle down. I have been the Duke of Blackmore almost half my life. It's time I looked to the future."

"You will have to do what I do and be discerning then," she advised. "Women will want you merely because you are a duke and possess fabulous wealth and estates scattered across England." Her intense gaze unsettled him. "You'll need to find a woman who wants you for yourself, Jon."

The carriage door opened and a footman said, "The driver is as close as he can get, Your Grace. You will have to walk a ways."

"Get closer!" he snapped. "I'm a bloody

duke."

Elizabeth punched him again, harder than before. "Get out," she ordered.

Jon did as she requested and helped her to alight.

She turned to the footman and said, "His Grace is not one to apologize, so I will do so for him. He was late this evening, which caused us to depart later than usual. I know you have gotten us as close as you can and it is appreciated. I am sorry he shouted at you. We will see you after the ball ends."

With that, his sister took his arm and pulled him along.

"Never apologize to servants," he admonished.

"It's not a habit of mine but, then again, I rarely lose my temper with them," she said sweetly, making him feel poorly for having done so. Then she brightened. "Tonight is the first night of a brand-new Season. One which we both may find our future spouses. To us, my sweet brother. May our searches prove fruitful."

Jon only hoped that would be the case.

CHAPTER FIVE

A RABELLA HAD NO desire to attend the opening ball of tonight's Season. The idea of making her come-out at four and twenty seemed ridiculous. She watched as Annie, her new lady's maid, arranged her hair. Annie had been a parlor maid who had insisted to Arabella that she had higher aspirations and could do hair, something that must seem important in society. She had granted the girl a promotion and had to admit that her golden curls looked better than they ever had.

She gazed into the mirror as Annie worked, still surprised to see the sapphire necklace around her neck and the earrings hanging from her lobes. They were family jewels and had been given to her by her father to wear tonight. The gesture was sweet but wouldn't work. She would never feel at home amidst the *ton*. At least she had a new wardrobe, thanks to the local seamstress near their country estate in Wiltshire. Oh, that sounded so pretentious. A country estate.

At least the estate had saved Arabella's sanity.

The news that her father had become the Earl of Barrington surprised all three of them. Papa seemed dazed. Mama walked about with a smile on her face and a spring in her step. For Arabella, it had sounded a death knell. Her father finished that week's term at Oxford and resigned his position. They terminated the lease on their house early and had arrived at Barrington Hall, which was in terrible condition. It seemed the previous earl hadn't cared for country life and hadn't visited the estate in years. The steward was ancient and only had a foggy idea of what went on so Arabella had convinced her father to gift the man with a cottage and pension in order to allow her to see to running things.

Then her mother had fallen ill. She had fought for several weeks but she'd never been a strong woman. Poor Mama had always wanted to move among Polite Society. She died less than a month after their arrival, only being a countess for a few weeks. On her deathbed, Mama had made Arabella promise to make her come-out once the mourning period had passed. Reluctantly, she had given her word.

And now regretted it.

Papa had been beside himself with his wife's death. He'd gone from being surprised at becoming an earl—and totally unprepared for it—to drifting through life as a sleepwalker. Having given up his lifelong profession to become a gentleman, he had no roots. Losing Mama only deepened his anxiety and he fell into a deep depression. Arabella had the local doctor visit but the man had done Papa no good, resorting to leeches and bloodletting, which seemed to only exacerbate the problems. She'd finally put a halt to that process but for months, her father never stepped outside his bedchamber, having all meals sent up and rarely wishing to see his only child.

With all that time on her hands and having also lost her own purpose in life, she fearlessly attacked all the mounting problems at Barrington Hall and their estate and spent months learning what the house needed to have done in order to bring it up to speed. She had walked the estate from end to end, visiting countless tenants and getting to know them and learn of their needs, as well.

Six months into her campaign to shore up everything, her father had seemed to awaken to his responsibilities and joined in her endeavors. Between the two of them, it took another six months until everything met their satisfaction and lived up to their expectations. Now, though, the house sparkled, all its repairs completed, while the land and cottages were in excellent shape. The year had taught Arabella much about managing both a household and estate and keeping busy had helped her time of mourning pass quickly. With the mourning period completed now, she unfortunately had to fulfill her promise to Mama and make her debut into society.

Gazing at her reflection as Annie put the finishing touches on her coiffure, she dreaded tonight. She would rather be sitting in her study at Barrington Hall, reading over crop reports or learning more about livestock issues. Instead, Mr. Barley, their new estate manager, had taken over the space she had occupied and was now in charge of the land and their tenants. While she liked him and found him to be experienced, Arabella couldn't help but think she could do a better job.

"There, my lady. You look right nice. You'll shine at the ball tonight," Annie said.

"Thank you. My hair has never looked more lovely. I must compliment your skill."

"Oh, I can do much more. You'll need to give me time to play with it a bit. I have all sorts of ideas I'd like to try out for you. Is there anything else you need?"

"No, thank you. You may go."

"I'll wait up for you and help you from your gown."

"That's not necessary, Annie."

The maid sniffed. "It most certainly is, my lady. I know we're both new at this but I know enough to know that."

After Annie left, Arabella rose. Nerves rushed through her. She would know no one at tonight's ball. It was hard for her to understand how or why they had even been invited but her father explained that there would be certain social events the Earl of Barrington and his family would always have been invited to. It didn't matter who the earl might be. He assured her she would be fine, knowing how she loved to dance and had done so at local assemblies in Oxford for several years. She did worry that she didn't know how to waltz, a dance she'd heard talk of. It was said to be most scandalous and wasn't danced outside of London.

Papa also said once she made friends, she would be invited to other events, which he would be happy to escort her to. He referred to afternoon tea parties and musicales and even invitations to the theatre. While her mother might have enjoyed the social whirl, Arabella couldn't help but secretly wish that the former earl was still alive and she was back at Oxford, helping Papa with his lectures and having Mama still alive.

Rising, she knew she couldn't put it off anymore. She supposed once tonight was over and she saw what a ball was like and had met people in Polite Society, it might not be as difficult as she thought. Holding on to that bit of hope, she descended the stairs, where her father awaited her in the foyer.

"Ah, but don't you look lovely, my dear," he said, his eyes shining with love. "I am glad you chose pale blue for tonight. It helps set off the sapphires."

"They do look lovely with the gown, Papa. Thank you again for providing them for me to wear."

"Remember, there are more jewels you can choose from. Rubies. Diamonds. A wonderful set of emeralds." A shadow crossed his face. "I only wish your mother could have worn them."

Arabella slid her arm through his. "She is with us tonight in spirit, Papa. Watching over us from heaven."

He patted her hand. "I am sure she is, my dear. Come. The carriage had been brought around for us."

Once inside the vehicle, her nerves didn't diminish. They only increased until she had trouble breathing. Where was the confident woman she knew? The one who had foraged through libraries and debated with university students. The one who had learned how to command an entire staff of servants and settled tenants' disputes. In her heart, she knew she was still that woman but going into a ballroom of hundreds of guests she had never met had Arabella ready to leap from the coach and run home.

The carriage slowed and came to a halt. A footman opened the door and aided her and her father. Once on the ground, Papa tucked her hand through his arm and they started toward Lord and Lady Kennedale's townhouse. She tried to avoid puddles of water and the mud surrounding them and found it hopeless. Her new satin shoes would be dirty by the time they arrived. They were her only dress shoes and she hoped Annie would be able to somehow clean them.

Once inside, they joined the receiving line. As Arabella glanced around, heat rose in her cheeks. Her gown was woefully plain compared to the others she saw. She'd had three dressier gowns made up for evening events and five day gowns, thinking that to be plenty. Observing the women surrounding her, she knew using the local seamstress had been a mistake. She should have insisted they come to London early, in time for her to see a London modiste and have gowns created in town. Perhaps she could still do so and have one or two made up.

They met Lord and Lady Kennedale and the countess' eyes raked over her judgmentally, causing Arabella's cheeks to pinken even more. Escaping the line, her father guided her to the ballroom's entrance and stopped.

"I am off to the card room," he said. "You know I don't dance. I never was good at it. I certainly didn't need it all these years."

"You're . . . leaving me?" she sputtered.

He smiled benignly. "You look lovely, Arabella. Your dance card will fill quickly. I will see you at ball's end."

With that, he walked away.

She had never felt so inadequate or alone as she stepped inside. A crowd already gathered. A footman handed her something. Glancing at it, she saw it was a programme for her partners to fill. What if no one asked her to dance?

Fighting her growing fears, Arabella moved through the room. As she passed groups of people, she saw their eyes move over her and knew every one of them found her gown lacking.

Mustering her courage, she stepped to a group of four women who chatted. When she joined their circle, they fell silent.

"Good evening. I am . . . Lady Arabella Jennings. Daughter of the Earl of Barrington," she remembered to add.

It still baffled her why she had to introduce herself as a lady. Nothing but ladies had been invited to this event. Still, she did her best to take this new title in stride.

She smiled and glanced about the group, waiting for them to introduce themselves to her. Only silence reigned.

Finally, one of them, a tall brunette, spoke. "We haven't been properly introduced. I'm afraid you must leave."

Suddenly, the circle tightened, squeezing her out.

"But . . . I did just introduce myself," she insisted, trying to move back into their ranks.

No one spoke to her. It was as if she didn't exist. They continued conversing as she stood there awkwardly, quickly learning from their conversation that the brunette had had sixty ballgowns and one hundred gowns suitable for day wear made up for this Season. Appalled at the outrageous number, Arabella moved away. That would mean the woman wore a different gown practically every night, plus she would have to change dresses numerous times during the day. And that was to wear her new wardrobe. What of her old one? Did no one in London repeat a gown?

A sick feeling grew within her as she continued through the room. Twice more, she tried to join a group and was told they hadn't been introduced. Finally, she asked a rather sharp-tongued woman how she was supposed to be introduced when she didn't know anyone in London.

The woman had looked Arabella up and down and finally said, "If you know no one among the *ton*, then you aren't worth knowing."

Humiliated, she moved to a far corner, hiding behind a tall, potted plant, her cheeks ablaze. She watched as various people came up and introduced others to a group, seeing that there always was a common connection. That's how introductions were made in Polite Society. Had her father not known this? She realized that he had never attended social events and at six and forty, he wouldn't have a clue his only child struggled, not knowing a soul.

But she did know some people here. They all just happened to be men. As she observed things, though, she saw it would be a terrible mistake for her to approach a man she had known at Oxford, men who were Papa's students. Some particularly snobbish rule was in place that prevented that. Since she knew no women present, she was a social pariah.

The orchestra, who'd been tuning their instruments, now appeared ready to play. Suddenly, men approached women and couples paired off, filling the ballroom floor. Arabella remained behind her plant until the music began and couples commenced dancing. A lump formed in her throat, filling it until it became hard to breathe. She was a failure. A total failure. She would never be accepted by the *ton*. Hanging a title in front of her name didn't change who she was. How she had been raised. She had no way to make friends—and no desire to be in the presence of any of these horrible people.

Skirting the edge of the room, she made her way from it and went in search of the library. She would find a book to read and pass the hours that way until it was time to rejoin her father. Hurt filled her, knowing how disappointed her mother would have been with her actions, but Arabella couldn't remain and become the first wallflower of the Season. She'd rather escape the crowd and read.

Finding the library, she entered and closed the door. She skimmed the shelves until she found a book of Shakespeare's comedies. After her disastrous experience tonight, she needed something to make her laugh. She went to the far end of the room and sat in a wing chair. Opening the book, she began reading, hoping she could lose herself in the pages.

CHAPTER SIX

J ON HAD ENTERED the Kennedale ballroom with high hopes after his discussion with Elizabeth in the carriage. He had decided to be choosy in whom he asked to dance, only considering women who might make for a potential Duchess of Blackmore. Most importantly, there would be no flirting. Unless something remarkable stirred within him. Usually, he flirted without thinking, lining up assignations as he danced with women willing to meet him—either somewhere during the ball or at a later time. If he truly were looking for a wife, though, he had no need to go hiking skirts in alcoves or plotting some future rendezvous. Tonight would be different.

Until it all seemed very much the same.

He had circulated around the ballroom to see who was present, stopping and chatting for a few moments with acquaintances here and there, some of whom he hadn't seen since last Season ended. Eventually, he made his way around to his friends, easily spotting George's tawny mane of hair, and joining him and Samantha.

"How is it to be attending your first ball as a married couple?" he asked.

George and Samantha glanced to one another. Jon swore the electricity in that one look almost caused the room to go up in flames. He chuckled, while secretly pining for something like the two of them had. He doubted he would find it but it wouldn't stop him from trying.

"I think we'll enjoy ourselves for a bit," George said. "And then leave after supper."

"Leave?" he asked. "Why do that?" Then seeing the sheepish look on George's face and the hot blush that rose on Samantha's cheeks, he began laughing. "Oh, I see," he said, knowing exactly what the pair would be up to after their departure—most likely in their carriage.

Weston joined them. "Anything going on?" he asked casually, his eyes searching the ballroom.

Jon saw Weston's gaze landed on Lady Ruthersby and said, "How goes your pursuit of the beautiful widow?"

His friend scowled. "I signed her programme twice and then she urged me to go do the same for the three candidates of her choosing."

He chuckled. "Oh, are these the ones she and Elizabeth and Samantha have been perusing to be the future Duchess of Treadwell?"

Weston's scowl deepened. "Yes," he said bluntly.

"Why don't you just declare your intentions to her?" Jon asked, perplexed why his confident, bold friend was hesitating.

Weston shrugged. "I don't know. I want to. I feel I need to wait. I can't afford to scare her off, though. Not when I know that she is The One."

He shook his head. "So, you'll dance with the women she believes will make you a good wife and mother to your children?"

"Yes. I only signed the three cards. I will dance once with each of the women Elise chose."

"And with Elise twice," Jon prompted, calling the Dowager Duchess of Ruthersby by her Christian name, wanting to poke Weston a bit further. "If you'll excuse me. I think I will go sign her dance card, as well. I'm sure she'll be happy to see a friendly face since we've already met."

"Leave her alone," warned Weston with a low growl.

"I know. She's *your* future duchess. Not mine. Don't worry, my friend. Elise will be in safe hands with me," he promised.

"That would be a first," George quipped, causing Weston's face to darken in anger.

Jon left and went in the direction of the breathtaking widow his friend had chosen to marry sometime in the future. He still didn't quite understand Weston's reluctance to speak to Lady Ruthersby about his feelings but it was obvious they ran hot and deep for her.

Reaching her, Jon gave his most charming smile and said, "My dear Lady Ruthersby. You've had such a crowd surrounding you. Might there be room on your programme for my name?"

She returned his smile, one which was warm and reached her eyes, unlike so many other women of the *ton*.

"I'd be delighted to partner with you, Your Grace."

Once he scribbled his name, he told her he would soon return. He moved about the room, signing his name to two other dance cards, one a young, dark-haired beauty making her come-out and the other a woman who had seemed reserved when they'd previously danced at events last Season. Those two dances were early and ended without him wishing to pursue anything further with either.

Then his time came to dance with Elise, whose cheeks were flushed from having partnered with so many other men. He noted that Weston had already left the ballroom, probably bothered by seeing her having such a good time. Jon had to admit that Weston had chosen well. Elise was not only stunning in face and figure but had a sweetness about her that wasn't forced and a true interest in those around her.

As they danced, he said, "You look most beautiful tonight, my lady."

"Thank you, Your Grace. It has been a good while since I have attended any social event. I didn't realize how much I'd missed doing so. How is Lady Elizabeth getting along tonight? I've grown quite fond of her."

"She talks about you and Samantha constantly. I am glad to see such remarkable women have such a good influence on my little sister."

"Lady Elizabeth is a good friend and will make for a good wife and mother," Elise said.

"I think so, too, but I am probably prejudiced," he admitted. "I am over a decade older than Elizabeth. Our father died when she was only six so I have been a little of a brother and more like a father to her. I am quite proud of the woman she has turned out to be."

Their dance ended and Jon spoke to a few other people, finding he was already bored. This wasn't a good sign. To feel so passive and uninterested on the opening night of the Season did not bode well regarding his hunt for a wife. He thought how Andrew had met Phoebe away from London, in Cornwall. Of course, Andrew had just been shot by his loathsome half-brother but he had Phoebe to help nurse him back to health. George and Samantha had grown up on adjoining estates and though she had wed someone else and then been widowed, the two had found their way back to one another. As for Weston and Elise, her carriage had broken down directly in front of his estate. With none of his friends meeting their spouses—or future spouse—in a London ballroom, Jon decided maybe he was looking in the wrong place. He would have to continue attending *ton* events in order to escort Elizabeth to them but perhaps his future duchess would be found in an unusual place. He would cling to that hope.

Jon decided to go to the card room but when he reached there, gambling held no appeal for him. He was a man tightly in control of his emotions, as well as his finances. He didn't believe in Lady Luck and, consequently, he spent little time at the gaming tables. Bored, he wandered the house, snickering to himself because usually at these events he roamed about because he'd planned a clandestine meeting with some pretty female and was in search of her and a place of quiet in order to amuse himself.

He passed what he thought was Lord Kennedale's library and doubled back. A closed door could mean the earl wished people to stay out—or it could mean a tryst was in progress. If it were the latter and he spied an amorous couple, he would leave. If the former, he would simply close the door behind him. At the moment, passing a couple of hours by reading held greater appeal to him than any of the featherheaded, gossiping ladies of Polite Society.

Opening the door, Jon stepped inside, his eyes skimming the room. No couple engaged in a kiss was in sight but something did intrigue him.

A very beautiful blond sat curled up in a chair on the far side of the room, engrossed in the book in her lap. He couldn't remember ever having seen her, which seemed impossible since he was a frequent guest at most events during the Season and had a sharp eye for faces. She looked to be in her early to mid-twenties. Perhaps she'd been one of those vapid creatures who'd made her come-out years ago and made no impression on him, a young lady who'd married after that first Season and then retreated from London's social scene. She might even be a widow returned to town, ready to make another match.

No, he didn't think so as he continued to study her. He closed the door softly behind him and took in her appearance. Her gown, pale blue in color, was almost dowdy, much as one would expect some type of companion to wear. Gems glittered at her throat and ears, though the jewels might have been borrowed. Most likely, she was a poor relation and companion to someone attending tonight's ball. A woman of no means or social standing whose relative or employer had urged her to come and then dropped her the minute they'd left the receiving line.

No wonder she'd come in here to hide. She wasn't properly dressed. For that reason alone, the women of the *ton* would savage her with their gossip. Obviously, she had no social connections or even a handful of friends she could have stood with to pass the time. Instead, she'd retreated to a quiet world of books, where she probably felt most comfortable. He should leave her to her solitude and find somewhere else to go.

Then she smiled at something she read on the page, her face lighting up. Jon could have left—except for that radiant smile. It intrigued him. The book she held was monstrously fat. He ascertained that she must be educated. Well-read since a book of that size didn't put her off. Suddenly, he wanted to know what she was reading. Discuss it with her. He was a great lover of books and could talk about them all day long, having read everything he could get his hands on as a boy. His love of reading and gaining knowledge had followed him into manhood. Wouldn't it be wonderful if he could talk to this woman about what she was reading and not have the usual, dull conversations that surrounded a ball? It would be novel to find a woman with not just outstanding looks but brains to accompany them.

That would be not only an intriguing woman, but a dangerous one.

Her smile widened and he knew what she

read amused her. A deep laugh followed, much deeper than any woman's he'd heard before. It was rich and vibrant and drew him in. He wanted to hear that laugh again.

And he wanted to know the woman behind the laugh.

CHAPTER SEVEN

ARABELLA QUIETLY LAUGHED to herself. She hadn't picked up a Shakespeare comedy for a few years and *A Midsummer Night's Dream* had been the perfect solution to the storm clouds that had gathered inside her. Who needed the members of the *ton* when she could read of the jealous fairy king, Oberon, who was angry at his wife, Titania, and had sent his servant on a mission in the forest to solve the problems of the Athenian lovers wandering in the forest. Puck's antics were much more entertaining than dancing with some silly peer who was thick between the ears and would step on her already-ruined satin slippers.

She continued reading and then found herself laughing aloud as Puck exchanged poor Nick Bottom's head with one of a donkey. She hadn't remembered that and it made her wish to do the same. She would replace the mean-spirited woman's head, the one who had told her that she wasn't worth knowing, with that of a donkey. Or a goat. Definitely a goat, because they also smelled to the high heavens.

"Take that, Lady Whatever-Your-Name-Is," she said aloud.

Then suddenly, the air in the room changed subtly. Arabella glanced up and saw a man coming toward her. He had hair black as a raven's, thick and plentiful, and dark blue eyes that stood out in his handsome face. She struggled to untuck her feet from underneath her and tried to stand quickly. All she accomplished was tripping as he reached her, the heavy tome falling squarely on his right foot.

Large, warm hands clasped her elbows and easily lifted her to her feet. As Arabella looked up—and up—she realized he must be over six feet, his frame solid, his shoulders broad. His lips were sensual, a smile playing about them. He looked brash and bold. Larger than life. The kind of man who did whatever he pleased and didn't care if he hurt others in the process. She had known his type among the students at Oxford and hadn't cared for them. A man like this would know he was good-looking and expect everyone to do as he ordered simply because of who he was. Most likely, this man held an esteemed title and possessed a grand estate, both going back several generations, passed along from male to male within his family.

She didn't care. He might be handsome as sin and wealthier than Midas but he was just a man. She wouldn't fawn over him. Nor would she apologize for being in here. Unless it was his library. In that case, she would have to apologize. No, he wasn't Lord Kennedale. That was the peer hosting this ball. She had met him and his wife in the receiving line. Perhaps, though, this was Kennedale's son. She bristled, not wanting to apologize when she was the one that had been wronged by so many in the ballroom.

He ascertained that she was steady and released her, reaching for the book and handing it to her, his long, elegant fingers grasping it with ease.

"I believe you dropped this, my lady."

Oh, dear Lord. His voice was as smooth as silk, like a caress against her skin. She'd already warmed with his touch but his voice was one that could lead her to unknown places. The slashes of black that were his eyebrows arched slightly and she caught amusement in his eyes.

"I did. Thank you, my lord."

Arabella held the book tightly in front of her, glad it was a barrier between them because she felt the heat radiating from this powerful man. He was still standing far too close to her. She moved to take a step back and found she already was next to the chair she'd been sitting in. There was simply nowhere to go. With determination, she stood her ground, gazing up at him.

"I fear that look on your face is quite judgmental, my lady. Not quite one of contempt for me but perhaps a bit of defiance lurks there?" he asked.

She steeled herself. "I am not one to judge, my lord. Unlike the people in the ballroom beyond us." She hadn't meant to add those last words and regretted they'd slipped out.

A thoughtful expression crossed his face. "Polite Society is, for the most part, quite critical of others. The women, in particular. They find fault with everyone and everything." He paused. "Something tells me you aren't like them, though. That you would wait before making a rash call."

Her cheeks heated at his words. She felt chastised but refused to be apologetic.

"Might we sit a few minutes, my lady? I'd like to make a good first impression on you."

"Why ever would you want to do that?" she asked, bewildered. "You don't know me, my lord. I am no one. At one glance, I could tell you are an important member of society. I doubt you even think about the impression you make upon others because, in your world, it simply doesn't matter to you."

Surprise filled his face. "Ah, I see you have begun to judge me already. Is it my looks? My posture? Do I appear haughty? Forceful? Influential?"

"My opinion makes no difference, my lord."

"Because you are no one."

She felt the flush creep up her neck. "Yes."

But suddenly, she wished she were someone. Someone that would interest this man, if only for a little while. In a way, he was like one of those Oxford students who had dismissed her with a single glance. She needed to prove to them she was a woman of keen intelligence.

Arabella wanted to prove it to him, too. Why, she didn't know.

He looked to his right. "There. In the corner. A settee. Might you join me for a conversation that goes beyond discussing the decorations or commenting about the weather?"

When she only looked at him dumbfounded, he added, "Please?"

It was the please that got to her. She didn't think he was a man who used the word very often.

"Yes, I would happy to join you. Let me replace this volume of Shakespeare first."

Arabella went to the bookcase and slipped the volume into its proper place. She turned and found he'd followed her. He offered his arm and escorted her to the corner of the room. The light was dim. Suddenly, she stopped in her tracks and pulled her hand from his arm.

"I am not that kind of woman, my lord."

His lips twitched in amusement. "And what kind would that be, my lady?"

"The kind you think I am."

She started to go around him but he stepped in front of her. "Then what were you doing alone in the library?"

She snorted. "Well, I certainly wasn't waiting for a man. I was reading. Shakespeare."

"Shakespeare?" His lips twitched in amusement.

"Shakespeare," she repeated, the word laced equally with anger and defiance. "I find books make for better companions than the vipers out there."

He grunted, as in if agreement. "Then we should talk Shakespeare." He held out a hand, indicating the settee. "That's all we'll do. I give you my word."

Reluctantly, she took a seat. He had already disturbed her peace and quiet. She glanced at the clock on the mantel and saw the ball had only begun an hour ago. She might as well stay. If he proved himself to be a rake, she would soundly box his ears and leave.

"What amused you?" he asked. "You were laughing as I came in."

"Puck."

"Oh, *A Midsummer Night's Dream*. Robin Goodfellow. He certainly delights in pranks and separating the wandering lovers of the forest."

"You know it?" she asked, amazed he knew Puck's true name, much less anything about the play. Perhaps he had seen it on the stage and the plot had stayed with him.

He grinned. "You sound surprised, my lady."

She shrugged. "Many claim to know Shakespeare but I find them to be hopelessly ignorant of the bard's works."

"Well, I am quite familiar with them. I enjoyed reading as a boy and that joy never left. In fact, I read daily."

"Shakespeare?" she asked, doubt creeping into her voice.

"Sometimes," he admitted. "Though I prefer his other works instead of the comedies."

"The histories? Or the tragedies?"

"Both. Give me interesting, scheming people, whether in *Macbeth* or *Henry the Fourth*. The comedies seem to be dominated by the theme of love." A look of distaste crossed his face. "You know, lovers separated and overcoming obstacles in order to reunite. They always end in marriage and everyone goes on their merry way, love having saved the day."

Arabella could hear something in his voice and dared to ask, "You don't believe in love, my lord?"

"No," he said frankly. "At least, I didn't until I witnessed a few of my good friends fall in love.

They are deliriously happy with their spouses." He gazed intently at her. "What of you, my lady? Do you believe in love?"

The question startled her. "I . . . I am not sure. No one has asked that of me before. I would have to say that it is certainly possible but not very common."

"Were your parents in love?"

"No. No, they weren't," she replied. "Papa was kind to Mama and respectful but they had very little in common and spent practically no time together. Mama married him because she longed to have a title. Her father was a doctor, you see, and she had aspirations of coming up in the world."

An inscrutable look crossed his face. "Did she enjoy being a titled lady?"

"She was a countess for less than two months and then passed away." Arabella's throat grew tight.

Suddenly, he took her hand and it seemed like balm which calmed her. "I am sorry to hear of your loss." Those blue eyes penetrated her, seeing into her soul. "It seems a recent one."

"It was but I wasn't very close to her. I helped Papa with his work."

"An earl worked?" he asked, a puzzled look crossing his face.

"Papa was a fourth son. He wasn't ever meant for the title. He is now the Earl of

Barrington."

The stranger nodded. "Yes, I remember Barrington passing. Around the Christmas before last, I believe."

"Yes. My two uncles, Papa's other brothers, also passed away near the same time, leaving him as the new earl." She frowned. "And now I'm making my come-out because it's something Mama wanted for me."

His hand tightened imperceptibly on hers. Butterflies began beating inside her, a warm fluttery feeling unknown to her.

"You didn't want to make your debut into society?"

Arabella bit her lip. "Not really. The *ton* had no interest in Papa. His three brothers had no need of him. They were strangers to one another for decades. We only came to London to fulfill Mama's wish to see me make my come-out." Tears filled her eyes. "And that has been a complete disaster."

"Why do you say that?" he asked, his voice low and tender, causing her throat to swell further.

She pulled her hand from his. "You don't need to pity me, my lord." She took a deep breath and exhaled. "I had no idea of the rules of society before tonight. Papa must not have, either. I know he never went to social events."

He took her hand again and held to it more

tightly when she tried to pull away. "Tell me."

She swallowed. "I needed to have someone to introduce me to others, for one thing. I tried to go up to various groups tonight and meet people."

He winced and she saw how wrong that had been.

"No one would have anything to do with me. Except for one woman. She told me if I didn't know anyone, then I wasn't worth knowing."

A tear cascaded down her cheek. He wiped it away with his thumb and took her chin in hand.

"I am sorry you were abused by those vile women. Yes, it's true that introductions must be made by others and that is how various connections come about."

"I do know some people who are present tonight but they are men."

His brows rose. "How?"

"They are my father's former pupils. Papa was a don at Oxford and I recognized some in the ballroom. Having made the mistake of trying to approach different women, though, I didn't want to blunder further by going up and speaking to a man." She sighed. "They probably wouldn't have spoken to me if I had."

Arabella looked down, feeling miserable. He raised her chin until their gazes met.

"You are someone, my lady. An interesting, kind someone. Don't let others make you feel inferior. We shall return to the ballroom and I will make sure you meet others, especially my friends. They are kind and will welcome you."

His words startled her and she pulled away from him. "You don't have to do that, my lord. Why, from what I can ascertain, your actions might damage your own reputation."

He chuckled. "I'm afraid both our reputations would be ruined if anyone came through those doors and found us here alone together. That is why I wished to sit in this darkened corner so we wouldn't easily be seen if someone entered."

"Why?" she asked, perplexed by his statement.

"A young woman making her come-out should never be alone with a man. If she is, she is compromised and he should do the gentlemanly thing and ask for her hand in marriage."

Arabella shot to her feet. "You mean if anyone walked in on us, you would have to marry me?"

"I wouldn't have to—but I would."

Her face flamed. "That is out of the question!"

He rose and gave her a rueful smile. "Am I so terribly ugly and dull that you wouldn't wish to wed me?"

"No. It isn't that at all. But to force us into matrimony simply because we had a brief conversation is absurd."

He shrugged. "Polite Society does have some unusual rules."

"Then you must leave at once," she told him. "I will give you time to get away and then I, too, will leave. I should never have come in her alone. I understand that now and I thank you for cluing me in to the error of my ways."

"Where will you go?"

She frowned. "I suppose back to the ball-room. Papa is playing cards and will do so until we leave. I'll simply find a seat and officially become the first wallflower of the Season. I'll explain to Papa that I cannot return since I have no acquaintances. He'll understand. He knows I dreaded coming tonight anyway." She gestured to her gown. "My dress is all wrong. I look ghastly compared to the other beauties sporting their finery. My heart wasn't in it, anyway. Perhaps Papa will let us return to the country."

"What would you do there?" he asked.

"Why, help run the estate. That's what I have been doing ever since Papa became Barrington," she proclaimed. "I find it much more productive and interesting to help our tenants and make the estate profitable than wiling away my time being snubbed by people I don't know and probably will never know—much less like."

His face grew thoughtful. "I see. Well, you should at least meet a few people since it is your first ball."

"And my last."

"Once you return to the ballroom, I will come to you and take you around. We can even dance. If others see you dancing with me, they'll want to dance with you, too. If it's the only ball you ever attend, you might as well dance a few numbers." He hesitated. "You do dance, don't you?"

Arabella laughed aloud at the concerned look on his face. "I did at the assembly rooms in Oxford. Quite often. They didn't dance the waltz there, though, so I won't be able to partake in that particular dance."

He smiled at her. "I can teach you the waltz. There's nothing to it. You merely follow your partner's lead." He cocked his head. "What do you say, my lady? Will you let me present you to some of society tonight?"

CHAPTER EIGHT

J ON WATCHED THE woman's face carefully to see how she responded to his question. She had no guile and made no move to hide her emotions. Or her opinions. He'd never met a female who was so outspoken. It was something that delighted him. The few minutes he'd spent in her company had been more interesting and entertaining than any ball he had ever attended. He didn't know what would come out of her mouth.

Oh, that mouth. Lush, pink lips that begged to be kissed. He would do it, too, if not for the feeling that she would slap him if he attempted to do so. She was rash—despite what she'd said earlier. Bold. Intelligent. And his heart went out to her. The *ton*, vicious and quick to judge others—especially outsiders—had already ostracized her for her manner of dress and the fact she'd had no chaperone who'd taken her about and seen that she was properly introduced. Her father should have known better but she'd said he was a fourth son. A man that far from the title would have had to make his own way in the world. The army was meant for second sons. The Church for third ones. Any sons beyond that had a rough go of things.

She had mentioned Oxford and her father being a don. Jon decided to seek out the Earl of Barrington and come to his own conclusions about the man. He certainly hadn't seen that his daughter curbed her tongue.

The sudden thought of his tongue entangling with hers had his blood heating. Jon was physically attracted to her but it was much more. He wanted their conversation to go on and on. He wanted her opinions and ideas. To hear what her life had been like before she became the daughter of an earl. He especially wanted to hear about why she ran an estate. That was a man's job. Something told him, though, that this pert young woman would take on the world without a second thought. She brimmed with confidence. Yet he saw how she'd been hurt by those guests present tonight. All he could say was they were fools. She was a diamond of the first water. They had all been idiots not to recognize her value.

He had—and found his duchess.

He awaited her reply and finally received it. As he'd known, various emotions flitted across her face. Uncertainty. Defiance. Acceptance.

"I suppose it would be wise to try and meet a few others," she said. "If only to share a few names with Papa. I will tell him I didn't care for any of them. He knows I am more like he is than my mother. Mama lived for the day to take her place in society."

"While you would rather retreat to the country."

She shrugged. "Can I help it if I find livestock and crops more interesting than a ballroom of emptyheaded men and women?"

"Now, you are not being fair," he chided gently. "I am not emptyheaded at all. Far from it."

"You are most certainly the exception, my lord," she said graciously.

"My friends and their wives are also rather clever. And kind, I might add. So is my sister, Elizabeth. I certainly want you to meet her."

"You've a sister?" she asked.

"Yes, one who made her come-out last year."

The woman grew thoughtful. "Did she wed?"

"No." He chuckled. "She is looking for that elusive thing. Love."

"Ah," she said knowingly, her head nodding as a smile played about her lips. "Then I hope she will find it. It would be nice if one person in your family did."

"Have you brothers or sisters?" he asked.

"No. It is only Papa and me. I was his shadow growing up. I was never interested in clothing or hair or domestic duties. I preferred to spend time with Papa and his pupils."

"You mentioned knowing some of them."

"Yes, I was a frequent visitor to his lectures, sitting in the back and taking it all in."

"A woman in the lecture hall?" He was astounded, knowing what a stir that would have caused at Cambridge.

She grinned. "I even wrote some of his lectures for him as I grew older."

Jon was now utterly fascinated by her. "You don't say."

"Other dons had research assistants. I served as Papa's. And I also ate dinner regularly with him and his pupils at their college. We had all manner of discussions."

He could see young men totally captivated by the blond beauty.

"So you are well educated."

She nodded. "Extremely so. I've read extensively. The discussions with Papa's students over the years helped me see events from many different points of view." She sighed. "I only wish I could have gone to university. I would have become a don as Papa did if I'd been born male."

"I didn't know they could wed. None of mine at Cambridge were allowed to do so."

She mulled over his words. "I certainly never

knew any other dons who had a wife. Funny, it never occurred to me until you mentioned it. I suppose it did make Papa unique. He has a brilliant mind, however. Perhaps he convinced the head of his college to allow him to do so. I suppose I can ask him about it."

"Perhaps we can do so over supper," he suggested. "We could partner for the supper dance and then dine together. I am eager to meet your father."

"Why?" she asked, puzzled by his statement.

"Because you've piqued my interest more than any woman of my acquaintance. I want to meet the man who raised such a remarkable daughter."

She blushed to her roots. He saw she was trying to maintain her composure and decided he should offer to leave.

"Let me depart now. I will find you in the ballroom and help present you to a select few. Hopefully, your opinion of society might change if you meet the right people."

She chuckled. "I doubt it but you have been most gracious to me, my lord. I will gladly meet a few of your friends."

"And dance with me? Sup with me?"

Her blush deepened and he saw she wasn't unaffected by him. It pleased him.

"I will."

Jon reached for the programme tied about

her wrist and wrote his name beside the supper dance. It upset him to see the card entirely blank. Society didn't know what they were missing. Their rejection of this woman had turned into something wonderful for him, though.

The chance to meet his future duchess.

"There. I will see you inside." Reluctantly, he moved away from her and toward the door.

"My lord?" she called.

He halted and turned. "Yes?"

"If you're going to introduce me around, might it be a good idea to actually *know* my name?"

Jon roared with laughter. "I am sorry, my lady. You are certainly correct on that matter." He went back to her and lifted her gloved hand. Kissing her fingers, he asked, "And you are?"

He sensed the shiver that ran through her. "Arabella Jennings. Lady Arabella Jennings."

Oh, he liked the name. It suited her.

"It is an honor to meet you, Lady Arabella." He continued to hold her hand, gazing into her sky-blue eyes.

"And?" she asked.

"And what?" he replied, not breaking the gaze.

"You are?" she prompted.

He grinned. "I am Blackmore." He released her hand.

"Blackmore," she repeatedly thoughtfully.

"Are you an earl like Papa?"

"No." He continued staring at her, wishing to unpin her golden hair and run his fingers through its waves.

"A viscount, perhaps?"

"No." She had the smoothest complexion, milky white. He imagined the skin under her dowdy gown. His hands caressing it.

"Then what *are* you? Surely, you have a title since you are here tonight." She paused. "Unless I have been conversing with the haughtiest valet I've ever met."

"I am haughty?"

"I believe you pointed that out when we first met," she swiftly replied.

"How many valets have you met?"

"None up to this point. That may change, however, if I find you are a valet."

Jon liked her more and more. She was quick-witted and had a keen sense of humor. Life would never be dull with this duchess.

"I am not a valet. Not a baron. Not a marquess. I am . . . a duke."

Arabella began laughing, that low laugh that sent tingles racing down his spine.

"Why not tell me you're the Prince of Wales? I would sooner believe that."

"I am a duke, my lady. I assure you I will never lie to you."

"Pish-posh," she said dismissively. "I don't

know who I've been speaking to but I can tell you this. No duke would have spent a tenth of the time with me that you have. Dukes, with their lofty positions, do not deign to speak to their inferiors. I fear you are having fun at my expense, my lord." Her cheeks now spotted with anger. "I doubt you have a title at all. You are most likely a second son, full of pride and arrogance. You have beautiful posture, you know, and I am sure that was drilled into you in the army. Though I cannot understand why you would be in a London ballroom versus where you ought to be—out on the field, kicking Bonaparte's scrawny arse all the way back to prison."

Arabella huffed. "I would say it has been a pleasure but you ruined it for me with your little game, Sir. Goodnight."

She strode across the room and flung the library door open, sailing through it, her head held high.

"Oh, you impertinent female," he said to himself. "You have everything I want, Arabella Jennings."

The pursuit would be infinitely challenging. She would not make it easy on him. Especially when she learned he truly was a duke. He'd been wrong. He had found his future wife at a London ball. Just not in the ballroom.

And now he was ready to go get her.

ARABELLA HURRIED FROM the library, angry at having been taken in by the man. Damn him and his good looks!

She paused in the corridor and tried to even her breathing. His audacity was unparalleled. Some of her father's students had been incredibly arrogant but none of them matched Blackmore. Or whatever his true name was. To think she might believe him a duke.

"Hah!" she said aloud.

He had been right, though, about them being caught alone together. She had always been with her father whenever she encountered one of his pupils. He'd either been in the classroom as one or two might approach her and ask a question. Or Papa had been present at supper and would have gladly stepped in if something untoward had been said or done in her presence. Arabella didn't know the rules—written or unwritten—as far as Polite Society went, but what Blackmore said about them being found alone and being forced to wed rang with truth. Everyone had been so stilted in their behavior in the ballroom, not even wanting to speak to her since they'd had no formal introduction.

How much worse would it be to be caught alone with a man?

He had said they would have to wed. Or no, he'd said the honorable thing to do would be for the man to extend a proposal. Blackmore, for all his smooth ways and killer looks, most certainly would not have done the gentlemanly thing and asked Papa for her hand in marriage, despite what he'd told her. Not that she would wish to be encumbered for life with a man of his ilk. True, he was most pleasant to look upon. He spoke with confidence and was learned. But why was a man such as that in a library in the middle of a ball? Most likely, he had been scouting for a place to have a tryst with some willing female. His type would be bored with social conventions and seek out adventure, the more risqué, the better.

She wondered what it would be like to kiss him—and gasped.

Where had that thought come from? She had never kissed anyone before. Never had the inclination, much less the opportunity. Though she had been exposed to many men over the years, thanks to her father's occupation and the fact she was always near him, she had never once felt an urge to kiss a man.

Until now.

Suddenly, it occurred to Arabella that Blackmore, a rake if ever there was one, hadn't taken advantage of her. Hadn't kissed her. Hadn't even made a move that would lead to a kiss. It caused her face to burn even hotter than before.

He hadn't because he wasn't attracted to her. She glanced down and saw what she now knew was a dowdy gown. She wanted to strangle the village seamstress who had made up the dresses for her. Yet she couldn't blame the woman. Barrington lands in Wiltshire were far away from fashionable London. How was a seamstress in her late fifties to know what the fashionable styles were in one of the most cosmopolitan cities in the world?

Still, weren't rakes supposed to compromise women, even if they were unattractive and dressed drably? She had overheard enough gossip at the college supper table to know about rakes and what they did. To think Blackmore found her so homely and unappealing that he didn't even attempt to make a move on her made Arabella feel more insecure than she ever had been—and that included those horrible minutes in the ballroom before she'd retreated to the library.

She pushed away from the wall she was leaning on and headed down the corridor at a brisk pace, not wanting to encounter the scoundrel again. But where could she hide?

The retiring room.

She didn't know how large it would be or if she could settle in there for any length of time. At least it would give her a place to go for now. If she had to double back and retreat to the library again later, she would, for she doubted Blackmore would go there twice in the same evening.

Arabella stopped a footman and he directed her to her destination. She entered, finding it probably served as a parlor when a large social event was not in progress. The room was filled with women, their conversation buzzing as bees around a hive.

Then it stopped.

All eyes turned to her and she felt her face burn with the unwanted attention. Quickly, she retreated to the far side of the room and scurried in to where a chamber pot sat. Drawing the curtain around her for privacy, she slowly exhaled, tears stinging her eyes.

Everyone knew who she was. She wouldn't even have a chance to be a wallflower. Instead, Arabella Jennings had been marked as a social pariah on the first night of the Season. Her mother would have been so ashamed. Arabella wouldn't cry, though. She blinked back the tears. She would not allow the lot of them to see her in defeat or let them know how deeply she'd been wounded by their dismissal of her. She didn't care for the *ton* or its customs. They had written off her father years ago and now did the same to her. It didn't matter. She had tried. That was what was important. She would tell Papa London held no appeal for her and ask that they return to the country at once.

She counted to one hundred. Then five hundred. Then a thousand. She made use of the chamber pot and then calmly exited from behind the curtain, certain that most of the women who'd been their earlier had now gone. The room was definitely emptier than when she'd arrived. Before, ladies primped at a large mirror and gossiped in clumps. Only a handful of women remained. She supposed that supper and the supper dance would be coming up soon and that was why they had vacated the room.

Arabella went to wash her hands and thanked the servant who handed her a towel. By the look on the young girl's face, she didn't receive many thank yous. Who were these people that they couldn't even treat someone with common decency?

"Oh, blast!" said the woman next to her.

She turned and saw the woman digging through her reticule. She looked at Arabella and said, "I know my lady's maid put extra pins in here but for the life of me, I cannot find them."

Arabella saw several strands of hair had come lose from the elaborate raven coiffure and said, "I have extra pins. My hair is thick and often needs more pins in it, especially once I've left the house."

The woman's face lit up with a smile that reached her dark blue eyes. Arabella couldn't believe someone was responding to her nicely instead of acting as if she were invisible.

"Oh, you are an angel for letting me borrow them," the woman said as Arabella reached inside her own reticule and withdrew several.

"May I help you?" she asked, handing them over.

"No, I can do so. I prefer doing it myself rather than asking others to do so for me."

Quickly, the raven-haired beauty lifted the stray curls into place and repaired the damage, smoothly sliding the pins into her abundant hair. She smoothed it. "There, I think that's done the trick."

"I am glad to be of help," Arabella replied, wondering why this elegant beauty hadn't heard the gossip and shunned her instead of conversing with her.

"We haven't met," the woman said. "I can't believe I've accepted help from a stranger and neglected my manners."

"I could have introduced myself. I will now. I am Lady Arabella Jennings," she said, waiting for the reaction that would have the woman snub her.

Instead, the woman smiled. "Oh, what a lovely name. I am Lady Elizabeth Sutton and terribly happy to have made your acquaintance."

Then the young woman slipped her hand through Arabella's arm. "I am so glad we met. Are you going back to the ballroom? We can accompany one another."

Lady Elizabeth tugged her along. Somehow, Arabella's feet moved but she remained in a daze as they made their way to the ballroom, still astounded that someone had acknowledged her.

"You must come to tea tomorrow," Lady Elizabeth continued. "It will be my way of thanking you for coming to my aid."

"Tea?" she croaked, thinking although she had a few new gowns she actually possessed nothing to wear that would be acceptable in a London drawing room.

By now, they had reached the ballroom and entered it. Couples moved about the dance floor, dresses swirling as the musicians played a lively tune.

"Where is he? I would like you to meet my brother." Lady Elizabeth scanned the room. "Perhaps he's on the far side of the room. Come along, Lady Arabella."

She didn't have a choice. The insistent young woman pulled her along. As they passed the few not on the dance floor, Arabella saw looks of astonishment on each face.

"Oh, there's Lord Atterby. We're to dance the supper dance together. It's almost time for that now."

They reached the peer, who was of average height and had brown hair and brown eyes. Nothing distinguished him from any other male in the ballroom. Or perhaps it was because

Arabella still had Blackmore on her mind. No man could compare to the rake's dark looks, with chiseled cheekbones that looked as if they could cut glass and dark blue eyes that danced with mischief.

"Good evening, Lord Atterby," her companion said. "Have you met Lady Arabella Jennings?"

"I have not." He took her hand and bowed over it. "Atterby, at your service, my lady."

She supposed the gossip regarding her hadn't reached this lord's ears. "It is a pleasure to make your acquaintance, my lord."

"Oh, here's Jon," Lady Elizabeth said, a pleased look settling across her face.

Arabella looked up as a man joined them. She felt the blood drain from her face.

It was Blackmore.

CHAPTER NINE

HE WAS MORE handsome than she'd remembered from their earlier encounter. This time, she took in the immaculate black evening clothes and snow-white cravat tied to perfection. The tall, powerful frame that hinted at the strength within him. The thick, midnight black hair and dark blue eyes. Arabella felt herself go lightheaded and panicked. She'd never fainted in her life and she wasn't about to start now. She had already drawn enough attention to herself this evening. She refused to attract more.

"Lady Arabella Jennings, I'd like to introduce you to my brother, the Duke of Blackmore."

No no no no! He *was* a duke. A bloody duke. A rake of a bloody duke.

"Lady Arabella," he said, sweeping her hand to his lips and pressing a kiss against her gloved fingers. "I am delighted to meet you."

She grew dizzy at his touch. Heat filled her

and she sensed her cheeks heating.

"Lady Arabella helped me with my unruly hair, Jon. You know how pins always seem to go missing from it, especially if the dancing is energetic. She provided me with additional ones."

He chuckled and the deep sound caused a chill to run through her. "Thank you, my lady, for helping my sister tame her hair. While I think it is one of her best features, her hair does seem to have a mind of its own at times." He smiled, his even, white teeth only drawing attention to his perfect lips.

Lips that she wanted to touch. To kiss. Lips she needed to feel against hers.

"I've asked Lady Arabella to tea tomorrow to thank her for helping me," Lady Elizabeth told her brother.

She protested, "Lady Elizabeth, you mustn't think—"

"No, I insist," her new friend said, cutting Arabella off. "Are you wed? Your husband is most welcome to escort you."

She shook her head. "No, I am not married. I live with my father, the Earl of Barrington."

"Barrington?" the man she now knew as a duke asked. "I knew Barrington before he passed away. Last year, wasn't it? And you are the daughter of the new earl?"

Oh, he was being clever. She'd already told him this—but he was pretending this was their first meeting. A part of her wanted to throttle him. Another part found it quite sweet that he refrained from embarrassing her by noting their prior encounter.

Her head held high, she said, "I am, Your Grace. Papa was an Oxford don before he came into the title."

"Is this your first time in London? At the Season?" the duke asked nonchalantly.

"It is, Your Grace. We've only recently come from our country estate in Wiltshire."

"Oh, that's marvelous," he said. "Elizabeth, perhaps you and Lady Arabella can strike up a friendship since she is new to town."

"Oh, no," she objected. "That wouldn't be appropriate."

"Why not?" Lady Elizabeth asked. "I would love to become friends with you, Lady Arabella. I could also introduce you to a couple of new friends to me. Lady Ruthersby and the Duchess of Colebourne."

Blackmore laughed. "Ah, yes. The three of them have become as thick as thieves. They're trying to marry off the Duke of Treadwell, the duchess' brother."

Couples began moving toward the dance floor and Lord Atterby finally spoke. "Lady Elizabeth, are you ready for our dance?"

"Yes, my lord. Lead the way," she said airily. As the couple moved away, Lady Elizabeth turned over her shoulder and said, "We'll talk about tea tomorrow."

Arabella smiled weakly as the pair departed. She'd been left with the Duke of Blackmore, the last person she wanted to be around at this moment. She kept her eyes on the dance floor, afraid to meet his gaze, which she sensed lingered over her.

"Lady Arabella, would you care to dance the supper dance with me?" he asked.

She finally faced him. "You shouldn't be seen with me, much less offer to partner with me, Your Grace."

"Why not?"

"You know why," she hissed as the musicians began to play.

His eyes gleamed. "You know my sister and Lord Atterby. Now, you know me. Come, the music has started. Dance with me, Arabella."

His gaze pinned hers and she felt her resistance begin to crumble.

"But . . . it's a waltz," she said.

"I know. And if you remember, I told you that I am the perfect teacher."

Without waiting for her to reply, he led her onto the floor and took her in his arms. Her heart began beating at twice its normal rate. Her mouth grew dry.

"Follow my lead. You'll catch on. I know you will."

With that, he swept her away.

Arabella stumbled a few times early into the dance but she caught on quickly, feeling the rhythm as Blackmore swept her around the dance floor. Her confidence grew as the colors of the room blended into a blur behind him and they continued to move gracefully, as if some unspoken language occurred between them. She had never felt a man's arms about her in such a manner and despite feeling free and alive for the first time in her life, it was causing havoc with her insides. They fluttered madly, as if a parade of butterflies batted their wings throughout her. The blood pounded in her ears, almost drowning out the music itself. She began to focus on Blackmore's face, a mixture of encouragement and arrogance, as if he'd known all along he could take her under his wing and make her feel like she was floating through the air.

The music ended and the last note hung in the air. His arms lingered about her and then released her. Suddenly, Arabella felt bereft, as if she'd experienced some great loss. She shook her head, trying to rein in these wild emotions raging within her. Glancing about, she saw curious looks in her direction as her partner took her hand and placed it upon his arm.

Bending until his lips grazed her earlobe, causing a sensation of electricity to ripple through her, he said quietly, "Would you do me the honor of allowing me to escort you to supper?"

His lips lingered, his breath warm against her skin. Then he pulled away.

"Yes," she said breathlessly and then with more control, "Yes, Your Grace. That would be quite agreeable."

Chuckling, he tucked her hand through the crook of his arm and they began to follow the mass exodus from the ballroom toward supper.

"You picked up the steps quickly," he praised. "Once you've danced the waltz another time or two, you will be more than proficient. You will be perfect."

"It felt like soaring," she admitted, sounding girlish. She reminded herself not to act the fool around him and added, "You were an excellent partner."

"You have a natural grace about you, Lady Arabella."

She frowned. "Do not lay compliments on too thickly," she admonished. "I was merely adequate."

"More than adequate," he corrected. "I'll broker no argument from you."

They reached the hall where a buffet supper had been laid out. She saw tables laden with so much food, the feast might feed all of London.

"I would ask if you wish to sit with my sister and Atterby but I'm sure you would say yes." He glanced around. "I would introduce you to my friends, Treadwell and Colebourne, but I see they are already sitting with the Ruthersbys and have no room at their table."

"You don't wish to sit with your sister?"

"I wish to sit with you." His direct gaze caused her to warm. "Ah, I see a table for us."

He led them to a small table in the corner, one meant for only two. She halted as they approached it.

"No, that isn't appropriate. It might give people the wrong impression."

"What? That I have found a delightful companion who not only dances well but one I wish to spend time in deep conversation?"

He moved her toward it and seated her before taking a seat himself.

"You deliberately misinterpret my words, Your Grace."

"And you deliberately ignore mine." He paused. "I thought I indicated to you earlier in the library that I find you fascinating, my lady. I wish to extend our earlier conversation."

"But . . . you're a duke," she hissed.

He looked taken aback. "Do I carry some rare disease that you fear I will spread to you?"

"I have told you that I have already been ostracized by the *ton*. You won't be helping your reputation by sitting with me."

Blackmore laughed heartily. "Oh, you should be the one fearing your reputation being stained,

Lady Arabella. I am known as quite the rake and so overbearing that my nickname in the newspapers is the Duke of Arrogance."

She could understand that. He had more than confidence about him. It was in his posture, a conceit and hubris that declared to others he was better than they were and would be the first to tell them so.

"I suppose all dukes are arrogant," she quipped. "It must be in the breeding. Ducal lines are blue-blooded ones. You are far superior to most everyone sitting in this room."

"I am glad you recognize my superiority. That goes in my judgment, as well, my lady. I tell you—I want to be with you during this supper, Arabella Jennings." He rose. "I'm off to fill two plates for us. Do you have anything in particular you might wish to consume?"

Arabella gave him a wry smile. "Considering I have never supped at midnight, much less from such a sumptuous buffet, I will allow your superior judgment to select items you feel to be remarkable and will dine upon whatever you bring back."

A slow, seductive smile spread across his handsome face. "I like it when you fight back. Verbal sparring with a clever companion will make this supper pass far too quickly."

With that, he bowed and left her alone for a few minutes. Arabella gazed about the room, seeing surreptitious glances in her direction. She knew the *ton* must wonder why the Duke of Blackmore was favoring her with such attention. She supposed they would think her naïve and his latest conquest but she didn't care. The fact was that it was exhilarating to be in his company. To have a man of his looks, title, and charm pay a small bit of attention to her was wonderful. If this were to be the only ball she ever attended, at least it was becoming a memorable one.

He joined her again, the plates he brought overflowing.

"I'll never eat all of that," she said, laughing.

He grinned. "I didn't think you would. I have a large appetite and box frequently in order to be able to eat all that I want. What you leave on your plate, I am hoping you will graciously allow me to finish for you."

Arabella swallowed, thinking of him boxing. Her father had once taken her to a boxing match because one of his favorite students was a sparring partner of the boxer featured on the bill. She had been wide-eyed seeing men stripped to the waist as they viciously duked it out.

"You box?"

"Yes. Are you familiar with the sport?"

"I have been to one bout."

"Have you?" He eyed her with interest. "Women aren't allowed."

"I know. Papa took me. He thought it would

be educational," she said primly.

Blackmore laughed loudly, drawing eyes to them. "I still want to meet the earl. Is he at supper?"

"I looked about the room and didn't see him."

"If he enjoys cards, the host usually has sandwiches brought to the card room in case players would rather remain at the tables there."

"I am sure he's still there. He does enjoy cards."

"Ladies aren't allowed in the card room." His brows arched suggestively. "Would you like to go there and seek him out after we sup?"

Arabella had a feeling he wanted her to say no, thinking her too meek to rise to his challenge. She wanted to surprise him. Put him in his place. Knock him down a few pegs.

"Yes. I'd be delighted to accompany you to the card room, Your Grace," she said sweetly.

CHAPTER TEN

J ON LIKED LADY Arabella more and more. However, he didn't want to see her gossiped about any more than she already had been this evening. A trip to the card room, where women never ventured, would not only be unwelcomed but set the tongues of the *ton* wagging even more than they had. He couldn't see her ruined over something so trivial.

Seeing that couples were beginning to leave the supper room, he said, "Before we do so, I would like to introduce you to my friends. I don't hold many close but they are as dear to me as brothers."

He caught George's eye and indicated for him to join them. George leaned over and said something to Weston and the two men, accompanied by Samantha and Elise, headed in their direction.

As they arrived, Elizabeth and Lord Atterby

came over, as well. Jon helped Lady Arabella rise.

"I'd be honored for you to meet my friends," he said. "Lady Arabella Jennings, this is the Duke and Duchess of Colebourne." He indicated George and Samantha. "Her Grace's brother, the Duke of Treadwell. And Lady Ruthersby."

Jon liked that Arabella maintained her poise as she greeted not one but two dukes.

He added, "Lady Arabella is the daughter of the Earl of Barrington. This is her first Season."

Weston said, "I met your father in the card room tonight, my lady. Barrington is an astute player."

She smiled. "He would be happy to hear the compliment, Your Grace."

"I have not been in London for many Seasons myself," Lady Ruthersby shared. "I am a widow."

"I am a widow as well as a new bride," Samantha said. "I find I know very few people. I am sure since this is your first Season, tonight must seem overwhelming with so many new people to meet."

Jon noted Arabella's wry smile but she politely responded, "It has been a most interesting evening."

"Well, Lady Arabella saved my evening," Elizabeth proclaimed. "My hair went awry from all the dancing. Who knows where the missing pins wound up? Lady Arabella graciously loaned me some of hers. I have asked her to tea tomorrow to show my gratitude. You all should come, as well."

Jon knew Weston had Elise Blakeney on his mind and quickly said, "I believe Treadwell and Lady Ruthersby already have a prior commitment tomorrow afternoon but surely the Colebournes can join us. You, too, Atterby," he added, hoping Elizabeth liked the young man enough to include him in the invitation.

"We would be delighted to come," Samantha replied.

The women, including Atterby, began talking about tonight's buffet, allowing Jon to turn to his friends.

"What do you think of her?" he asked quietly.

"What do we think of her?" Weston echoed. "Are you saying what I think you are?"

"Yes." Jon glanced to Arabella and back. "I am interested in her."

"I didn't know you were interested in any woman—other than bedding them," George quipped.

Anger flashed through him. "I need a wife. You and Andrew have seemed to make fine matches for yourselves and if Weston will get his head out of his arse, he will do the same with Lady Ruthersby. Why not wed? I'll be thirty this year. I will need an heir."

"The point isn't if we like her. It's if you do— and obviously you do," Weston said.

"I do," he admitted. "Very much."

"Well, she's a comely woman. Curves in all the right places," George noted. "I can see why you're attracted to her."

"It's more than that," Jon insisted. "I had the most interesting conversation with her in the library."

"What were you doing in the library?" Weston demanded. "Alone with her?"

He shrugged. "I was bored. I found her with her nose buried in a tome of Shakespeare. The *ton* did not take well to a woman whose dressed was so unadorned and who had no chaperone to introduce her about. The women were rather cruel to her."

Both his friends nodded, knowing how vicious Polite Society could be.

"We talked. I mean, we really talked. It wasn't meaningless conversation. She is spirited. Intelligent. I am drawn to her mind as much as her body," he admitted.

George laughed. "I never thought I'd hear that from the Duke of Arrogance."

"Oh, hush, Charm," Jon teased, calling George by society's nickname for him.

"No, I am pleased for you," George said. "I am deliriously happy with Samantha, as I know Andrew is with Phoebe." He looked to Weston. "And I have the same hopes for you and Elise."

"I'm getting there," Weston said and grinned.

"Don't think you will beat me to the altar, Jon."

"I doubt it. But I did want your opinion of Lady Arabella."

"If you like her, we also will," George assured him.

"Enough to dance with her?" Jon asked. "She's only danced once and that was with me. Being seen dancing with two other dukes might take the sting out of the evening and help others to notice her. I know you said you and Samantha were leaving after supper, though."

"I'll be happy to dance with Lady Arabella before we go. And we will be at tea tomorrow," George assured him.

"You take the next dance and I'll partner with her for the one that follows," Weston said.

"Thank you both. While she is in good hands, I think I will go and meet her father."

He turned and saw most everyone had left the supper room and suggested, "We should return to the ballroom."

George whispered something to his wife. She nodded and he said, "I would love a dance with you, Lady Arabella. Are you free for this next number?"

As the group moved back toward the ballroom, Jon peeled away and retreated to the card room, where he'd briefly visited earlier. It was about half-full but he knew more would return now that supper had ended. He spoke to an acquaintance and mentioned the Earl of Barrington.

"He took me for a pretty penny earlier this evening," the viscount said.

"Which table is he sitting at?"

"There. Talking to Welles."

"Perhaps I can win a hand from him," Jon said and headed in that direction, seeing the large stacks of chips in front of the man.

The seat next to the earl was empty so he took it. Lord Welles and Barrington conversed for another minute and then Welles excused himself, giving the Jon the opportunity to speak.

"Lord Barrington?"

"Yes?" the earl said, turning to face Jon.

"I am the Duke of Blackmore. I've heard you have had a run of luck this evening, my lord."

Barrington laughed. "I haven't played cards since my university days. My father didn't see the need to pay for the education of a fourth son, which led to me applying and winning a scholarship to Oxford. A young man has to eat, though, and so I supplemented my meager income with winnings from card games. I am a cautious player but when Lady Luck smiles upon me, I take her in hand and conquer my opponents. Fortunately, she has been with me tonight. I know to fold, though, whenever she deserts me for another."

No wonder Arabella had such a poor view of

society. Her own father had to scrape by to become educated and had been ostracized by his own family.

"I hear you recently came into your title," Jon said, prodding the man a bit so he could learn more about him—and his daughter.

"I did. I stayed at Oxford for years, serving as a don. My three older brothers all died within a month of one another, making me a surprise earl."

"I believe I danced with your daughter earlier this evening."

"Oh, Arabella does enjoy dancing. I am glad to hear she is having a good time. I myself never attended any social events, going straight from the classroom as a pupil to an instructor."

So it was true that the man hadn't deliberately abandoned his daughter. He simply lacked knowledge of the social graces and blithely thought all would be well tonight because he had a clever, beautiful daughter who was used to taking care of herself.

"How have you found your country estate? Where is it?"

"In Wiltshire. A little over twenty miles from Salisbury. Frankly, it was in deplorable shape," he confided. "My eldest brother rarely visited his seat. Arabella had to take it in hand and get it up and running again."

"She did?"

"Yes. Unfortunately, I was at sixes and sevens. I resigned from my college in order to take up the responsibilities of the earldom but grieved for the life I had made for myself and had to abandon. Then my wife passed after a sudden illness and I was no good to anyone. Arabella took care of everything. By the time I roused myself from my melancholy, six months had passed. My daughter already knew the names of all our tenants and their family members. She had seen to repairs on the estate and within Barrington Manor. She'd researched crop rotation and had a plethora of knowledge regarding livestock. If not for her, I am afraid the estate would have not only fallen into disrepair, but it no longer would have generated any income at all."

Jon liked what he heard. If Arabella could take over the responsibilities of an earldom and meet with success, becoming his duchess would be like a walk in the park.

"Your daughter did a kindness to my sister tonight and Elizabeth has asked Lady Arabella to tea tomorrow. I came to invite you, as well, so that you would escort her."

"Oh, I'm to come, as well?" the earl asked. "I suppose I should though I'm not used to escorting Arabella about at her age. Life for a middle class woman living a quiet life in Oxford is far different from the glittering ballrooms of London."

"Yes, it is," Jon agreed. "Your daughter will need an escort to whatever social events she attends. Will that be many?"

The earl shrugged. "I've received a handful of invitations. I really don't know many who inhabit this stratosphere, other than having tutored some of them over the years. They've been welcoming. I suppose Arabella and I might be invited to a few of their gatherings."

"I hope more are to come," he said. "And Lord Barrington? I would like your permission to court your daughter."

"Oh!" The earl appeared flustered. "Well, I suppose if it is all right with Arabella, it should be with me." He paused and then said, "Be kind to her, Your Grace."

He wondered if Barrington had heard of his Duke of Arrogance moniker and decided it was merely a father cautioning a suitor to do right by his daughter.

"I will, my lord." He offered his hand. "It has been a pleasure to meet you. I look forward to seeing you at tea tomorrow afternoon."

He provided the earl with his address and excused himself. Returning to the ballroom, he scanned the room for Arabella. She was with Elizabeth—and surrounded by a bevy of men. Jealousy soared within him and he strode toward the group. Someone touched his arm and he stopped. It was Weston.

"It seems a metamorphosis has taken place in your absence. Lady Arabella has suddenly emerged from her cocoon and is considered a brilliant butterfly," his friend said.

"Where did all these men come from?" he asked, bewildered by the attention she was receiving.

"I believe part of it stems from having danced the last two numbers with dukes. And the supper dance beforehand. The rest? It seems they are former pupils of Lord Barrington's and knew Lady Arabella during their university days."

"I wanted her to be accepted," Jon said, shaking his head.

Weston laughed and slapped him on the back. "It seems you're going to have competition. Heavy competition from the looks of it. Of course, you can challenge a few to a boxing match and beat them to a bloody pulp as you're so wont to do at Gentleman Jack's. I doubt they'd show the lady their faces after that, all bruised and battered and missing a few teeth."

"Don't push me, Weston," he warned. "I may do that very thing."

He looked as Arabella's dance card was being passed from man to man. Without a goodbye to his friend, he muscled his way into the circle and snatched the card before its holder could sign it. Thank goodness he had for only one slot remained on it.

Marking his name in the last spot, he said, "Lady Arabella, you almost forgot that you had promised to save the final dance for me."

He returned the now-filled programme to her with a smile and saw the pink flush on her cheeks.

"Thank you, Your Grace," she said as Elizabeth helped attach it to her wrist again.

Couples moved toward the dance floor and Lord Atterby offered his hand. Arabella took it and they moved onto the floor, where a lively country reel began. The group of young swains melted away and Elizabeth said to Jon, "It seems our wallflower has become the belle of the ball."

CHAPTER ELEVEN

ARABELLA TRIED TO maintain her composure as she danced with the Duke of Colebourne. To think she had only danced twice this evening—and both times she partnered with a duke. Colebourne was warm and funny and had her laughing. He didn't seem like a duke at all, more like a naughty, charming schoolboy. After their dance, he returned her to the sidelines where his wife awaited with her brother. The two were quite striking with their aquamarine eyes and raven locks.

"My duchess and I are off for the evening, Lady Arabella, but we will see you again at tea tomorrow. In the meantime," Colebourne turned to Treadwell, "my good friend wants your next dance."

"Thank you, Your Grace," she told him, saying her goodbyes to the duchess and then turning to Treadwell once they'd departed. "You don't have to dance with me, Your Grace. I fear the Duke of Blackmore put the both of you up to it."

"What if he did?" Treadwell said, placing her hand on his sleeve. "Yes, Blackmore asked us to look after you for a few minutes but I don't see it as a chore. More a delight."

She pursed her lips. "Are you trying to be as charming as Colebourne?"

He laughed as he led her onto the floor. "Did you know that the Duke of Charm is Colebourne's nickname?"

"No. I'm not party to any *ton* gossip." She paused. "Do you have a moniker?"

"The Duke of Disrepute," he said with a wide smile.

"Oh, dear. Then I may be damaging my reputation by partnering with you," she said saucily. "Then again, it was already in shreds."

Treadwell leaned close and whispered in her ear, "The shifting winds in Polite Society may soon turn in your favor, Lady Arabella." He then stepped away and faced her as the music began and she whirled about the room, eventually returning to him by song's end.

As the duke escorted her from the ballroom floor toward Lady Elizabeth, he said, "Be prepared for the onslaught you will face."

His cryptic words caused her to frown. Arabella had no idea what he meant by them. Then suddenly, she was surrounded by a bevy of men. Familiar men. Ones she had known at Oxford as students of her father's. As the sea surrounded her, Treadwell winked—and moved from her sight.

"Do you remember me, Miss Jennings? It's been five years since I graduated from Oxford."

"I thought it had to be you, my lady. I'd heard your father had come into the earldom."

"What about me, Lady Arabella? Your father was my favorite don. Oh, how I remember those suppers, debating every topic under the sun."

"Good evening, my lady. Might you have a dance free? I would love to continue our discussion regarding the Peloponnesian Wars."

She recognized and called every one of them by name. Some were familiar faces from just over a year ago, while others she hadn't seen in almost a decade. One asked for her programme and suddenly it was being passed among them.

Then instinctively, she knew the Duke of Blackmore was nearby. Funny how she could sense his presence in such a crowd. He moved through it and plucked her programme from a man's hand and glanced at it quickly.

Then he raised his eyes, pinning hers in a heated gaze.

"Lady Arabella, you almost forgot that you had promised to save the final dance for me."

The duke handed her the programme, his

name boldly scrawled next to the last dance of the evening.

"Thank you, Your Grace," she said politely, finding Elizabeth suddenly by her side and aiding her in attaching the card to her wrist again.

She still sensed Blackmore's eyes upon her as Lord Atterby told her their dance was about to begin. He led her onto the dance floor. Arabella was grateful the country reel prevented them from chatting—and kept her too busy to think.

They finished their dance and then the remainder of the evening passed quickly, as she danced every number and then talked with former students about the past between dances. Arabella couldn't help but wonder if these men would have sought her out if she'd remained in the ballroom instead of cowering in the library or if they only wanted to speak to her since she'd danced with three powerful dukes.

Her partner returned her to the edge of the dance floor and asked if he might call upon her tomorrow. He was the fifth man to do so.

"I am engaged for tea with Lady Elizabeth Sutton but you are welcomed to visit before then."

"Then I will certainly call upon you in time to visit. Perhaps we might go for a drive in the park the day after?" he asked hopefully.

"Could we speak of this tomorrow?" she asked, her head still reeling from the sudden change in the evening.

He brought her hand to his lips and kissed her fingers. "Of course, my lady. Until tomorrow afternoon."

Arabella watched him depart and sensed Blackmore behind her.

"I thought he would never leave," he grumbled.

She turned. "Why would it matter to you, Your Grace?"

Looking displeased, he took her arm. "Come along," and pulled her toward the center of the room.

Arabella sensed the eyes upon them and wished he hadn't taken them to stand in such a prominent place. The musicians struck up the waltz and his arms came about her, drawing her near. A little too near as her breasts brushed against the wall of his muscled chest.

"I suppose you always want to dance in the center of everyone," she said. "Being a duke and thinking it your privilege to do so."

He pulled her closer, his hand tightening around hers, the other splayed against the small of her back. Her breath caught as she gazed into his eyes. She had never seen a man look at her in such a way. It was thrilling. Upsetting. A little unnerving.

"I am a duke, after all," he said. "I am due the very best."

"Merely because you were fortunate enough to inherit a lofty title from your father doesn't make you better than everyone else here."

A shadow crossed his face and he gazed out across the room as they continued to dance.

"Did I say something wrong, Your Grace?" she asked quietly, hoping he could hear her words over the soaring music.

"Not at all, Lady Arabella. I am merely being the Duke of Arrogance."

He remained silent after that, twirling her about, the heat radiating from him, the spice of his cologne tickling her nose. She gave herself over to the dance since he didn't seem to want to converse any longer and found it liberating to move to the music.

When the last notes were struck, a wistfulness passed through her. She had started the evening as an ugly duckling and had ended it as a beautiful swan, dancing with the most handsome man in the room, albeit the most arrogant one.

"Let me take you to your father," the duke said, tucking her hand through his arm and holding on to it possessively.

"I must thank you, Your Grace. If not for you and your two friends dancing with me, no one would have paid the least bit of attention to me tonight."

"They might have if you hadn't been a coward and hid in the library."

Immediately, her hackles went up but her sharp retort died upon her lips. "You are right, Blackmore. I was foolish to let the women of the *ton* fluster me."

He smiled down at her. "You certainly made up for it. You had gentlemen falling over themselves wanting to converse and dance with you."

"All of them Papa's former students, so we had a previous acquaintance. I doubt they would have shown any interest in me if three dukes hadn't done so."

"You should receive several invitations to social occurrences after tonight," he predicted. "And I am sure more than a few might angle for a visit."

"Yes, five gentlemen already have promised to come see me tomorrow even though I explained I was to be gone for tea in the afternoon. I asked them to come beforehand."

His thumb stroked her fingers, causing her belly to flip on its end.

"I suppose I should be glad that I will see you at tea tomorrow."

"Just because your sister asked me to tea does not mean you are required to attend."

Blackmore halted. His gaze penetrated her. "I want to take tea with you, Arabella."

She noticed he used her Christian name and wanted to chide him for doing so but she was incapable of forming words as he looked at her.

"There you are, my dear," her father said. "I see you're with His Grace."

"Yes, Papa. Have you met the Duke of Blackmore?"

"I have, indeed, and he asked me to tea tomorrow," her father replied.

Arabella looked up. "That was very thoughtful of you, Your Grace."

"I can be upon rare occasions," he said glibly. "Now that I have returned you to your father, I must go in search of my sister. Until tomorrow." He released her and bowed to her and then her father before striding away.

"Well, he certainly is a force of nature," her father said. "One hears the phrase *larger than life* and Blackmore certainly makes that true."

"I agree."

Papa escorted her outside and they moved through the crowd until they found their carriage. A footman opened the door and set the stairs down for her to ascend. They sat for some minutes, Papa talking about meeting up with acquaintances from decades ago, as well some of his former students.

As the carriage finally set in motion, he said, "The Duke of Blackmore asked my permission to court you tonight, Arabella. I told him it was up to you."

ARABELLA ALLOWED ANNIE to help dress her and told the maid that she wanted her to work on embellishing all of Arabella's dresses, especially the ones for evening.

"Not fancy enough for the likes of Polite Society?" the servant asked, a knowing look in her eyes.

"Yes," she said curtly, not wanting to elaborate on how unsuccessful the first part of her evening had gone last night. "I also may purchase a few new gowns here in London."

Annie nodded. "A good idea, my lady. I'll get to work seeing what I can do. You can count on me."

Arabella went to the breakfast room and found her father already there, sipping his coffee and reading the morning newspapers. She took a seat to his left and Stone poured tea for her as a footman brought her a plate with her usual toast points. Her favorite marmalade already sat on the table in front of her and she generously slathered the toast with it.

She took a bite and savored it as she tried to collect her thoughts. Ever since her father had told her that the Duke of Blackmore had sought permission to court her, it had been hard to do so. She thought logically in all matters, her emotions never swaying her. But the image of the impossibly handsome duke, all tall and broad and muscular in his tailored evening wear caused rational thought to fly out the window.

Why would a well-known rake wish to court her?

"Papa, did you enjoy yourself last evening?" she began.

He set his newspaper aside. "I did. I fear being a country earl can be a bit lonely, especially with your mother gone. I was used to interacting with numerous students and colleagues on a daily basis. It felt good to sit and talk with a large group of men who circulated through different tables in the card room. Why, I spoke to some gentlemen I hadn't seen since my own schoolboy days."

"So, you wish to remain in London for the rest of the Season?"

He studied her a moment. "You do not?"

"I don't know," she admitted. "I have very mixed feelings about it at this time."

Stone returned to the room with a silver tray stacked high. "The post, Lord Barrington."

Papa swept up the myriad of letters and what Arabella supposed were invitations. Looking at the large stack with distaste, he said, "Might you sort through these for me, Arabella?"

"Of course."

He went back to his paper and she began opening invitations, placing them in various stacks according to the type of social event they described. When she finished, she counted twenty-two of them, a staggering amount in her eyes.

"Papa, we have received a large amount of invitations. To balls. Routs. Garden parties. The theatre."

"Hmm." He glanced at the piles and then to her. "Do you wish to attend any of them? I feel it would be rude not to do so. Especially since Blackmore is interested in you. I am certain he will be at a number of these events."

"What if I don't want his attentions?" she asked, wishing to see his reaction.

He looked perplexed and then said, "Arabella, Blackmore isn't the sort of man who will accept a no and then move on."

She sniffed. "You're saying that merely because he's a duke, I should allow him to court me?"

His brows arched. "I am saying that he seems a most determined man. One who will not let anything—or anyone—get in his way. You must have made quite an impression on him for him to declare his intentions so soon to me."

"I don't like this new attitude in you, Papa. You disappoint me. Just because a man is a duke doesn't mean he gets his way about everything."

He shook his head. "That *is* the point, my dear. Dukes can do whatever they want. They are forgiven for any mistakes they make. They are placed upon pedestals by the *ton*."

"But you have never been one to bend to Polite Society," she pointed out.

He chuckled. "I was never around Polite Society, Arabella. My father and brothers washed their hands of me. I had to make my own way in the world. Now that I am a part of it—and you, as well—I must adhere to their rules. After all, we must find you a husband."

She gasped. "What did you say?"

"You heard me. You need a husband. That is what a Season is for. It is the very reason your mama wanted you to partake in it and find a titled gentlemen to wed you."

She crossed her arms, knowing her jaw set stubbornly. "What if I don't wish to wed?"

He sighed, running a hand through his thinning hair. "My sweet girl, what else are you going to do? I am no longer a don. You have no lectures to write for me. We have hired Mr. Barley to manage the country estate. I know you still want to make a few improvements to the London townhouse but, after that, what do you plan to do with your time?"

Arabella hadn't thought about it. She had been busy for over a year getting Barrington Hall and the estate to rights. It had taken up all her waking hours. He was right, though. She needed a purpose.

But to wed?

She decided to broach another matter. "Papa, I know I already had the village seamstress create a new wardrobe for me but, after last night, I find that it is somewhat lacking."

"Hmm?" He took a sip of his coffee and tore his eyes away from his newspaper. "New gowns, you say?"

"Yes. Mine appeared rather shabby alongside other ones." She indicated the invitations in front of them. "If I am to accept these invitations, I will need new clothes to wear."

"Buy whatever you like. I meet with Malcolm Price yesterday."

"You did?" Surprise filled her. "Why didn't you mention it to me?"

"Oh, he gave me some papers that are on my desk. I was going to ask you to go through them. You know I haven't a head for numbers. Still, he seemed to believe we are in very good financial shape. He even helped me set aside money for your dowry."

"Dowry!" And this was before Blackmore had even mentioned anything to Papa. "How much?"

"Twenty thousand pounds."

"What? We have that kind of money?"

"Yes. Oh, you have the Wiltshire estate running quite well now. It will pay for itself and any needs that arise. Price went over my business holdings. He'd done so when I first became the earl."

"I remember him visiting again when we moved to Barrington Hall. I was tending to Mama. It was when she'd first fallen ill."

"True. Anyway, we met again yesterday and things look quite well. Feel free to purchase the wardrobe you need."

Arabella still couldn't believe that twenty thousand pounds had been set aside, all just to get someone to marry her. It was a great deal of money and if word got out how large her dowry was, fortune hunters would invariably come sniffing around her.

"Papa, please don't share how much my dowry is with anyone."

"Why not? It might attract the right kind of husband for you."

She glared at him. "The right man will want me for me. Not for my dowry. I'd prefer you not make known its size. Allow me to go through the Season and get to know others. If I develop feelings for any gentlemen, I may send him to see you."

"Well, you already have Blackmore interested. Either others will follow suit—or he'll frighten them all away."

She snorted. She was not going to allow that overbearing man to make the most important decision of her life for her. If she had to wed—and it appeared to be her destiny from what Papa had just revealed—she would be the one to control her choice.

Arabella doubted she would ever choose to be the wife to a well-known rake such as Blackmore.

CHAPTER TWELVE

"YOU TALKED TO Cook about what to serve at tea?"

Jon looked up from his correspondence and found Elizabeth standing in front of his desk. He'd been so involved in his business correspondence that he hadn't heard her approach.

"When do you care what we serve at tea?" His sister smiled. "Or is it because of *who* is coming to tea that you suddenly care so much what is served?"

He shrugged. "This will be Lady Arabella's first outing in London to take tea with friends. I merely wanted to make certain there would be something provided that she would enjoy."

"You brought her enough food last night from the buffet," Elizabeth said. "Did you find out some of her favorites?"

"I did. And when did you have time to see what our plates contained? I thought Lord

Atterby was keeping you occupied."

She rolled her eyes. "Atterby is nice. But extremely boring. I need someone more exciting than Atterby to keep me entertained."

Jon was glad to hear it. He had thought the same about the bland man and how he wasn't nearly good enough for Elizabeth. He also hadn't minded seeing Arabella dance with Atterby because he knew young Atterby wouldn't be any competition for him. Not that he was competing for Arabella. In his mind, things were already settled. He was the best choice for her. Period.

"Cook said that you specified which scones and which cakes were to be served. That you even mentioned what she should fill the tea sandwiches with and which blend of tea to send in." She pursed her lips. "You really do like her, don't you, Jon?"

He nodded. Before he could say anything, she raced around the desk and flung her arms about him.

"Oh, I do like her myself. Truly. I am sure I will like her even more once I get to know more about her. She seems so clever and she is very beautiful."

Elizabeth released her hold on him. "It's almost time for our guests to arrive. I need to change my gown."

She breezed out of the room and he leaned back in his chair. He wondered what god-awful gown Arabella would wear today. Perhaps he could get his sister to speak to her about her apparel. Even have Elizabeth take Arabella to her modiste. Not that he cared what she wore—but the *ton* would. As he pursued her, he would already be fighting all the rumors about him, which she was bound to hear, sooner rather than later. His reputation as a man about town and utter rake might have others thinking poorly of Arabella herself merely for being in his company. Her atrocious gowns would only add to the gossip.

He steepled his fingers. It had been less than a day since he'd decided to make her his duchess and yet the idea pleased him. Moreover, he wanted to please her, which is why he had spoken to Cook about what to serve at tea today.

A firm knock sounded at the door and he said, "Come."

Thistle came into the room, a silver tray in hand. "This came for you, Your Grace," the butler said and Jon took the note.

"Thank you. Let me know when our guests for tea arrive. It will be the Colebournes and Lord Barrington and his daughter."

"The one who favors cinnamon?" the butler asked.

"Blast! How did you know that?" he demanded.

"Cook told Mrs. Thistle. Mrs. Thistle told

me. Let me assure you that there will be both cinnamon cakes and buns at tea today, Your Grace." The butler's eyes gleamed with mischief.

"Stop that," he chided.

Thistle's brows arched, an innocent look on his face. "Stop what, Your Grace?"

"You know what."

The butler stood silently but bit back a smile.

"Yes, I am interested in the woman," Jon blurted out.

A grin spread across Thistle's face. "That's very good to hear, Your Grace. It's about time you considered taking on a wife and providing an heir. Winspeth agrees."

"Winspeth? What are you doing gossiping with my valet?"

A sage look appeared upon Thistle's face. "Gossip is the lifeblood of a household, Your Grace. Surely, you realize we have your best interests at heart."

"Then do let me know if Lady Arabella passes muster," he said, his voice laced with sarcasm.

Thistle smiled sunnily, obviously ignoring it. "Very well, Your Grace." He left the room.

Jon glanced down at the letter in his hand and broke the seal.

Your Grace –

I am writing to inform you of the dire condition of your uncle, Ambrose Sutton. Colonel

Sutton has been in poor health for a good number of years but his condition has taken a turn for the worse. He is not expected to live beyond this week, according to his doctor.

While the colonel realizes his long estrangement from your father, the previous Duke of Blackmore, may have colored your opinion of him, he would like to inform you that he has had legal documents drawn up giving you guardianship of his son, Arthur, upon the colonel's death.

I realize the Season has begun and you may have social obligations to fulfill, but I urge you to come and see your uncle at your earliest convenience and take custody of your young cousin upon the colonel's death.

I have enclosed directions to Mr. Sutton's residence. You may also call directly at my office, which is in the same village and can easily be pointed out by anyone since we are a small community.

Your faithful servant,
Milford Milligan, Esq.

Jon placed the letter on his desk. He only had a vague recollection of Uncle Ambrose from his childhood. He and Arch couldn't have been more than six or seven when the man had appeared at Blackstone Manor, resplendent in his military uniform. Jon remembered lurking outside the door as his uncle and father talked, their voices raised. Arch had quickly become bored and left, preferring to get into some mischief rather than linger to see what the result of the conversation was between their father and a relative they had never seen before.

Finally, the door had swung open and Uncle Ambrose appeared. He'd looked down and ruffled Jon's hair and told him to always be a good boy, especially since he was a second son. The words that had stuck in Jon's head were, "You are meant for the army, Jonathan. Don't wish your life away wanting to be the duke. That's for your brother."

Little did Uncle Ambrose know a little more than a decade later Jon would murder his twin and quickly become the duke when his father passed. As he pushed aside his ever-present guilt, Jon wondered what had become of Ambrose during all these years. His uncle would have been kept busy with Bonaparte making a run here and there, trying his best to grab power. Jon wondered what role his uncle had played in the war. When he'd married. How old this cousin Jon was supposed to take under his wing might be.

Leaving London to go to Suffolk to take care of this matter was the last thing he wished to do, especially now that he'd met Arabella. He decided to put off leaving for a couple of days. It didn't matter if he reached Uncle Ambrose before he died. If he were truly so bad off, he might not even be conscious, much less be able to carry on a conversation with his nephew. Jon would leave at the end of the week. He only wished he knew how old his cousin was. If he were away at school, surely this Milford Milligan would have sent for the boy in order for Arthur to tell his father goodbye. Besides, any funeral would wait until the Duke of Blackmore arrived. No event, even a funeral, would be held without its most esteemed mourner present.

Jon dashed off a quick note to Milligan, informing him he would leave London early Friday morning and should arrive by late Saturday evening. Any decisions that needed to be made could take place after his arrival. He signed and sealed the letter and rang for Thistle.

"See this is posted at once."

"Yes, Your Grace. And your guests should be arriving within the next five minutes."

"Very well. I'll make my way to the drawing room now."

Jon rose and went upstairs, eager to see if Lady Arabella Jennings held as much fascination for him this afternoon as she had the previous evening.

ARABELLA TOOK HER father's hand and alighted

from the carriage. She saw another carriage pull up behind theirs and the Duke of Colebourne bounded out, handing down his wife. The two women spied one another and went to greet each other.

"I am so glad to see you again, Lady Arabella," the Duchess of Colebourne said, looking a bit wan. "We will have a better chance to become acquainted in a quiet drawing room versus a noisy ballroom."

"I think so, too, Your Grace. May I present my father, the Earl of Barrington? Father, this is the Duke and Duchess of Colebourne."

The duke offered his hand. "Glad to make your acquaintance, Lord Barrington. I hear you are quite the card player."

Arabella's father laughed. "I am afraid no one will want to play with me anymore, Your Grace. I had a run of luck last night. That's all. Who knows if or when Fortune might smile upon me again?" He turned to the duchess and took her hand. "Your Grace. My daughter has told me very good things about you."

"Lady Arabella is a delight," the duchess said. "I haven't been to London for several years and am eager to make new friends." She smiled warmly at Arabella. "I know we are going to enjoy getting to know one another."

"Shall we go inside? I see Thistle hanging about the door, eager to get us in off the pavement," Colebourne said.

The duchess slipped her hand through Arabella's arm and they entered the townhouse. Her jaw dropped at the opulence of the foyer alone. She had thought their Wiltshire estate lovely and had been surprised at the elegance of the London townhouse Papa had inherited, but this was astounding. The art on the walls alone were worth hundreds—no, thousands—of pounds.

"If you'll follow me," the butler said.

They went up a grand staircase. Arabella found her heart hammering. This was the home of the man who wished to court her. She could actually live here one day. Shaking her head, she tried to bring herself back to reality. She was not going to marry Blackmore. She still believed he played some game with her. She was different from his other conquests, a quiet country mouse who had book smarts but knew very little of the ways of the world. Because she was so unlike the other women he mingled with—and bedded— she had merely caught his eye for the moment. It would be a passing interest. She should think nothing of it. Instead, she would concentrate on other gentlemen she'd become newly-acquainted with, including several from their Oxford days. She'd had seven stop by this afternoon, two whom had been unexpected guests. Arabella had insisted that Papa be present in the drawing room as she entertained their company. She had suspected most of their guests came to visit with him but found that she garnered most of the attention. Two gentlemen had seemed to particularly favor her. It would definitely be worth getting to know those two better and see if they might make for her future husband.

They reached the drawing room and the butler announced them. As they entered, he gave her a warm smile.

And then winked.

Startled by such a cheeky move, especially by a servant, she stumbled a moment and then found her footing. She and the duchess crossed the room to where Lady Elizabeth and the Duke of Blackmore awaited them. She tried to ignore how immaculate his clothes were. How his buckskin breeches clung to muscular legs and the bottle green jacket made his shoulders look broader than any other man's.

They exchanged greetings and she introduced Papa to Lady Elizabeth, who put everyone at ease with her gracious manner.

"Shall we sit?" their hostess asked. "Lord Barrington, I am sure you would favor this chair. My father called it the most comfortable in the room."

"Why, thank you, my lady."

As they all began taking a seat in the grouping of furniture, she realized she would be sitting next to Blackmore. Arabella perched upon the settee, which had seemed large enough when she first seated herself. It then miraculously shrank in size once the duke sat next to her. He took up an inordinate amount of space, thanks to his large frame. She glanced down because their thighs pressed against one another's, causing her to go hot inside. His long, elegant fingers rested upon his thigh. She remembered they'd taken her chin in hand, bringing a rush of . . .

She told herself to stop it. At once. She would not sit here and fantasize about the Duke of Arrogance. Or moon over him. He would like that far too much. He already thought he was incredibly special merely because he was a duke. She didn't need him to know how jumbled her thoughts were whenever he came near. Drat! Even when he wasn't near. She'd thought off and on about him all day long and had looked forward to attending tea with him. This wouldn't do. Arabella decided to pay him scant attention and focus on the others present.

Lady Elizabeth poured out and handed the duchess the first cup and then Arabella the second one.

"Shall I fix you a plate?" the duke asked. "I think I did a rather good job of it last night."

"Of course," she said breezily, feigning a confidence she didn't feel.

"I hear you enjoy the taste of cinnamon," Lady Elizabeth said.

"How did you know?"

"My brother told me. In fact, I believe our cook has included a few items with cinnamon in them."

She watched Blackmore fill a plate for her. He moved with a catlike grace. He placed a sticky bun on her plate and handed it to her.

"I hope you'll find everything to your liking," he said, smiling at her.

The smile caused her belly to flip several times over and made her heart race. "Don't look at me like that," she murmured quietly as the others began filling their plates.

"How?" he asked innocently.

"Like I am a biscuit to be gobbled up," she retorted.

He laughed. She liked his laugh. It came from deep within his chest and bubbled forth. His eyes crinkled up and his beautiful mouth looked even more irresistible. She'd heard the Oxford students talking about a schoolboy crush. Well, she seemed to have a schoolgirl one on His Grace. She had better keep it quiet, else he'd puff up larger than a cloud and float away.

"I already have a biscuit on my plate, my lady," he said jovially. "However, I am more than willing to sample whatever you offer."

She felt her cheeks singe with heat and quick-ly looked down at her teacup. Bringing it to her lips, she decided to keep to her original plan and ignore him.

Turning to the other duke present, she asked, "The duchess said you were newly wed. How did you meet, Your Grace?"

Colebourne flashed a tender smile at his wife. "Sam was my neighbor growing up. I was best friends with her brother, Weston. You remember meeting Treadwell last night?"

"Yes, I do. Please, go on."

"Sam—Samantha, that is—used to follow us around, thinking she could do everything we could."

"I could," the duchess proclaimed. "Thanks to you. My husband taught me how to ride and fish. I was quite the tomboy in my youth."

"Unfortunately, I am an idiot of the first order," the duke continued. "I let her get away, ignorant of the fact she had blossomed into a beautiful, caring young woman. She married and moved to the far north."

The duchess took up the story. "I was widowed and decided after a few years not to remain with my husband's family. I longed to come home to the south of England." She glanced to her husband, her eyes glowing with love. "This time, George noticed me. We wed rather quickly, last October, after having become reacquainted at a house party held in September by the Duke and Duchess of Windham. Windham is friends with my husband and brother and with Blackmore."

"The Eton Three—Windham, Colebourne, and Treadwell—all attended school together," Blackmore said. "At Cambridge, they allowed me and the Marquess of Marbury, currently Colonel Marbury, to enter their circle. We are fairly inseparable." He chuckled. "At least we were until the women came along. The Duchess of Windham is set to give birth any day now to their first child and she and Windham remained in the country instead of coming to London for the Season."

Arabella wondered if there were some unwritten rule that dukes only associated with other dukes. She'd thought it was the case and here was another duke being mentioned and the marquess would at some point become a duke himself. It made her feel very small and insignificant, wondering why she was truly here.

"Where do the Windhams reside?" she asked politely, trying to carry on the conversation as she looked at the Duke of Colebourne.

"Windowmere is in Devon. Colebourne Hall is about thirty miles from them. Treadwell Manor, my wife's childhood home, is but two miles from her current one."

"Where is your country seat, Your Grace?" her father asked of Blackmore.

"Blackstone Manor is located in Dorset, about three miles northwest of Dorchester. Though we're approximately sixty miles from

Windowmere, we are only ten from Hardwell Hall, where Colonel Marbury lives."

"I assume he's at war?" her father continued.

"He is. I can only hope our troops will defeat that mad Frenchman and lock him away for good this time," Blackmore said. "I am longing to see my friend and have him safely back in England once more."

They spent a pleasant hour at tea. Arabella did her best to avoid looking at or speaking to the man next to her.

Finally, he asked, "Do you have an engagement this evening, Lady Arabella?"

"No, it will be a quiet one for us. Papa and I did receive several invitations in this morning's post, however, and we will be attending a ball tomorrow night."

"Ah, my sister and I will be at that ball. Perhaps you would do me the honor of dancing the supper dance with me again. I so enjoyed your company last evening."

"Oh, do so, Lady Arabella," encouraged Lady Elizabeth. "And let's make plans for us all to sup together."

She gazed into the dark blue eyes that seemed to cast some spell over her. "Yes," she said faintly. "I will reserve the dance for you, Your Grace."

"We must be going," the Duke of Colebourne said and rose, signaling to the others present, who followed his lead. "We have a musicale to attend this evening." He smiled at her and her father. "I look forward to seeing you tomorrow night, Lord Barrington, Lady Arabella. Perhaps I might even try to play a hand or two with you in the card room."

"Let us walk out with you," Blackmore said, offering Arabella his arm.

She took it and that jolt attacked her again, like a lightning bolt that raced through her each time he touched her. The spice of his cologne made her grow lightheaded and she gripped his arm more tightly than she wished to do.

As they descended the staircase, he asked, "Did you have many callers this afternoon?"

"Yes, quite a few," she said. "Seven, to be exact."

He placed his free hand over the one that held his arm. His thumb languidly stroked it, causing a frisson of pleasure to ripple through her.

"I see the number of rivals for your hand grows."

"I am not some prize to be won, you know," she snapped.

He paused as they reached the foyer, ahead of the others. "No, Arabella. You are a treasure. Someone to be admired. Cherished."

His low voice—and what he said—made her knees grow weak. She licked her lips and could think of no retort.

"May I call upon you after teatime tomorrow?" he asked. "I'd like to take you riding in the park."

"I don't know how to ride," she admitted, embarrassed at not possessing a common social skill of a typical London lady.

"Then we will go driving in the park. I will call for you at five."

"All right," she said faintly and he led her across the foyer and out the front door to their waiting carriage.

Before the footman could clamor down, Blackmore opened the door and his hands clasped her waist, causing her to grow faint. He swung her up.

"I will see you tomorrow, my lady."

Arabella fell back against the seat, swallowing. Her father climbed inside and sat across from her. Blackmore closed the door and signaled their driver and the vehicle started up.

"Your friends are very nice, Arabella," Papa said. "I thought dukes were quite stuffy but both Blackmore and Colebourne seem like decent chaps. And Her Grace and Lady Elizabeth are lovely women."

She looked out the window as the streets of London passed by. So many conflicting emotions ran through her. She didn't want to like Blackmore. She still didn't trust him.

But she was afraid she might be in danger of losing her heart to him.

CHAPTER THIRTEEN

J ON DIDN'T WANT to waste his time going to tonight's musicale since Arabella wouldn't be there. It was an exclusive event, with a very limited guest list. George and Samantha would be there and he'd learned from George that Weston and Elise would also attend. Jon had a feeling Weston might actually offer for Elise tonight. He'd been like a caged tiger last night, pacing about and glowering as Elise danced with numerous men. Jon would nudge his friend to do that very thing when he saw him tonight. Weston, known as the Duke of Disrepute, was actually one of the most decent men Jon knew. He was also impressed by Elise Blakeney and thought they would make for an excellent couple. Elise was kind but she seemed to have a spine of steel. She would not let Weston push her about— and in fact, might do a little pushing of her own. Just the thing to keep Disrepute in line.

The carriage slowed and he prepared himself for the evening. He wished he were in a position where he would not have to accept future invitations unless Arabella and her father would also be in attendance. He'd gone to *ton* events for almost a decade now. They had all become the same.

Until Arabella came along.

Unfortunately, he was committed to escorting his sister to *ton* events this Season. Knowing Elizabeth, she would need to be chaperoned on a daily basis because she would insist upon attending every affair under the sun.

He alighted from the carriage and offered Elizabeth his hand. Once she was on the pavement, he told his driver to park a few blocks to the south.

"I may be leaving tonight earlier than other guests and want to be able to get out with ease."

"Yes, Your Grace," the coachman replied and flicked the reins with his wrist.

Offering his sister his arm, they began down the street toward their destination.

"You didn't say a word in the carriage, Jon."

"I suppose I had no meaningful conversation."

She smiled. "Might you have been thinking of a certain blond of our mutual acquaintance?"

He arched his brows. "And if I were?"

"Then I would be exceedingly glad. I've told

you. I like Lady Arabella. I am sure given the chance to know you, she will like you, too."

"That's the plan. She won't be here tonight, though."

"I know. And I heard you tell the coachman we might not be staying the entire time."

"You know I'm not much on a musical evening, Elizabeth. If I am ready to go and you wish to stay, I'll have George escort you home."

They entered and found no receiving line, which was to his liking. Elizabeth saw a friend and excused herself as he spied Weston and headed in his direction.

"You look glum."

"Elise is insistent in having me talk with . . ." His voice trailed off. "Whomever. I can't even remember the names now."

He laughed. "I am sure Lady Ruthersby would gladly remind you. If not, my sister or the Duchess of Colebourne have also been in on the selection process to find you a bride. They would be familiar with the names."

"Hell and damnation!" Weston hissed. "I don't care about the names. I don't care about these women. I only care about Elise."

"I saw how popular she was last night."

Weston frowned. "George thinks I should wait a week and then offer for her."

"What does George know?" Jon challenged. "He already landed his duchess. I say strike while your iron is hot and make sure she is yours."

His friend nodded with grim determination. "Thank you for your support."

"Elise is a lovely woman and will be your perfect match."

Weston looked pleased hearing the words and then said, "What of you and the divine Lady Arabella? I enjoyed my dance with her last night. Are you still determined to make her your duchess?"

He nodded.

"Do you love her?" Weston asked.

The question startled him. "No, of course not. Am I attracted to her? Most assuredly so. She is beautiful to look at but there is also substance beneath that beauty." He chuckled. "I will never be bored with her, I'll tell you that. In or out of the bedroom."

"Did I hear someone mention the bedroom?"

Jon turned, having already recognized the voice. He saw Lady Walton standing there. They had engaged in a brief, intense affair two Seasons ago.

"If you will excuse me," Weston said, bowing to her and quickly exiting.

"That was rather abrupt," Lady Walton purred, her fingertips sliding down Jon's chest.

He turned away as if to watch Weston but it was an excuse to break the contact between them.

"I spent a night with Disrepute, you know," she said, her voice sultry. "He is a masterful lover but he has nothing on you, Blackmore." She sidled up to him and placed her hand on his sleeve. "I rather enjoyed our nights together. Are you still behaving yourself these days?"

"What do you mean?

"Oh, I heard tale that you'd calmed down a bit last Season. I suppose it was because your sister made her come-out and you thought you had to behave. She didn't wed, though, did she?"

"No. No one caught her attention."

"You certainly caught mine," she purred, her fingers stroking his arm. "Then . . . and now. I assume you will want us to be discreet since Lady Elizabeth is still on the Marriage Mart." She licked her lips sensually. "I suppose we could slip off to—"

"No, thank you," he said abruptly.

Anger flashed in her eyes. "Don't tell me it's because you are involved with that Barrington woman. Everyone saw you dance with the chit last night. The two of you put your heads together for a good half-hour over supper."

He didn't want to cause more trouble for Arabella. "Yes, I danced with her. What of it? I danced with others, as well."

"You really should think twice before doing so again, Blackmore. She was the object of a good deal of opening night's gossip. That horrid gown she wore was enough to keep tongues wagging half the night. Did you know her father was a fourth son? Imagine him inheriting the title. Why, he will have no idea how to conduct himself. His daughter is simply common. You can slip the word lady in front of her name but she will never be one."

Anger surged through him but he didn't want to let Lady Walton see it and realize he had feelings for Arabella.

"Why are wasting so much time speaking of her then? She means nothing to you."

"You are right," she said. "We should be chatting about where we will meet later."

"I don't wish to renew our acquaintance again, Lady Walton. In—or out—of the bedroom."

Jon nodded curtly and strode off. Women like her with too much time on their hands and too much money from their dead husbands could prove deadly. He knew there was already enough gossip that circulated about him that would eventually reach Arabella's ears. He didn't need his name to be coupled with Lady Walton's again. He'd striven to keep his affairs quiet last year, for Elizabeth's sake, and had no intention of engaging in any more now that he'd decided to make Arabella his wife.

"Blackmore, a word?"

He halted and frowned as Lord Farrow approached. The viscount had outstanding markers at two gaming hells and had managed to gain a substantial loan from the bank where Jon sat as a director. Instead of paying the debts off with the loan, he'd dug an even deeper grave by losing the entire amount.

"I say, Blackmore, I know you have a bank director's meeting coming up."

"What of it?"

"Well, I thought if you pressed the other board members, I might be allowed a bit more time in which to repay my loan." Farrow paused and then said, "And possibly you could help me take out an additional one."

"Why would I do that? You have gambled away the first one. The bank expects to be paid. I will vote with the majority, whom I am sure will call it in. No further loans should be expected, Lord Farrow."

"But . . . I will have to sell my two unentailed properties to raise the funds to cover the loan. Surely, you can—"

"I have no intention of coddling you, man. Sell the land and pay your debts."

The viscount's eyes narrowed. "You are as cold-hearted as they say you are, Blackmore. Your soul is blacker than night."

He glared at Farrow. "My friends call me Blackmore. You may refer to me as Your Grace."

With that, he turned his back and continued

across the room. He saw others were making their way to the rows of seats and slid into the next to last row, taking the seat on the end. He sprawled, forcing others to go to the other end of the row to fill it in. He didn't care. He was a duke. Let them be the ones to move.

Musical evenings ordinarily seemed interminable but this one went on far too long. He left before the songstress finished her first set and wandered about. A late night supper was offered and he went in and ate quickly, not speaking to the people who joined him at his table. He saw Weston with a pretty girl who was not Elise and shook his head, wondering why his friend continued squandering time. As far as Jon was concerned, this entire evening had been a waste. He was bored and ready to go.

He rose and found George.

"Will you and Samantha see Elizabeth home?"

"Lady Walton still trying to sink her talons into you?" George asked.

"She tried and failed. I merely am weary of the entire evening. You know musicales are not my cup of tea."

"We will be happy to make sure Elizabeth gets home safely," George promised.

"Thank you."

Jon left the supper room, coming across his hostess, who must be returning from the retiring room.

"Oh, Your Grace, have you enjoyed this evening's entertainment?"

He knew she wouldn't care for the truth so he smoothly lied. "The woman is a remarkable singer, my lady, however, I have another event I must get to." He smiled charmingly. "I wanted to come to yours first because it was more important to me. You and your husband are always so hospitable."

Her eyelids fluttered and she held her hand over her heart. "Oh, thank you, Your Grace. We are delighted that you could attend tonight."

She was gracious enough not to point out that he'd been leaving without stopping by to let her or her husband know he departed. Dukes could be poorly behaved in every situation and still be forgiven for their lack of good manners merely because they were dukes. Arch would have loved being a duke, with his blatant disregard for rules. Jon, however, had tired of the games and the empty life of chasing skirts and juggling the parade of various lovers and mistresses. He wanted what George and Samantha had. What Andrew and Phoebe had. What he knew Weston would have with Elise.

The Eton Three had fallen hard and fast. He might not be in love as his friends were but he did know quality when he saw it. He would be proud to make Arabella Jennings his duchess. She was totally ignorant of men, however, and he knew he couldn't offer for her too quickly, as he had encouraged Weston to do. Lady Ruthersby had had her Season and wed. She might be close to Arabella in age but Elise had much more life experience than the earl's bluestocking daughter. He would have to take his time and court her properly before he asked for her hand in marriage.

The only thing he worried about was the fact that Arabella would certainly have other suitors lining up at her doorstep. Deciding when to offer for her would definitely be a balancing act. While he couldn't keep eligible bachelors from calling upon her, he would—after a very short while—find a way to subtly discourage them until he was the only one courting her. For the first time in a long time, he was happy about being a duke. A raised eyebrow or condescending look and most bachelors would turn tail and run. If any were foolish enough to keep pursuing Arabella, then he would make certain they understood it was a duke who wanted this woman as his duchess. That would cause his competition to dissolve.

Jon left the townhouse and went to find his carriage. In the past, he would have gone to his mistress' house or one of his lovers. He'd paid off the current mistress before last Season began and hadn't retained a new one since. And there were no lovers he wished to tangle with in the sheets.

He would go home and think about his upcoming drive in the park with the blond beauty who fascinated him.

And at tomorrow night's ball, he would steal a kiss from her.

Not that he needed to know how she kissed. He doubted she had ever been kissed before. Kissing was an art form in which he excelled. He would teach Arabella everything she needed to know in order to please him and herself. No, he was gripped with desire and yearned to place his lips on hers. To taste her. Breathe in her scent. Skim his hands along her skin.

Smiling, Jon flung open his carriage door and hopped inside.

CHAPTER FOURTEEN

ARABELLA WAS TOO nervous to take tea, knowing the Duke of Blackmore would arrive within the hour.

"Papa, I think I will go to my bedchamber."

"You don't want any tea?" he asked. "Cook made some of the raisin scones you like."

"No, you go ahead without me. I wish to change my dress."

She would do that—and probably throw up from sheer nervousness.

As she made her way to her room, she worried how one man could have such an effect upon her. She had always lived in an orderly world. She liked a place for everything. She was highly organized. She made logical decisions based upon facts. Within a space of a few days, though, Blackmore had slammed into her life and made her question everything about herself. Usually, she brimmed with confidence. But around the duke, she found herself unsure about how to even hold her teacup. She knew she was his intellectual equal but he was so far above her socially. Not only in rank but in knowledge of the manners and unspoken rules of the *ton*.

She still found it a bit hard to believe that he wanted to woo her. She was the daughter of an Oxford don, even if Papa had since become an earl. She had no background in how to speak to such a man, much less move through the society he kept. Part of her believed he was simply toying with her and, because of that, she must guard her heart. At his core, Blackmore was an arrogant rake who might be trying to compromise her. Many men enjoyed the chase—or so she'd been led to believe by eavesdropping on some of the personal conversations at the college supper table. She did not want to be hunted. Teased. Embarrassed. In fact, today's drive was probably a mistake because she would be seen in public with a notorious scoundrel. She should have thought of that and turned him down flat.

Yet how was she to say no to those dark blue eyes that drew her in? The Duke of Blackmore seemed to see through her, straight to her very soul. She seemed to have no willpower where he was concerned.

"Develop a spine, Arabella," she told herself as she entered her bedchamber.

Annie sat, a needle in hand, working on

another of Arabella's gowns. This was the one she would wear to tonight's ball. She hadn't had a chance to investigate finding a modiste and should have asked either Lady Elizabeth or the Duchess of Colebourne at tea yesterday who created their gowns. With one wed to a duke and the other a sister to one, she doubted she could afford their modiste, no matter what Papa had told her. Obtaining a name from either woman, though, would at least be a start.

"How are you coming along, Annie?" she asked.

"Look at the two day dresses I've laid out on the bed," her maid said. "A few embellishments was all it took, my lady. I think you'll be pleased."

Arabella went to the bed and gazed upon the servant's handiwork. "Oh, Annie! You did such a nice job." She lifted one from the bed and held it to her. Crossing the room, she looked into the mirror and said, "This is more like it."

"This one's almost done, too, my lady, but I still think you need to see a London dressmaker. I can only do so much with what I have to work with. You need more luxurious fabrics."

"I have plans to ask a couple of friends to-night who they use to design their gowns. I'll only need a few."

Annie snorted. "You need more than a few. Most London ladies change their gowns five times a day."

She sniffed. "I am not in the habit of doing so. Except for now. I think I'll wear the yellow to go driving with His Grace."

Her maid set aside the sewing. "I can work on this while you're gone and it'll be through in plenty of time for tonight. Let me help you change."

Within a few minutes, Arabella wore the newly-adorned gown.

"I like the lace at the collar and upon the sleeves. It adds a bit of sophistication to it."

"You need a few fichus," Annie suggested. "They can help change the look of a gown."

"I'll remember that. You'll have to accompany me when I land an appointment with a modiste."

"Of course, I'll go with you. I'm your maid, my lady. You must be chaperoned around London when you go places."

"Except for this drive."

"Yes. That's different," Annie said. "The duke is courting you. The park is full of swells at that time of day. You'll be in the public eye. Just don't go getting out of the carriage to investigate pretty flowers or something of that sort if he suggests doing so."

"Why not?" she asked, baffled by the comment.

The maid shook her head. "You're plenty smart when it comes to your books, my lady, but not very wise in the ways of the world. The duke could pull you behind a tree and try and kiss you."

Arabella thought that sounded extremely interesting but kept her thoughts to herself.

"Let me fix your hair. Sit at your dressing table."

She let the servant fuss over her and had to admit that she looked very good once Annie had finished.

"Be sure he gets you back here by six o'clock. I'll have a tray for you to nibble something and then we'll need to see to your bath so you can dress for the ball."

She sighed. "I seem to spend a large portion of my time undressing and redressing. And bathing in-between."

"That's what ladies do."

Crossing to the door, she opened it and found a maid with her hand raised, about to knock.

"My lady, His Grace is here. He's in the drawing room with Lord Barrington."

"He is? Why, he is early. He didn't seem to be the early type to me," she murmured.

"Maybe he's eager to see you, my lady," Annie called out from the chair she was again sitting in, needle once more in hand.

Arabella felt a blush stain her cheeks. "Thank you," she told the maid and began making her way to the drawing room.

When she entered, she paused a moment. Blackmore was in deep conversation with Papa and she took a moment to study him. It was sinful how handsome the duke was. Everything about him appealed to her, which worried her.

And truth be told, it frightened her a little bit.

As Papa said, it would be hard to tell this man no. If he pressed her for a kiss, she would willingly allow it for she was curious about the process of kissing, especially with him. If he pushed her to go further, it would take a great deal of determination and control to tell him no.

Her father looked up and spied her. "Ah, Arabella, do come in. His Grace is here."

The duke rose as she approached. "It's nice to see you again, my lady, especially turned out in such a lovely gown."

He took her hand and brought it to his lips. Even though she'd already put on her gloves, she could feel the heat of his fingers burn through them. She blinked, trying to stay focused.

And wary.

"You look well turned out yourself, Your Grace. I hope you and Papa have had a pleasant conversation."

"We have, my dear. His Grace was telling me about his horses. I used to love to ride but had no reason—or enough income—to maintain one in Oxford. We lived close to the university and walked to it daily," he told Blackmore.

The duke addressed Arabella. "I was telling your father that if he is in need of quality horseflesh, I would be happy to accompany him to Tattersall's on Hyde Park Corner."

"I explained to the duke that I had inherited my brother's stable of horses both here and in Wiltshire. They seem adequate to me."

"I would be happy to look over the ones in your mews and advise you," Blackmore said.

"That's very decent of you, Your Grace."

"In the meantime, will you excuse us? The park gets crowded as five o'clock approaches."

"And I have strict instructions from my maid to return by six o'clock in order to prepare for tonight's ball."

Blackmore offered his arm. "Then we had better take advantage of the time we have. Good day, Lord Barrington."

Arabella noticed how firm his arm was beneath her fingers. His tailored clothes allowed her to see how well-built he truly was. She remembered he mentioned that he boxed and, for a moment, she longed to see him stripped to the waist, all those lovely muscles on display.

They went outside and she saw a fancy vehicle at the pavement in front of the townhouse, which she assumed was the height of fashion.

"Is this yours?"

"Yes. It's my barouche."

"I don't think the previous earl had one of

these. It's very sleek. And your horses are so well matched."

"They are bays I purchased from Tattersall's. Come, let's get you in."

He helped her up and climbed in beside her. Arabella turned over her shoulder. "Does that come over us?"

"Yes, the hood is collapsible. Since it turned out to be such a fine day, I decided to push it back for a better view."

He took up the reins and eased away from the curb, heading toward Hyde Park. As they went, he pointed out the sights to her. A bookstore he frequented. A tearoom his sister favored. The place where he had his boots made. By the time they reached the park, her previous nerves had calmed and she realized she was enjoying herself.

Turning into the park, she saw the road lined with carriages.

"How many people are here?" she asked, amazed so many vehicles clogged the road.

"It is the fashionable hour and place to be seen," he said. "We will have to stop and visit several times."

He was right. They barely went ten feet before he stopped the vehicle. This occurred over and over. After half an hour, she said, "Enough. You have introduced me to so many people, my head is spinning. I will never keep all their names straight. At least I am good with faces, though."

Blackmore turned down a side road less traveled. "Did you recognize any who were rude to you at your first ball?"

"Yes. I took the high road and was coolly polite to them."

He roared with laughter. "That's what I like about being in your company, Lady Arabella. You are refreshingly honest. Never boring."

"Ought we be getting back?" she asked, noting the traffic had thinned some.

"We will. I'm taking what would be termed the long way. Although with so many carriages on the main path, this way will most likely take less time."

"There won't be any stopping, will there?"

"Why? Do you need to stop?"

"No. It's just . . ." Her voice trailed off and she sensed her cheeks pinkening. She seemed to do nothing but blush around the duke.

He laughed. "Oh, I see. Your lady's maid warned you off."

Arabella sniffed. "I did come driving with you. Even if you are a well-known rake. But yes, Annie did expressly tell me to keep within view of others and inside the carriage at all times. Or barouche. I do like the sound of that word. It rolls off the tongue."

Blackmore groaned beside her.

"Is something wrong, Your Grace?"

"Nothing that won't be corrected by this evening," he said, laughter in his voice. "Do you remember you're to reserve the supper dance for me?"

"I will this time since you've asked so nicely. In the future, though, you will have to sign my programme as the other gentlemen do. Assuming they'll sign."

"Oh, I am sure a horde will beat their path to you at any ball you choose to attend." He paused. "Did you have many callers this afternoon?"

"I don't think that's any of your business," she said smartly.

"Didn't your father tell you what we spoke of the other night?"

Arabella began fidgeting. "I am not sure what you mean."

He chuckled. "Oh, you know exactly what I mean, Arabella."

She sighed. "I wish you wouldn't call me by my Christian name. It isn't proper. You slip and do so at times."

Blackmore glanced at her. The heat in his eyes startled her and she gasped.

"I never slip, my lady. Especially where you are concerned. And I am speaking about my interest in courting you. Which you knew that was what I meant."

She glanced away, unnerved by what she'd seen in his eyes. "Papa said it was my choice to let you court me or not."

"He did, did he?"

"I am sure you are not used to anyone refusing you anything but—"

"There'll be no buts, Arabella. I am going to court you. You are going to allow it. I'll even allow you to play at talking with others, thinking it will make me jealous."

"You'll *allow* me? Did you really say that, Blackmore?"

"You may call me Jon when we are alone like this. It's short for Jonathan."

"I will call you the Devil Himself if I choose," she said angrily. "You have no rights or control over me. I will speak to whomever I wish. Whenever I wish. I will dance with the men I want to. Or I won't dance at all. It is my choice. Mine. Mine alone."

He turned the horses and they came out of the park. Silence reigned between them until they reached her home. Blackmore jumped to the ground and then grasped her waist, lowering her to the pavement.

And kept his hands there.

"Let go," she said firmly.

"I apologize," he said. "I was wrong to say what I did to you."

His words mollified her slightly but he needed to release her. Those large hands covered far too much of her. And his thumbs had started stroking her. Stroking her—in broad daylight! They danced along her ribcage, coming perilously close to the bottom curve of her breasts.

"I accept your apology," she said briskly. "I must go inside now to prepare for tonight's ball."

"Arabella." His voice was tender. "Please, don't be mad at me."

She forced herself to look him in the eyes. She did see regret—and something else. It was the something else that made her shiver. Or those maddening thumbs.

"I am not angry," she said evenly. "I will see you this evening. Please, Your Grace, release me."

His hands left her. Suddenly, she felt a yawning emptiness and wished he'd put them back on her. Anywhere on her. Everywhere on her.

Offering her his arm, he escorted her to the open front door, where the butler now stood. He raised her hand to his lips and pressed a kiss upon her fingers.

"Until tonight."

CHAPTER FIFTEEN

J ON TAPPED HIS foot as Elizabeth sailed down the stairs.

"I thought you would never be ready," he complained, taking her arm and escorting her to the waiting carriage.

"You don't have to be so grumpy," she admonished. "Besides, I am actually ready early tonight. Whenever have you been worried about arriving at a ball on time?"

Her grin, though, told him she knew exactly why he was out of sorts.

He had blundered badly this afternoon with Arabella. He knew he could act in a high-handed manner and it had come back to haunt him with his remark regarding whom Arabella could speak with. She was right. He had no hold on her.

Yet.

Perhaps he should go ahead and declare his intentions and see that no one else tried to claim her. That wouldn't be fair to her, though. She was new at all of the social swirl. Her confidence had been badly damaged with the way she had been treated on the opening night of the Season. She needed to have time to recover it and enjoy herself. He would keep a careful watch upon her and if he saw any gentlemen becoming too close, he would step in and see that the man made himself scarce. After all, he was a duke. No lower-ranking gentleman would dare cross him if he made known that he'd set his sights upon Arabella.

They arrived at the ball and he left Elizabeth at the receiving line, too impatient to wait through it in case Arabella was already inside the ballroom. He was glad he skipped it because she was, talking to two gentlemen. Quickly, Jon strode over. His presence alone caused the other two suitors to give her a quick goodbye.

"You needn't have frightened them away, Your Grace. I have already written your name beside the supper dance."

"Can I help it if they are intimidated by me?"

She batted her lashes coyly at him. "Well, you are a duke. They would be regardless of the circumstances."

"Are you still angry with me?" he asked bluntly.

She considered his question, leaving him nervous. "I was put out with you. You can be overbearing at times."

"I know. I will work on that. For you."

Her cheeks filled with color. He wanted to kiss her, here and now, but it would lead to a scandal so great they would have to wed by special license by week's end if he did so. Instead, he took her hand and raised it to his lips.

"I will see you later this evening, my lady," he said and took his leave.

Jon didn't bother asking for dances with any other women. The *ton* would notice, of course. Let them. He passed Lady Walton and nodded courteously. She glared at him and turned away. He wasn't in favor of making enemies and Lady Walton was not one to have, with her vicious tongue and love of spreading gossip. He saw no way of making any kind of amends between them, other than going to her bed, and that wasn't something he was willing to do. Already, he felt a deep loyalty to Arabella. He knew once wed that he would never stray.

But could he learn to love her? That was the question. He was amused by her. Intrigued with her. Taken with her beauty and grace. Love, though, was some ephemeral thing. He decided they didn't need it. They would have passion. Desire. The strong physical attraction which he knew smoldered between them would only grow once they consummated their marriage. Jon was certain Arabella would suit his every need.

He went to the card room and promptly lost both hands to her father. Lord Barrington gave him an apologetic look as he raked in his winnings.

"I see Fortune still keeps company with you, my lord," he told the earl. "I think I will leave before I lose anything further to you."

He rose and Lord Farrow immediately took his seat, ignoring Jon. He retrieved a brandy and talked to a few acquaintances and then found himself going back to the ballroom. It was far too early to do so but he itched to see the men Arabella danced with.

A scotch reel was just finishing and he spied her, her cheeks flushed with color from the exertion. What troubled him was that Lord Kenyon, a known rake, took her arm and guided her from the dance floor. They must have partnered for the reel. Anger seethed within him and multiplied a thousandfold as he saw Kenyon usher her through the French doors that led to the balcony. While he knew the viscount must have suggested some fresh air after such exertion, Jon knew the man would take the opportunity to kiss Arabella.

That wasn't going to happen.

He would be the first and last man she ever kissed. Jon realized that jealousy, an unfamiliar emotion, rippled through him. He had never experienced it before but he recognized it for what it was as he hurried toward the doors and stepped into the cool evening with its light breeze. He glanced from left to right and spied the swirl of mint skirts that Arabella wore, hurrying after them.

The viscount had led her to the far end of the balcony and now placed his hands on Arabella's bare shoulders.

Rage seethed through him but Jon stepped forward and calmly said, "Ah, there you are, my lady."

Her eyes were large as she recognized him. Kenyon turned and blanched. Jon assumed the viscount was remembering their boxing bout of a month ago, where he had left Kenyon with a blackened eye and broken nose.

"Good evening, Your Grace," Lord Kenyon said. "You were looking for Lady Arabella?"

"Yes. I was." He glared at the rake and Kenyon mumbled something before curtly nodding to Arabella and fleeing.

"Why did you scare him off?" she demanded. "We were merely taking in some air."

He placed his hands on her shoulders as Kenyon had and squeezed briefly. Her eyes widened and she licked her lips.

"The viscount didn't bring you out here for air, Arabella. He meant to kiss you."

"He did?"

Oh, her naivety was charming—but it would

land her in trouble. Jon had planned to kiss her tonight and decided he should do so immediately, the better to give her something to think about.

He slid his hands along her shoulders and slowly down her arms, seeing her shiver. He laced his fingers through one of her hands and said, "Come along."

He took her further into the shadows to the edge of the balcony, where a set of stone steps led down to the lawn. He knew they were there because he'd used them before, taking more than one woman to the place nestled underneath this balcony. It had included Lady Walton, which left him feeling awkward for a moment, but he would create a new, lasting memory with Arabella.

Their first kiss.

Only a glimmer of moonlight reached this nook. He released her hand and slipped an arm about her waist. His hand seized her chin.

"Have you ever been kissed, Arabella?"

"No." Her voice was but a whisper.

"Then it is about time we remedied that."

He bent and touched his lips to hers. He had to remind himself to hold back. She had never been kissed before. Despite the fact that blood pounded in his ears and he felt like some eager schoolboy wanting to gobble her up, he knew he must practice restraint. He forced himself to merely brush his lips against her soft, pliant ones, allowing her to get used to him. He cupped her cheek as he kissed her, marveling at the soft, floral scent that wafted from her skin.

She sighed and he pressed harder against her lips, his arm tightening about her waist, pulling her closer. His thumb caressed her cheek as he kissed her over and over. Her palms slid to his chest and captured his coat, bunching it as she pressed near. Jon sensed she was ready for more. He flicked his tongue, touching her bottom lip, allowing it to glide back and forth. She made a sweet sound and he began outlining her lips with his tongue. She shivered and clung to him.

Gently, he ran his tongue along the seam of her mouth, urging her to open to him. Like a flower opening to the morning sun, she did.

Heaven lay inside her mouth.

She must have sipped on ratafia at some point this evening for he tasted it on her, a mixture of lemon peel and nutmeg and, of course, cinnamon. His tongue swept along hers, drawing on that sweetness, teasing the roof of her mouth. He moved his hand from her cheek to her nape, steadying her and tilting her head for better access. Jon drank of the nectar that was Arabella, his hand caressing the small of her back. The little noises in her throat grew louder and he groaned, deepening the kiss. Her heady floral perfume drove him mad as her breasts pressed firmly against his chest. God, how he wanted to strip the dress from her and suckle them!

He kept from doing so and slowly retreated, gentling the kiss before finally breaking it. He gazed down at her and saw the dazed expression she wore.

She looked up at him in wonder. "People kiss . . . with their tongues?"

He chuckled. "I suppose your mother didn't tell you that."

Arabella's eyes widened. "I doubt she knew of it. I cannot imagine her . . . and Papa . . . oh, my."

Her innocence touched his heart and he couldn't stop himself. He kissed her again, sweetly at first and then softly biting into her full, bottom lip. He sucked on it and felt her tremble as her hands clung to his shoulders. He broke the kiss, resting his forehead against hers.

"So, how was your first kiss?" he asked quietly.

"It was perfect."

"Good." He gave her a hard, swift kiss, one so possessive that she had to know he branded her as his with it. "Be sure you don't kiss any other gentleman."

"Why would I? You do it so marvelously," she said in wonder. "Perhaps we should kiss some more?"

Jon laughed. "No, my delectable little sweet."

"Was I . . . did I . . . I mean . . . I didn't really

know what I was doing. I'm sorry if I didn't please you."

He kissed her lightly. "You did please me, Arabella. Very much. I have much to teach you about kissing but I believe you will catch on quickly. Just as you did the waltz."

"When?"

"When what?"

"When will you teach me?" she asked eagerly.

"Soon." He kissed her a final time. "We should return to the ballroom. You've probably missed your next partner."

"I don't care," she declared. "Kissing is infinitely more fun than dancing—and I am one who has always loved to dance."

He took her hand and brought it to his lips, turning it over and placing a kiss in the center of her palm.

"Let me take you upstairs. You'll slip in first. I will find another entrance."

"But . . . Lord Kenyon knows you came after me. He'll know what we were up to."

"Kenyon would have done the same thing if I hadn't come along. He is a scoundrel and you'd do well enough to stay away from him. Still, he won't say a word."

"Why not?"

"Because he knows I'll beat him to a bloody pulp if he did. I have before and wouldn't hesitate to do so again."

"Jon!"

He took her face in his hands. "I like hearing my name on your lips, Arabella." He chuckled. "Even if you're upset."

"It was a mere slip of the tongue," she retorted.

"I do like tangling with your tongue."

"Jon!"

"Quiet, now. Let me take you back to the balcony."

"Will you kiss me once more?"

He bent and touched his lips to hers for a sweet kiss. Reluctantly, he broke it.

"Come along, Lady Arabella, else you'll get into trouble."

"I think I already am," she admitted softly.

Jon thought the same true for himself as he took her hand and led her back to the balcony.

"Go," he urged and watched her until she slipped through the French doors.

He waited several minutes and then entered from the opposite side and skirted the ballroom. He stopped a footman and inquired what dance the musicians were on and learned the supper dance was next. When it arrived, he went to Arabella and took her onto the dance floor. It was a waltz and he eased her into his arms, wishing he could do much more than dance with her.

They twirled passed Lord Dorsley and Elise,

who'd stopped dancing because Weston stood beside them. Jon decided his friend had exercised all the patience he had and was ready to declare for Elise.

"What do you think is happening?" Arabella asked, her eyes turning toward the threesome who stood while others twirled about them.

"I believe Treadwell is about to make his intentions known. To Lady Ruthersby and everyone in this ballroom," he replied, watching Dorsley step away and Weston sweep Elise into his arms.

Moments later, they stopped and Weston's voice carried through the ballroom as he said, "It's one of the things I love about you. There are many things that make me love you."

Jon stopped dancing, knowing this show would be too good to miss. Other nearby couples also halted, looking on in curiosity.

Elise stammered, "I . . . surely . . . I mean . . ."

Weston pressed a finger to her lips. "No more talking. Listen."

Now, the musicians became so interested that they lowered their instruments.

Weston took Elise's hands and declared, "I love you, Elise. Madly. Deeply. Passionately. Maturely. That is what matters. I thought once, long ago, that I was in love but after knowing you, I finally know what true love is and that I could only love you. I asked you to help me find a wife this Season—when all along I knew *you* would be that woman. Every characteristic I gave you to search for in my future duchess was one you already possess. Intelligence. Compassionate. Kindness. Humor. I wanted a woman who loved children. No one is a better mother than you are to Claire. I need you to be my friend. My conscience. My everything."

His friend's words seared into Jon's soul. Weston leaned in and said something privately to Elise and then he tenderly kissed her hands.

"Please, love. Say you'll marry me. Be my companion and lover. The mother of my children. Grow old with me, Elise. Our lifetime will be an adventure."

Suddenly, Elise was telling him yes and they kissed in front of the entire ballroom. Jon sensed the shock pouring through those gathered as Weston broke the kiss and lifted Elise in his arms. They stared at one another a long moment and then kissed again before he marched through the parting sea of still dancers and left the room to the sound of thunderous applause.

The moment moved Jon—and also broke him.

He looked back at Arabella, who gazed after the couple with a tender smile upon her rosy lips. He didn't love her. He lusted after her, especially since the taste of her was still upon his lips. But he didn't know if he could ever love anyone and he certainly didn't think he deserved love. Not after what he had done to Arch.

With a weight squeezing his heart, he knew this beautiful, kind, wonderful woman deserved better than he could ever give her. She deserved a good man. An honest man. One who would love her completely. Love everything about her and give himself wholly to her.

He wasn't that man. He was an imposter. A pretender. A man who never should have been made a duke. He might become a better man if he wed her but guilt at murdering his brother would always plague him. Arabella deserved the best. He was far from that. She needed to know. Now. He must let her go before she gave anymore of herself to him.

"Arabella, we must talk," he said quietly.

She turned. "Oh, wasn't that wonderful? You can't say now that love doesn't exist, Jon."

"Come."

He led her from the floor, where voices buzzed, discussing the outlandish behavior of the Duke of Disrepute and Lady Ruthersby. Jon entered the corridor in front of the ballroom.

"I have misled you terribly, my lady," he said formally. "I should never have asked permission from your father to court you."

Her brows knitted in confusion. "I don't understand."

"You don't have to. I was a fool to think I

could be like my friends and find happiness."

He took her hand and brushed his lips to her knuckles. With regret, he met her gaze. "You are free to seek the company of others, my lady. I no longer will take up your time."

Jon turned and strode away, each step taking him away from Arabella breaking his heart.

CHAPTER SIXTEEN

ARABELLA STOOD FROZEN to the spot as she watched Jon abandon her. It wasn't that he physically walked away. It was also the swift rush of the emotional abandonment that cut her to the quick.

What had changed in the space of a few minutes?

Not half an hour ago he'd given her her first kiss, one turning into another and another. She hadn't a clue what was involved with kissing but he was obviously a master at it. His drugging, intoxicating kisses had swept her up high to the sky, where she felt as if she were running free, released from the bonds of Polite Society and discovering who she was—and who she might become.

With him.

When he'd joined her minutes later for their dance in the ballroom, nothing seemed to have changed. He had a playful, teasing light in his eyes as he'd taken her into his arms and they had begun to waltz. When they'd passed the curious trio of the Duke of Treadwell, Lady Ruthersby, and some unknown peer all standing in the middle of the dancers, Jon had seemed to know exactly what was going on. That Treadwell was declaring for Lady Ruthersby in the midst of the dance.

Treadwell's words had moved Arabella. His love for Lady Ruthersby shone in his eyes and through the magical words he spoke. Arabella thought Jon was pleased for his friend.

Then without warning, everything changed—and she had no idea why. He'd told her he'd misled her and he would no longer court her, pressing her to see others. His words baffled her, especially after the heated kisses they had exchanged below the terrace. Kisses that branded her as his.

She blinked back the tears that threatened to fall. That was the last thing she wanted to do, cry in front of the vipers of the *ton*. Fortunately, they were all still in the ballroom or would be going into supper. She decided to retreat to the retiring room as a few tears fell.

Once there, she washed her face and dried it, staring into the mirror. She didn't look different but she felt like another person after those kisses. She longed for Jon to come back and tell her everything he'd said was a mistake. She liked Jon. Not the haughty Duke of Arrogance who wore a mask when he stepped out into the world. Polite Society had no idea of the lighthearted, intelligent man Jon truly was, except for his small circle of friends.

Arabella wondered if she had done something wrong and decided she hadn't. Whatever had gone wrong between them wasn't her fault. She didn't think it was his, either. She had seen the struggle and reluctance in his eyes when they had parted. He hadn't wanted to go.

Then why had he?

She needed to be alone. To think. To reason. To see if she could discover what had happened and how she could repair the damage. Jon had mentioned that he was a fool to think he could find happiness as his friends had. She needed to mull over his remark. That meant leaving the ball. She had no taste now for gaiety and pasting on a false, social smile to the world.

As she started to exit, a woman brushed by her and then turned. She was an exceptional beauty, with dark hair and large, brown eyes and a complexion as smooth as milk.

"Lady Arabella, isn't it?" she said, judgment in her voice.

She didn't recognize the women as one who had snubbed her during that first ball but obviously the gossip about Arabella had reached this woman's ears.

"And you are?" she challenged, not willing to remain shy or timid when confronted by this type.

"Lady Walton. I noticed you've danced with Blackmore twice. And I saw you with him in the park, as well."

Just hearing Jon's name felt like a punch in her gut but Arabella stood her ground. "What of it? He asked. I accepted."

Lady Walton shook her head, pity in her eyes. "My dear Lady Arabella, I know you are new to London and the ways of the Polite Society. You would do yourself some good if you avoided the likes of Blackmore. He is a rake to the extreme. Your reputation is already in tatters, thanks to your ghastly wardrobe and lack of social graces. Don't harm it further by keeping company with such a blackguard."

She leaped to Jon's defense, despite the fact he had just abandoned her.

"First, I am not your dear lady. We are not acquainted and I can tell I would not wish to be so. What do you know of him, Lady Walton? Blackmore has been nothing but a gentleman to me. Very amusing and quite kind. His sister, too, has been lovely to me, as have his friends."

The woman's brows arched. "Oh, you seem quite protective of him. His beautiful manners and sinfully good looks can fool anyone, Lady

Arabella. Especially some naive country miss such as yourself. Let me be frank. Blackmore is interested in only one thing and that is to get into your bed. I should know. I am one of those who has tangled in the sheets with him."

Arabella felt her face flame.

"Blackmore is an expert lover. He has slept with half of the women in the ballroom tonight. He will merely add you to his conquests and then drop you. He is mercurial to the extreme. Cool. Wild. Moody. He never follows any rules. And if he does bed you, he'll soon tire of you."

Despite the sick feeling in her belly, she said, "As he did you? You sound jealous, Lady Walton. I'm sure Blackmore grew bored with you. He is a highly intelligent man. I can see where he would lose interest in you quickly. As for me, I have no intentions of sleeping with the duke. If I decide to seek a husband this Season, it is one who would be faithful to me."

The woman laughed harshly. "That certainly isn't Blackmore."

"Then I suppose he is not for me. You are welcome to him, my lady."

Without excusing herself, Arabella left the retiring room. Her legs shook something awful.

Jon had slept with that snake of a woman. And with a good many of the female guests here tonight. She'd known he must have a black reputation but she hadn't thought about him hopping from bed to bed. It bothered her that she still ached at his absence and that she needed to find out why he'd departed so abruptly, ending the chance of anything between them before it had a chance to flourish.

With a calming breath, she headed to the card room, knowing her father would be found there. She knew females weren't allowed inside but she didn't care. Let the *ton* gossip about her if they wished. She didn't want any other suitors coming to call. She only wanted Jon. Her Jon. Her duke.

As she tried to cross the threshold into the card room, a footman stepped in her path, blocking her from entering.

"How may I help you, my lady?"

His jaw set stubbornly and since he was as big as the side of a house, there would be no getting around him.

"I need to speak to my father, Lord Barrington. At once," she said crisply.

"I'll fetch him straightaway, my lady," the servant promised and turned away, his tone forbidding her to take another step before he returned.

Arabella saw him go to the table where her father sat, halfway across the room. The footman bent and whispered in her father's ear. The earl nodded and placed his cards face down, saying something to the other players at his table. He then whipped out a handkerchief, gathering up the winnings in front of him, scooping the pile atop the handkerchief and knotting it before placing it in his pocket. He bid his companions goodnight and came to her.

"What's wrong, my dear? Have you a headache? You look unwell."

She supposed she looked ghastly after having the man who held her heart break it in two and shove it in her face.

"I do have a headache, Papa. Could we leave?"

"Of course."

He led her to the foyer and said, "Wait here. I'll see that the carriage is fetched at once."

As she waited, she saw the Duchess of Colebourne exit the retiring room, looking even paler than she had at tea yesterday. The duchess spied her and crossed to her, smiling broadly.

Tamping down her hurt, she mustered a smile. "Congratulations, Your Grace. I know you are pleased about your brother's upcoming marriage."

The duchess laughed. "I most certainly am. The Duke of Disrepute gave the *ton* plenty to talk about tonight with his public proposal and declaration of love for Elise. I daresay they'll be wed before the week is out. George teased Weston that the special license is burning a hole in his pocket."

"Oh, so they will wed by special license?"

"Yes. I suppose I will need to throw together a wedding breakfast." The duchess sighed.

"Are you up to doing so, Your Grace? Are you in good health? You seem most weary."

"I am weary but for an excellent reason." She leaned close to Arabella. "We are going to have a child next fall."

Arabella smiled at her new friend. "That is most wonderful news."

"The sickness seems to come and go. More coming than going these days but I am assured that it will pass. I was returning to the supper room. We wondered why you and Blackmore had not joined us as planned."

She steeled herself. "Blackmore left the ball."

"He left? In the middle of a ball? How peculiar. Did he say why?"

Tears stung her eyes. "I only know he told me he was no longer interested in me and told me I was free to seek the company of others."

"He what?" Anger sparked in the duchess' eyes. "How dare he? George said Jon is quite taken with you. Why on earth—"

"I don't know," she interrupted. "I am leaving now. I need time alone."

The duchess nodded wisely. "You have feelings for him."

"I do," she admitted.

"Arabella?" her father called. "The carriage is

here."

"Coming, Papa," she said.

The duchess took her hands. "I will come see you tomorrow. We will talk about this and see if we can come up with why Blackmore would behave so oddly."

"You may not feel up to it, Your Grace. Might I come visit you instead? Of course, I have not had calling cards made up yet."

The duchess surprised Arabella by kissing her cheek. "Friends do not need a calling card. They are always welcome. Come for tea tomorrow. I will ask Lady Elizabeth to come, as well. She might have some insight as to why her brother is behaving so out of character."

"Thank you, Your Grace. I bid you a good evening."

Arabella joined her father and they went outside. In the carriage, he was quite chatty. She found she couldn't listen to him and only interjected a few murmurs every now and then, which kept him talking. They arrived home and she went to her bedchamber, where Annie helped remove her gown and dressed her for bed.

Alone, Arabella finally gave into her tears, soaking the pillowcase as she fell into a restless sleep.

ARABELLA RODE DRY-EYED in the carriage along with Annie. It still irritated her that at four and twenty she was expected to have her lady's maid act as a chaperone whenever she went anywhere in the city. There was something said for being middle class and living outside of London. She desperately missed her old life in Oxford but knew it was foolish to dwell on it. She was the daughter of an earl now and nothing would ever be the same.

What had changed most was how her heart could hurt so. She had never been one to allow emotions to dictate her mood. She had been proud of being self-reliant and not behaving as a typical female. She was intelligent and she used it without shame. Even when they had left the academic world of Oxford, she had been able to play to her strengths as she managed the Wiltshire estate.

Now, though, as a pampered lady of London, she had little to do other than make herself presentable to go to social affairs. The only thing that had made those seem worthwhile was seeing Jon. With him tossing her away as if she were rubbish, emotions she had never experienced came to the surface. He'd shown her a tantalizing glimpse of paradise—and then yanked it away. Perhaps his sister might shed some light on the reason why he'd chosen to part ways with her.

The carriage arrived at the Duchess of Colebourne's residence and a footman helped her and Annie from it.

"I'll go around to the kitchens, my lady," her servant said. "Send word when you're to leave."

"I will, Annie."

Arabella did her best to muster a smile and went to the front door. She was admitted by the butler and led not to the drawing room but rather a small, sunny parlor. The duchess sat at a writing desk and pushed aside her correspondence as Arabella entered.

"There you are," she said warmly, crossing the room and enveloping Arabella in a tight embrace. "It is so good to see you."

"It's very good to see you looking so well, Your Grace."

The duchess laughed. "I've only lost my breakfast today. I had several bites for luncheon and they stayed down. I hope that's a good sign. Please, come and sit, Lady Arabella. Elizabeth should be here shortly."

They had only just settled themselves when Lady Elizabeth entered the room, followed by the teacart. The duchess greeted her new visitor and then prepared the tea, passing each of them a cup and saucer as they both made up a small plate.

"Everything looks wronderful, Your Grace," Arabella said. "Thank you for having me today."

The duchess settled back and said, "First of all, I am to be Samantha. It is what Elizabeth calls me and I wish for you to do the same in private."

"Oh, that is quite an honor," she said, moved by the duchess' kind gesture. "And I am Arabella to you both."

"Elizabeth and I have gotten to know each other better as we've spent time with Elise—Lady Ruthersby." The duchess chuckled. "We were helping her to find suitable women to be my brother's duchess and have spent many hours on the endeavor."

Arabella was confused. "I am not sure I quite understand."

"My brother had already told our circle of his deep and abiding feelings for Elise. We knew all along that he would offer for her."

"And he did it in the most spectacular way at last night's ball," Elizabeth said. "It was the most romantic thing I've ever witnessed."

"Though the *ton* will wag their tongues about it for weeks to come, I am grateful that love has finally come into my brother's life," Samantha said. "He was to be married once many years ago. The marriage did not take place and he turned wild, earning his sobriquet the Duke of Disrepute. I think he'll sport a new nickname soon." She paused. "But we need to talk of another matter. That of Blackmore and Arabella. Do you have any insight, Elizabeth?"

"I wish I did," Elizabeth said.

Hearing her words, Arabella's heart sank.

"He had asked my father for permission to court me and then last night—immediately after the Duke of Treadwell proposed to Lady Ruthersby—he called me aside and, in private, told me he was withdrawing. That I should feel free to seek the company of other gentlemen."

"I truly don't understand why my brother would do such a thing, Arabella. And then he left abruptly this morning for Suffolk."

"Suffolk? Whatever for?" asked Samantha.

"That's a bit of a mystery. I confronted him at breakfast for leaving me stranded at the ball." Elizabeth smiled. "Thank you again for helping me to get home last night, Samantha. I accused Jon of forgetting about me. He admitted he had."

"But what is in Suffolk that would claim his attention?" Samantha asked.

"Our uncle and his son, our cousin." Elizabeth shook her head. "I never even knew we had an uncle. Jon had never mentioned him before this morning. He told me that Uncle Ambrose had come to the house once when Jon and Arch were very young, six or so, and that was the only time he'd ever seen him. Other than knowing Ambrose had gone into the military, Jon knew nothing about our uncle."

Arabella wondered who Arch might be, having never met him. From what Elizabeth said, he was a possible sibling. Perhaps being a second son, this Arch had gone into the military and was now at war against Bonaparte.

"Hmm," Samantha said. "Sounds like a falling out between your father and uncle."

Elizabeth continued. "Jon received word from some solicitor a few days ago that Uncle Ambrose was on death's doorstep and had named Jon as his son's guardian. The letter didn't mention how old Cousin Arthur is, only that Jon should come to Suffolk with haste to handle the affairs."

Arabella wondered why Jon hadn't left immediately upon receiving the news. As one who hadn't known her own uncles and had yet to meet the two daughters of the previous Earl of Barrington, she certainly would have gone quickly to see this dying uncle and meet her cousin.

"But would that have anything to do with Blackmore brushing off Arabella?" Samantha mused.

"I don't see why it would," Elizabeth said. "Jon said he might be gone a week or more, depending upon when Uncle Ambrose passed. He didn't know if Arthur was at school or if this solicitor had the boy brought home to see his father one last time before he passed. It's all very mysterious—but it shouldn't have affected his budding relationship with you, Arabella."

She found herself tearing up and hated that her emotions had such control over her.

Elizabeth took her hand and squeezed it. "I can tell you how excited Jon was about getting to know you. When the Season began, we both were quite honest with one another. I told my brother I was looking for love and that was the reason why I had not accepted any offers during my come-out. He shared that he was tired of the life he was leading and envious of his friends who had married and were building lives with their wives and hoping to start families. I know he has strong feelings for you, Arabella. I cannot imagine why he would break away from you, especially after seeing such happiness last night between Elise and Treadwell."

Arabella patted Elizabeth's hand before releasing it. "I will be honest. His words have left me in a quandary. He . . . well . . . he kissed me last night. It occurred before we danced and Treadwell proposed. I thought things were going splendidly between us, only to have my hopes dashed. Mind you, no promises had been given, much less broken, but I feel a sense of loss and betrayal all the same."

She took a sip of tea to calm her and then said, "I would never tell anyone outside this room but I am very hurt."

"And well you should be," Samantha agreed. "Blackmore has a reputation as a notorious rake but he has always acted very honorably in my presence. George considers him a dear, true friend, one who is loyal and would never betray him."

She looked to Elizabeth. "Do you think your brother . . . do you think he toyed with me? Being a rake, he may have wished to deflower me. If he had any feelings for me, might he have changed his mind about ruining me and that's why he said what he did?"

"My brother has had numerous affairs, I'll grant you that," Elizabeth said. "But he has never hurt an innocent. He has bedded only experienced, willing women. Widows who were free to do as they pleased or wives who had already provided their husbands with an heir and as many in the *ton* do, sought pleasure outside their marriages. Jon is a very good man, Arabella. When he returns to London, I will confront him and we will find the reason for his dismissal of you."

"No," she protested. "That is the last thing I want, Elizabeth. I don't want him to know I came to either of you regarding this matter. If he has decided I am not for him, I must learn to accept that and move on."

"But he cares for you," Elizabeth said passionately. "I know he does."

"Then he has an odd way of showing it," Arabella said. "I beg of you. Let the matter lie and don't involve yourselves."

"But what will you do, Arabella?" asked

Samantha. "I know from how you speak that you have developed feelings for Blackmore. Especially since you kissed him."

She shrugged. "My father expects me to wed after this Season ends. I suppose I shall have to investigate other men and get to know them."

But her heart told her that none of them would live up to the Duke of Blackmore. No man was as handsome or intelligent. None of them could stir her blood with his kisses. It didn't matter. She would shove her heart aside and lock it away, where it had remained all these years, allowing her to think rationally once again.

Placing her saucer down, she said, "If I am to look for a husband, I must be more presentable."

She saw the look exchanged between her new friends.

"I had a few gowns made up in Wiltshire before we came to London but I see now they are most inadequate. My maid has tried to do what she can with her needle to make them more presentable but I believe what I need is a good dressmaker here in London."

Samantha nodded. "Elizabeth and I share the most wonderful modiste. I will write to her now and see if she will grant you an appointment tomorrow. And the both of us will go with you to help you choose fabrics and styles."

Elizabeth smiled. "For now, you can come home with me. We are the same height and I believe I have several gowns that might fit you."

"I cannot take your wardrobe!" Arabella protested.

"I have too many gowns to count," her friend said. "And I am wearing none of those I did last year. You can take several of them and your maid can make them over so no one will recognize them."

Tears welled in her eyes. "That would be wonderful. How can I thank you both?"

Samantha smiled knowingly. "By looking spectacular in your new gowns. When Blackmore returns to London, he will salivate at your feet. And if for some odd reason he still wishes to keep to himself, then you will attract a good many men in his place. You are already quite popular. We will find you a husband, Arabella. I guarantee it."

Arabella smiled, knowing the only man she longed for had washed his hands of her. She would have to make the best of the situation, though. She couldn't wait around for the Duke of Blackmore to come to his senses. She would forge ahead and live her life the way she chose.

CHAPTER SEVENTEEN

Framington, Suffolk

JON ARRIVED AT Milford Milligan's office after stopping at the local tavern for a bite to eat since he had consumed nothing all day. Food held no taste for him ever since he'd left Arabella's side two nights ago. He forced all thoughts of her from his mind as he tried to down the bowl of stew and half a loaf of bread the tavern wench brought to him. Once he'd finished, he'd asked her where Milligan could be found and was directed here.

Framington was a small village about five miles north of Ipswich. He hoped his uncle's residence was nearby. He was weary from his journey and the sleeplessness brought about by letting Arabella go. It was for the best. She was a remarkable woman who deserved a man who would love her to the extreme. He had tried to convince himself he could be that man but only a cold lump resided in his chest where his heart should be. Arabella needed a husband who would make her the most important thing in his life. Jon didn't love himself and couldn't bring himself to drag Arabella into the mire he existed in.

He knocked on the door and entered when bidden to do so. A slight man with a trim moustache and sandy hair sat behind a desk. Kind, brown eyes hid behind gold spectacles.

"Mr. Milligan? I am the Duke of Blackmore."

The solicitor shot to his feet. "Oh, Your Grace. I only received your letter an hour ago. You almost beat it here," he exclaimed.

"My plans changed. I was able to leave London earlier than I expected. How is my uncle? And what of this cousin? You said very little of him, other than I would be named his guardian."

"Mr. Arthur Sutton has just turned sixteen, Your Grace. He is a delightful young man, though a bit lonely."

Jon frowned. "Has he no friends? Is he bullied at school?"

"No, there's been no school for Arthur in a good seven years or more."

"Why not?"

Milligan indicated a chair. "Might you have a seat, Your Grace? I can fill you in on what you need to know."

Jon took a seat and stared at Milligan. "Well?"

Nervously, the solicitor shuffled papers around on his desk. Jon tried to relax his features. He knew with his height and build that he cut an imposing figure. Throw the title of a duke into the mix, along with his innate arrogance, and he thoroughly intimidated people.

"I only met my uncle once and that was more than two decades ago. I was but a small boy. Tell me what you can of him."

"I see." Milligan adjusted his spectacles and calmed himself. "Being a second son of nobility, Colonel Sutton served in His Majesty's Army his entire adult life. That is, until he was injured in the Battle of Bussaco."

Jon had kept track of the many battles of the war, especially the ones of the Peninsular War, since Sebastian had been stationed there during that time. He idly wondered if his friend had encountered Ambrose while in Spain and Portugal.

"Bussaco? That is in Portugal, isn't it?" he asked. "I seem to recall that battle occurred a good five years ago."

"Yes, Your Grace. In the Portuguese mountain range of Serra do Bucaco. Lord Wellington's Anglo-Portuguese army defeated the French forces. Colonel Sutton was severely injured and not thought to live. He rallied and was brought back to Framington, where his wife and son lived. Mrs. Sutton was in delicate health, however, and died soon after her husband returned. Arthur was already living at home with his mother. He'd gone off to school, per his father's request, but his mother was lonely and had the boy brought home after only a few terms. Once the colonel arrived home, Arthur never left again. He was needed at home to help care for his father."

Jon pitied the boy, having to leave school to keep a sickly mother company and then remaining at home these past five years while his father obviously was in poor health. It was a heavy burden to place upon the shoulders of one so young.

"I would like to see my uncle now if he is still alive. If not, I wish to meet my cousin."

"I can take you there. Sutton Cottage is perhaps two miles from Framington."

"Good. My carriage is waiting outside."

They retreated to it, Milligan giving the coachman directions to their destination. On the way there, Jon reflected on the few times his father had mentioned his brother over the years. The duke claimed Ambrose unfit to do anything, saying horrible things about his own flesh and blood and remarking how their father had given up on teaching Ambrose anything. What Jon remembered most was how his father said because Ambrose lacked any kind of skill, Jon's grandfather had washed his hands of his second son, concentrating on teaching Jon's father all he would need to know to become Duke of Blackmore. It reminded him of his own boyhood and how his father had favored Arch over him to the extreme. Jon sympathized with his uncle and felt terrible for his much younger cousin.

The carriage came to a halt and they disembarked. Sutton Cottage was a small structure, probably all his uncle could afford after being pensioned off after his war wound. He vowed to do right by his cousin and help Arthur forge a good life once his father was dead.

The door opened and a short, stout man stood before them, his eyes wary.

"Ah, Mr. Randall," said Milligan. "This is His Grace, the Duke of Blackmore, and nephew to the colonel."

The man looked Jon up and down dismissively. "You took long enough to get here."

A sizzle of anger ran through him. "I did not know anything of my uncle nor his condition until I received Mr. Milligan's missive earlier this week."

Surprise filled the man's face and then he snorted. "Figures."

"Might we come in, Mr. Randall?" the solicitor asked.

"Suit yourself." Randall stepped aside and admitted the pair.

Jon looked about the cottage, seeing it was small and mostly bare. "I'd like to see Uncle

Ambrose."

"The doctor's with him now," Randall said.

"Good. I had planned to speak to the doctor," he added, "about my uncle's injury and how to make him more comfortable."

"I've been making him comfortable for years," Randall retorted. "Without the likes of you."

"Mr. Randall!" exclaimed Milligan. "You are to be respectful to His Grace."

"Why?" the surly servant demanded. "His father wasn't respectful of my master."

Jon spoke up. "I admire your loyalty to my uncle, Mr. Randall. And I apologize for my father's behavior. He was a hard man. As his second son, I received little of his attention."

Randall, who was gazing away, turned and met Jon's eyes. "Is that so?"

"Yes. My brother, who was minutes older than I, was the favored son. He died and I became the duke instead."

He wasn't sure why he was sharing this with such a belligerent servant but the man did seem protective of his uncle. That was something to be said in his favor.

"The colonel never got one letter from his father. I should know. I was his batman and with him from the beginning."

Jon saw loyalty ran deep with this man. "Uncle Ambrose came to the house once when I was a small boy. We spoke briefly—but he made a lasting impression upon me. I am grateful for your service to him all these years."

"It's been my pleasure to serve the colonel. In the army and now."

"Are you his valet?" Jon asked.

A harsh bark emitted from Randall. "His valet? I suppose so, Your Grace. I care for him and the house. There are no other servants. Only me and young Arthur. We see to the colonel."

Guilt rushed through Jon. He had unimaginable wealth and numerous properties. If he had known where his uncle and cousin were and that they were in such great need, he would have settled an income on them and given them an estate. Or brought them to live with him and Elizabeth. She would have liked that.

"Well, I am here now. I will do my part since I am finally aware of the situation."

"The situation, Your Grace, is the man is dying," Randall said bluntly. "He has been since I helped carry him off a battlefield five years ago. He's died a little each day. Suffered unimaginable pain."

Jon's thoughts turned to Arch and how he, too, had suffered terribly. "I am sorry to hear that. Truly."

"Are you the duke?" a voice asked.

Jon turned and saw a middle-aged man with light brown hair and a weary face.

"Yes. I am Blackmore," he confirmed.

The man crossed to him. "I am Dr. Smallwood, Colonel Sutton's physician. You have come just in time, Your Grace. I heard your voice and came to investigate. Come with me. I fear your uncle has only minutes to live."

Jon followed Smallwood up the narrow staircase. Two rooms were on the second floor and they turned to the right and entered the bedchamber. Candles burned on the bedstand and what had to be his cousin sat next to the bed, his face wet with tears. Jon nodded at the boy, who resembled him and Arch at that age, and then turned his attention to the man in the bed. He recognized the face from so many years ago but it was now deeply lined. His uncle's hair was sparse and what was left of it had turned an iron gray. He wheezed as he breathed. Ambrose was also missing an arm and both legs.

He went to the bedside and knelt, taking his uncle's hand.

"Uncle Ambrose, it is Jon. Do you remember me?"

Rheumy eyes turned to him. "Jon," he rasped. "You came."

"I did." He squeezed his uncle's hand. "I recall your visit to Blackstone Manor all those years ago. You were resplendent in your military uniform and made quite an impression upon me."

"I recall your brother was nowhere to be

found."

Instinct to protect his twin kicked in, even after so many years of Arch being gone.

"Arch hadn't the patience to eavesdrop at the door as I did while you and Father spoke."

"Argued, is more like it." Ambrose began coughing, the sound deep in his chest. "Thank you for coming."

"If I had known, I would—"

"I didn't want you to. Actually, I didn't want my brother to know anything. Especially after I came home from the war missing three of my four limbs. I'm also deaf in my left ear."

"I have been the duke for a more than a dozen years," Jon revealed. "Since I was sixteen."

Ambrose frowned. "I wasn't aware of that. As death approached, though, I had hopes that my brother already roasted in Hell and that my nephew would take on my son." He turned and smiled at Arthur and then returned his gaze to Jon. "What happened to your brother?"

"He died," Jon said succinctly, pushing away the memory of Arch drinking the overdose of laudanum. "His death killed my father."

"You've made a better duke than Archibald would have."

"You can't know that," he protested.

"I do. The way your father spoke about him that last time we were together, I could tell he had coddled the boy. Let him get away with too much. You, though, I could tell had a sense of right and wrong. I am sure you are a fine duke."

His uncle paused again, another coughing fit upon him. This time, he spit up vast quantities of blood and Dr. Smallwood moved in and fussed over him before finally stepping back.

"Will you take my Arthur in hand, Jonathan? Teach him to be a good man? Selfishly, my wife kept him home with her because she was lonely in my absence. When I came back to England, I fear I did the same thing. Arthur is woefully behind in his studies but he is a bright lad. Will you see he gets an education?"

Jon brought his uncle's hand to his lips and pressed a fervent kiss upon it. "I will, Uncle. Arthur will be treated as a brother by Elizabeth and me. He will be a valued member of the Sutton family."

"Ah, you have a wife? Children?"

Regret shot through him as he thought of Arabella. "No. Elizabeth is my sister."

Ambrose frowned. "You are old enough for a wife. You need one in order to get children off her. Do so soon, Jonathan." He closed his eyes and immediately fell into a restless sleep.

Randall stepped up. "The colonel's tired. You all should leave."

"I will stay downstairs," Dr. Smallwood offered. "I want to be here in case he needs me. He's due for another dose of laudanum soon."

"Arthur and I will remain by his bedside," Jon told the servant, daring him to say otherwise.

Instead, Randall nodded in approval. "I'll see you out then, Mr. Milligan."

"Have my driver return you to Framington."

"Thank you, Your Grace."

After everyone left, Jon turned to Arthur. "We have much to talk about, Cousin. I'd rather save it for another time. I want your father to get some good rest."

"Yes, Your Grace."

"No, none of that," he admonished gently. "I meant what I told him. You will be my brother. That means I am Jon."

Arthur swallowed. "All right, Jon."

They sat in silence until Ambrose began to struggle to breathe and Jon had Arthur fetch Dr. Smallwood. Randall came with the doctor and the four of them stayed until the colonel's breathing slowed and then stilled.

Dr. Smallwood checked. "He's gone."

"The colonel was a great man," Randall said. "He deserved a glorious end on the battlefield. Not lying in this bed, forgotten by the world."

"He may have wished for a different end," Jon said, "but it allowed him additional time with his son. I am certain that was more important."

He released his uncle's hand, which he had held for hours, the skin already beginning to cool. As he stood, he said, "You can help plan his funeral with me, Randall. You knew him best and will know what he would have wanted."

CHAPTER EIGHTEEN

JON THANKED THE clergyman who had conducted the graveside service for his uncle and then placed an arm about his cousin's shoulders.

"Shall we return to Sutton Cottage?" he asked.

Arthur nodded solemnly. The boy hadn't shed a tear for his father. Jon decided to dismiss his carriage and walk back. It was only a mile or so and would give them time to talk.

"I feel sorry for Papa," Arthur said. "Only the two of us, Randall, and Mr. Milligan came to the service. He was once an important man who commanded hundreds of troops. Helped the great Wellington plan his strategies. Then he wound up forgotten in a tiny English village."

"Such is the way of war, Arthur. Men—great and small—contribute to the war effort and then come home to lead quiet lives."

"Papa's was one full of pain. It wasn't fair."

"Sometimes life isn't fair." He hesitated and then added, "I had a brother once. My twin, born a few minutes before I was. We were the best of friends and closer than any two people could be. He got sick and died when we were sixteen. It was Arch who should have been the duke. Arch who should be living the life I live now."

"Do you miss him?"

"Every day. I swore to him I would live life to the fullest, for the both of us."

"Do you?"

Jon shrugged. "I could do better. We all could."

They walked on in silence for a few minutes and then Arthur said, "What am I to do now, Your Grace?"

"Jon," he prompted. "You will come to London with me, of course. Elizabeth, your other cousin, will be delighted to meet you. She is a few years older than you are and made her come-out to the *ton* last Season."

"What is the *ton*?"

Oh, this boy was ignorant of so many things.

"A come-out is when a girl makes her debut into Polite Society. They are the *ton*. It is a way for men to find wives. Various social affairs go on from after Easter through the end of summer. There are many balls and all kinds of parties. You are too young to attend these for now. Elizabeth will teach you to how to dance, though, so you can practice for when you begin attending events."

"When will that be?"

"When you finish your education. Can you tell me a little about your schooling?"

"I took lessons from the vicar for a few years and then Papa made funds available to send me off to school." Arthur brightened. "I liked it very much, especially math and history." Then he frowned. "But Mama missed me and had me return to Sutton Cottage to keep her company. Then Papa came home and Mama died. I couldn't leave him."

"So you had no lessons after that?"

"No," Arthur said, his head hanging in embarrassment. "Papa's military pension barely covered the cost of renting our cottage, much less food. Lessons and books were too great a luxury though Dr. Smallwood loaned me the few he has and I have pored over those."

Again, Jon felt guilty for not having known any of this. He could easily have had Uncle Ambrose moved to Blackstone Manor to be cared for while Arthur attended school.

"Instead, Papa tried to educate me the best he knew how. I have a slate and he would assign me sums or Latin verbs to conjugate and I would mark them there. Mostly, though, he talked of the war. He was away for years at a time, only coming home for short visits. He talked of his travels and the military. The strategies employed. What territories Bonaparte had tried to conquer and of the battles fought."

He didn't think sending Arthur away to school would prove to be very successful. It sounded as though the boy were woefully behind in his studies compared to others his age. University entrance exams would loom within the next year. Instead, Jon would need to hire a tutor to work with his cousin around the clock in order to prepare him for those exams. If he even wanted to go.

"Would you like to continue you education, Arthur?" he asked.

The boy's eyes lit up. "Oh, yes, Cousin Jon. Very much so." Then his shoulders sagged. "I know I haven't the background of other boys but I am a quick learner. If I have access to the proper tools, books and such, I could teach myself."

"No, I will find a competent tutor for you."

For some reason, Arabella came to mind.

Jon had spent hours thinking of the enchanting beauty ever since they had parted. He fell asleep to her image and dreamed of her nightly. Though he knew it would be wrong to take her as his wife, he thought of her intelligence and compassion. How she would be the perfect person to guide Arthur in his studies for a short time. Her knowledge would be put to good use and it would help Arthur to grow in confidence.

They reached Sutton Cottage and he said, "Pack your things. We will leave first thing in the morning."

"There isn't much to pack," Arthur admitted.

Jon knew that certainly was the case with the boy's clothes. The sleeves on his shirt and coat were too short and his trousers struck him just above the ankles. He would see that his cousin had a new wardrobe once they reached London.

"Well, get everything together that you need. We won't be returning to Framington."

"All right, Jon." Arthur scurried up the stairs.

He turned as Randall entered with several logs of firewood for the kitchen stove, taking it there and feeding them into it.

"I just saw the doctor," the former batman said, rising to his full height. "He apologized for missing the colonel's service. He had to patch up a boy who broke both his legs."

Jon wondered what Randall would do now that his master had passed on and felt responsible for the man who had taken care of Uncle Ambrose for so many years.

"Do you have plans, Randall?"

The servant shrugged. "I was hoping to stay here. The rent's paid for the quarter. It took up most of the colonel's pension. I'd hate to see it go to waste."

"What about after that?"

"Dunno," the servant said glumly. "Can't read or write. Now that Boney's entered Paris, I suppose I could go back to the army. If they'll have me. The colonel wrote me a reference before he died, in case I decided to do that."

Jon thought a moment. "It is going to be very hard on Arthur to leave everything he's ever known."

"The lad'll be fine. He's as bright as a shiny, new penny. He'll pick up all the airs and schooling." Randall stared at him. "That is, if you send him away. The colonel didn't have the money to do so. He wanted to do right by his boy and couldn't. It was his chief regret."

Randall looked away but not before Jon saw tears brimming in the servant's eyes.

"I don't think that would be in Arthur's best interest," Jon confided. "He has little formal schooling. He might be bullied for being so far behind his classmates. I was thinking of keeping him home and hiring a tutor for him. That way, he could prepare for his university entrance exams and get to know Elizabeth and me better." He paused. "But it would be good for him to have a familiar face about."

Randall rubbed his chin. "What are you saying, Your Grace?"

"I think you should come to London with us. You could act as Arthur's valet or I could find you another position in my household. I believe my cousin will make the adjustment to his new life more easily with you around to ease his way."

The man's face lit with a smile. "You mean it, Your Grace? I look upon the boy as family. I know he isn't but it would be good to see him have all the advantages his father wanted for him."

"Come with us, Randall," Jon encouraged. "It will ease Arthur's transition. Of course, we won't spend the entire year in London. We go to my main country holding, Blackstone Manor, as well as visiting other estates."

"I will come and serve you and young Arthur in whatever capacity you wish, Your Grace."

"Then you better go pack."

"Let me stir the stew and I'll do just that."

Jon saw the man had a spring in his step and knew he'd done the right thing by asking his uncle's loyal retainer to come to London.

ARTHUR COULDN'T CONTAIN his excitement as they drove through the busy streets of London.

"There are so many people, Jon!" he exclaimed. "The traffic. The buildings. I'll never find my way around."

"You won't be going out alone for some time. I will accompany you or Randall or a footman will do so. We wouldn't want you to get lost. London is teeming with people but there are large parts of it that you will not visit."

"Why not?" asked his cousin innocently.

"Let's just keep to our Mayfair neighborhood first."

"Don't forget about riding," Arthur prompted.

Jon had learned that the boy had never been atop a horse though he said his father had been a masterful rider before his war injuries. They simply hadn't had the income to buy and stable a horse. Framington was small and Arthur had walked everywhere, from church to the small village store where he purchased supplies such as flour for Randall to bake them their bread. The former batman had not only cared for Jon's uncle, bathing and changing him, but he'd also cooked all the meals and cleaned the small cottage. Arthur shared he sometimes helped in these duties but they had kept that hidden from Uncle Ambrose.

"What is Cousin Elizabeth like?" Arthur asked, his leg bouncing nervously.

"She is very kind and loving. She will shower you with both love and attention. You'll probably tire of it."

"I don't think so. Mama fussed over me but then always pushed me away. I never knew how to please her. Father was stoic and never demonstrative toward me. I never received a hug or kiss from him."

Jon's heart ached at the lonely, isolated life his young cousin had led.

"Things will change now. Elizabeth will smother you in kisses. She'll also teach you about society.

"The *ton*."

"Yes, that's correct. She will talk to you about good manners and teach you about music and dancing."

"What will you teach me, Jon?"

"I'll help fill in any gaps," he replied smoothly.

"When will you hire my tutor? I am eager to start my studies. Are you really going to pay for him—and for university?"

He smiled. "You need never worry about money again, Arthur."

He thought the boy too thin and now knew it was most likely because there hadn't been enough to eat. Jon planned not only to have Cook fatten up Arthur but once he completed his university studies, Jon would give Arthur one of his unentailed estates as a gift. He might have Arthur help run parts of Blackstone Manor before he did so, helping the boy gain confidence and knowledge. He only wished he could bestow a title upon him.

Then he realized if he never wed that Arthur

would become the next duke. As the closest male Sutton, he would inherit a wealth of titles and estates. Arthur was a sweet lad and would make for a good duke once given the proper training. Not the ridiculous mountain of information their father had foisted upon Arch, but enough so that Arthur would understand his responsibilities and be able to act accordingly. Jon relaxed, knowing he didn't have to worry about marriage now and providing an heir to the dukedom. He already had his heir in Arthur.

Then why did he keep thinking about Arabella? Seeing her with a baby on her lap, another child with her golden hair snuggled close to her, a content expression upon her face.

He cursed under his breath, which his cousin didn't hear because he was so taken by the passing scenery. He would take the boy out tomorrow for a drive and point out all the sights to him. They'd go to Hyde Park. The British Museum. For ices at Gunter's. He'd take Arthur to his favorite bookstore and let him choose however many books he wished to purchase. Already, he knew Arthur would delight in the library at the London townhouse, which rivaled that of the one at Blackstone Manor. Jon had always been a reader and his vast collection of books would please anyone with an intellectual bent.

He only wished he had shown the library to

Arabella before they parted. She would have been enamored with it.

"Damnation," he said aloud, causing Arthur to turn and stare at him.

"Is something wrong, Jon?"

"I just remembered I forgot to tell my solicitor something. I'll make an appointment with him."

He would need to see his solicitor in order to provide for Arthur. He would want it made known that his cousin was his heir apparent. Soon, all of Polite Society would know and he could go back to his nefarious ways, sleeping his way through the willing women of the *ton*. Yes, it would hurt Arabella when she heard the rumors but he hoped that in the ten days he'd been away from London that she had forgotten all about him. That she'd had numerous gentlemen call upon her and perhaps even found a few to her liking.

Men he wished to bash in their faces for even smiling at her.

He had to stop torturing himself. Arabella Jennings had been a fleeting dream. He had wanted her for her goodness, thinking she could change who he was. But tigers didn't shed their stripes. The Duke of Blackmore was who Jon was, whether he had wanted to be so or not. He would release the dream of Arabella and move on with his life, living it to the fullest, as Arch would have done. If at times he felt empty or shallow, so be it. By God, he was a duke of England, practically royalty. He didn't need to waste any time being wistful for what might have been.

The carriage turned onto their square and he pointed. "That is your new home, Arthur."

The boy's jaw fell. He tried to speak but no words came out. The vehicle slowed and then came to a stop. Jon saw a footman race from the door to open the carriage as Thistle looked on with interest. Jon had written to Elizabeth to tell him he would be bringing Arthur home and she, too, emerged in the open doorway and came to stand on the pavement.

He bounded out and then stepped aside so Arthur could remove himself from the coach.

"Cousin Arthur!" Elizabeth cried and came toward him with open arms. She threw them about him. "I am so glad to have you here. You will be another brother to me, a younger one so I may lord over you."

Arthur looked unsure and she said, "I am teasing you, Arthur. Have you never been teased before?"

She flung her arms about him again and soundly smacked him on both cheeks before doing the same to Jon. He kissed her in return.

"You are in time for tea," Elizabeth said. "It will be served in an hour. I have a few guests coming and they are eager to meet you, Arthur."

She slipped her arm through his. "Come and let me show you your rooms."

"Rooms?" Arthur squeaked.

"Yes. You'll have a sitting room, which can also serve as your place of study. Jon said he will be hiring a tutor for you and it will be a good place for you to meet. You also have a large bedchamber. Now, let me share with you about meal times."

Elizabeth led Arthur into the house. Jon turned and saw Randall had come down from where he had ridden with the driver and had removed his and Arthur's valises from the top of the carriage.

"Thistle?"

The butler scurried over. "Yes, Your Grace."

"This is Randall. He will serve as my young cousin's valet."

"I'll need more to do than that," growled Randall. "The lad won't need taking care of that much."

"I plan to take Arthur to my tailor's tomorrow, Thistle."

The butler nodded solemnly. "It's a good thing, Your Grace. It looks as if he grew four inches in his arms and legs since you left Ipswich."

Jon didn't bother telling his butler that all of Arthur's clothes were too small for him and instead said, "Perhaps there is something of mine from several years ago that he might wear? Just a few basics. Ask my valet. Winspeth might know where to locate something suitable."

"I'll see to it now, Your Grace, as well as have hot water for a bath sent up to you and Mr. Sutton. I am sure you are eager to wash the dust of the road from you before you take tea. Come along, Mr. Randall. I will show you to your room and we can discuss the other ways you can serve in His Grace's household before you aid Mr. Sutton in his bath."

He appreciated how Thistle—and all of his servants—seemed to anticipate his every need. He knew it would take Arthur some getting used to, living in such a grand house.

An hour later, Jon came downstairs with Arthur in tow. His cousin wore an outdated coat and pair of trousers Jon had discarded years ago when he'd gone through a growth spurt. The clothing couldn't have been worn more than twice. He had no idea where Winspeth kept such items but was happy the valet had located them. Arthur didn't seem to care about the style and kept raving how well the clothes fit him.

"I've never worn anything so nice before, Jon. Thank you again."

"It's only for a few days. I'll take you to my tailor and bootmaker tomorrow. They will see you properly attired. Until then, you can wear a few of my hand-me-downs."

"I cannot imagine wearing anything finer than this."

He chuckled. "You'll get used to it. Here is the drawing room. Let's see who Elizabeth is entertaining for tea today. Being unmarried and quite beautiful, she has attracted a good number of suitors."

"During the Season," Arthur added, showing off his limited knowledge of society.

"Yes."

Jon stepped inside and saw the backs of two women, realizing his sister's guests were not gentlemen callers but friends. His heart began pounding in his chest as they crossed the room. Samantha was one visitor.

And Arabella was the other.

CHAPTER NINETEEN

ARABELLA WAS PLEASED she remained poised as Jon appeared before them. She rose and smiled graciously, despite the thickening of her throat. She reminded herself to take slow, even breaths. She would get through this. It had been inevitable that she would see Jon once he returned from his uncle's funeral. In the time he'd been gone, she had been taken in by his circle of friends, especially the women, and there would be no avoiding him in the future. She hoped she could remain polite yet distant and wished Jon would be able to do the same.

No—Blackmore. She needed to start thinking of him as the notorious rake and unattainable duke.

Not the man who, for a brief moment, had her thinking foolish notions about a future together. About love. She knew now that their kiss, her first, had meant little to him. She was, as

Lady Walton put it, a mere conquest. Yet he hadn't deflowered her. Perhaps in some small way he did care for her. Or at least knew she was important to Elizabeth and had decided to keep his hands off her.

Even though he'd already broken her heart.

"Your Grace, Lady Arabella, I would like you to meet our cousin, Mr. Arthur Sutton."

Even his voice still made delightful shivers run down her spine.

Arthur stepped up and greeted Samantha first and then turned to her.

"It is very nice to meet you, Lady Arabella."

He was certainly a Sutton. He had the family's dark hair and blue eyes, though his were a lighter shade than his two cousins' were. Young Arthur also had the height, which the rest of his body hadn't grown into yet. The boy was all gangly arms and legs. When he put on weight and grew into his frame, he would be quite the heartthrob.

Just like his uncle.

Arabella stole a glance at Blackmore. Ooh, the big oaf and all his muscles agitated her. He had no right to look as handsome and wonderful as he did. She made a point to turn away. She wouldn't ignore him during tea but she most certainly wouldn't start any conversation with him. If he spoke to her, she would reply politely. That was all he was due.

"The teacart has arrived," Elizabeth said. "Shall we sit?"

Arabella took the same spot on the settee as she'd previously had and was grateful when Samantha sat beside her again. No more sharing it with a man who took up far too much room. Yet Blackmore sat directly opposite her, in her line of vision, making her uncomfortable. She squelched it. Plenty of young men at Oxford had wanted her to feel miserable as they sat near her in their superiority. She'd learned to be herself and shine. Her intellect and good manners always brought them around.

"Tell us about your life, Arthur," Samantha said. "Have you come from school?"

"No," said the boy, his index finger tugging at the cravat around his throat. "I spent the last several years at home with Father, helping him. His war injuries were severe."

"I am sure you were a huge help to your mother," Arabella said.

"Mother died soon after Father came home from battle. That's why I was needed at home," Arthur explained. "Father wasn't much on history but he did tell me about every campaign he ever fought in. He was on Wellington's staff, you know. A very valued member."

"That is something to be proud of," Elizabeth said. "I wish I could have known Uncle Ambrose."

"Besides all of the battles, he told me about why they were fought. The methods and means used. The strategy behind every move. It was the same when we played chess together."

"Ah, chess," Arabella said. "I play it with my papa. Chess is a great teacher. It helps you to solve problems, both immediate and long-range."

Arthur nodded enthusiastically. "That's exactly what Father said. He taught me to not only plan a move or two ahead but that I must always be thinking a dozen moves into the future. How to act and counteract my opponent." A sad look crossed his face. "We didn't play much the past few months. He was too ill to do so."

"I would enjoy challenging you to a match," she told him. "So would my father, Lord Barrington. You are welcome to come visit us anytime and test your mettle against the two of us."

Delight filled the young man's face. "That would be wonderful, my lady." He looked to his guardian. "May I do so, Jon?"

"Of course." He chuckled. "You had best be on your toes, though, Arthur. Lord Barrington is a former don of Oxford and Lady Arabella is quite knowledgeable herself."

"A don?" Arthur frowned. "A lord can be a don?"

"Papa was a fourth son," Arabella explained. "He never expected to become the earl and made his own way in the world. Through an unusual set of circumstances and the former earl only having two daughters, my father became Lord Barrington only recently."

Teatime continued in a pleasant manner. She noted how Blackmore made sure to include Arthur in their conversation and they talked of plans to take him about London to become acquainted with the city.

"Jon is also taking me to his tailor tomorrow," Arthur shared. "I seem to be growing overnight and nothing fits me. In fact, these are clothes of his that I have borrowed."

Samantha said, "I believe it's time for us to be going. The rout is at our house this evening and I need to make sure all is well with my staff."

"I look forward to seeing George again," Blackmore said. "And I must congratulate your brother and Lady Ruthersby on their betrothal."

The duchess chuckled. "You will have to congratulate them on their marriage instead. Weston had already purchased a special license and put it to good use two days after his very public proposal. I hosted their wedding breakfast. I am sorry you weren't able to attend."

"Then I will look forward to greeting the Duke and the Duchess of Treadwell tonight," Blackmore proclaimed.

Samantha rose and Arabella did the same. The others also stood.

"Might I see you home, Lady Arabella?" Blackmore asked, causing her belly to tighten. "I have a particular proposal to discuss with you."

She felt the color drain from her face and saw he realized how his words could easily be misinterpreted.

Before he could correct his mistake, she said, "I came with the duchess."

"This is something that cannot wait."

Samantha intervened. "Why don't you ride with us, Blackmore? I will have my driver drop me off and then continue on to Lord Barrington's townhouse so you and Lady Arabella have a chance to . . . discuss matters."

No, that wouldn't do at all. That would leave her inside the carriage with him. Alone.

And Arabella couldn't trust herself not to throw herself at him, kissing the life out of him.

That's the last thing she needed to do. Obviously, he had been unaffected by their kisses and had moved on. He'd told her so.

Then why was her stubborn heart refusing to yield? Refusing to recognize the facts?

"Thank you." He turned to Arthur. "I will let you and Elizabeth become better acquainted and see you for an early dinner before we leave for tonight's rout."

Blackmore escorted them downstairs and out to the waiting carriage. Fortunately, one of Samantha's footmen was prepared and had the steps placed down and helped the two women into the vehicle. Arabella quickly sat next to her friend, her heart pounding as Blackmore sprawled on the seat opposite them.

They reached the Colebourne townhouse and as Samantha started out, Arabella said, "It's only a few blocks to my home. Being that it is such a nice day, I'd rather walk."

"What a good idea," Blackmore said, following them out and then bidding Samantha goodbye.

He offered his arm and she took it, not wanting to seem churlish. It only angered her, though, to feel the marvelous muscles beneath her fingertips. She breathed in his clean, masculine scent and that irked her even further. She thought she should breathe from her mouth to avoid it but decided that would make her look like a dog, panting after him. Steeling herself, she fell into step beside him, wondering what he wished to speak to her about alone.

Instead of broaching the subject, he began speaking of his uncle.

"I have regrets in my life. One of them is not knowing Uncle Ambrose," he said, his tone thoughtful. "I only met him once when I was quite young but he made a lasting impression upon me. He came to Blackstone Manor in his military uniform, looking as tall as a mountain. I thought he was the most formidable man I'd ever seen."

"Why only once?" she asked, her curiosity getting the better of her.

"Uncle Ambrose and Father were estranged. My grandfather pitted them against each other, preferring my father simply because he would become the next duke. It was the only time I saw my uncle. I never knew what became of him, other than he was in the military. With Bonaparte keeping Europe busy for the last two decades, I assumed Ambrose fought against him."

"Arthur mentioned his father's war injuries."

The duke grimaced. "I learned a French spy blew up the tent he and several officers were in as they strategized for the upcoming battle. By the grace of God, Wellington had been delayed by an aide-de-camp else he would also have been present. Randall, my uncle's batman who came home to England with him, told me all but two men lost their lives that day. The first died of his injuries a day later. Only Ambrose survived. He lost both legs and eventually an arm and was deaf in one ear."

A shudder ran through Arabella. "How horrid. It must have been difficult for a boy so young to see his father that way."

"Arthur only saw Ambrose twice before when he came for short visits. He admits he didn't recall much of the first one because he was so young. Then his mother died and it only left him and Randall to care for my uncle. I wish I had thought to search for him and make contact sooner. I could have made their lives so much easier. Perhaps even gotten Uncle Ambrose medical help."

She halted and looked directly into his eyes. "You aren't to blame for the mischief your grandfather caused, forcing two brothers apart. I don't know when you became the duke but I know just from Papa becoming Lord Barrington how many responsibilities there are."

"I was young. Sixteen."

"Sixteen? Why, you were still a boy. You must have been overwhelmed."

"It was . . . difficult," he admitted and then urged her to continue down the street.

They turned the corner and her house came into view. Nothing was said as Stone admitted them. Arabella led the duke to the nearest parlor, not wanting to go all the way upstairs to the drawing room.

As they stepped inside the room, Jon looked about. The parlor was covered in bouquets and the cloying smell of flowers filled the air.

"I see you have been quite popular in my absence," he commented, trying to keep his tone neutral though jealousy gripped him in a vise.

"Oh, the flower arrangements," she said, carelessly tossing her hand. "I think every gentleman in London feels the need to send flowers to any woman he speaks to or dances with. I am sure those who sell flowers make more during the weeks of the Season than they do the rest of the year combined."

"So, you've been dancing while I've been gone."

"Yes," she said begrudgingly. "It seems I am not a wallflower, after all." She paused and then in her frank way said, "Why are you here, Your Grace? What is it you wish to speak to me about that couldn't have been said in front of others?"

He watched her deliberately sit in a wing chair and not on the nearest settee. Despite her actions, Jon still believed that Arabella did care for him. She was back to calling him "Your Grace", though, and he felt he'd been relegated to the starting line with her regarding their relationship. Glancing at the stern look on her face now, he decided perhaps he resided in a deep hole a good number of feet behind the starting gate.

"I have a favor to ask of you."

Suspicion filled her eyes. "What?"

"I wish to find a tutor for Arthur."

Surprise replaced the suspicion. "What?" she repeated, her tone decidedly different now.

"Arthur has very little formal schooling," he explained. "In fact, there are huge gaps that exist in his education. I find him to be bright and outgoing, however. His greatest ambition is to attend university. With the entrance exams for his age a little more than a year away, he needs intense tutoring."

"Why not send him to school?" she asked.

"He is sadly behind in so many areas. I fear since he lags that school wouldn't be the right place for him. With the right tutor, though, he could easily catch up. He is eager to be challenged."

"I see. You want me to recommend someone to you. I most certainly can do so. I can think of three or four men who currently tutor at Oxford but would certainly be willing to move to London in order to work closely with the cousin of a duke. Why it would be wonderful for—"

"I could think of no one better suited to the task than you, Arabella. Would you consider taking on Arthur? You are well versed in a variety of areas and have patience and compassion. I know my cousin would be in excellent hands with you guiding his studies."

He watched her mull over his offer and then her eyes lit with unbridled enthusiasm.

"You know, teaching might become my life's work," she proclaimed. "Of course, I understand tutoring one boy is but a start but you have given me a brilliant idea, Your Grace."

Jon glowed with pleasure. He had put that smile upon her face. It was like the sun, warm on his back, spreading through him.

Not wanting to dampen her enthusiasm but

trying to keep her from becoming an object of further gossip, he said, "I would keep our arrangement to yourself for now. With one pupil, you can school him in the mornings and still be able to accept social invitations in the afternoons and evenings."

Her eyes danced in delight. "If I am successful with Arthur, I might start a tutoring service. Or better yet, open a school for boys. Oh, it could be for the less fortunate. Bright, clever boys who wish to win scholarships to university." She laughed, joy on her face. "Why didn't I think of this before? Papa has scads of money. He would be in favor of this, I know he would."

He needed to stop her grand plans before she spiraled out of control.

"Arabella, your father has money now but once he passes, that money goes to the next Earl of Barrington. It is not yours to play with your entire life." He hesitated. "Do you know who inherits the title next?"

She waved a hand. "Some distant cousin. I think in Hertfordshire." Her brow wrinkled in concentration. "Papa's health is excellent now so I would have a good number of years to get this enterprise off the ground and see it become a success."

"Health is a precarious thing," he warned. "My own father was in robust health until out of nowhere, an attack of apoplexy came on."

She bit her full, bottom lip and desire swept through him. He longed to do the very same thing. He remembered her taste and how right she had felt in his arms. Though he didn't deserve someone as wonderful as Arabella, his miserable life would become more than tolerable if she were in it.

As his wife.

Jon suddenly wanted her with a fierceness that was all-consuming. And he wanted her to want him, as well. Having Arabella by his side would keep his demons at bay. He might not love her as Weston did Elise but he would worship her. Give her the stars. The moon. The sun. He convinced himself that would be enough. That love didn't have to play a part in the relationship. That passion between them and respect for one another actually could be enough.

"To guarantee this school of yours a steady income, you must wed, Arabella. A man of wealth. As a duke, I know who gambles and who invests wisely. I could introduce you to the right men to see you achieve your dream."

He could see the wheels turning inside her head and bit back a smile.

"You are right," she agreed, a thoughtful expression on her lovely face. "I need to wed a man who shares my vision and who would fund it willingly."

No man in his right mind would allow her to

participate in such a foolish scheme.

Except for him.

Arabella had intelligence and perseverance. Beauty and spirit. She would make for a marvelous Duchess of Blackmore and his life would never be dull with her in it. Jon planned to give Arabella whatever she wanted. If it was a school for underprivileged, intelligent boys, he would do so.

"I will need a partner, Jon," she said thoughtfully.

He noticed her slip, calling him by his Christian name, and knew he had already made progress.

Smiling at her, he said, "Then it is a partner you shall have."

CHAPTER TWENTY

ARABELLA FINISHED DRESSING with Annie's help and went to breakfast, eager to discuss her ideas with her father. There'd been no time at the Colebournes' party last night. She had tried her best to keep her eyes off Blackmore, as he was greeted by his friends and caught up on news of the Duke and Duchess of Treadwell's wedding that had occurred during his absence.

She sailed into the breakfast room and dropped a kiss upon her father's brow before taking her seat.

"You seem to be in an excellent mood this morning, Arabella."

"I am, Papa. I have something particularly exciting I wish to discuss with you."

He set aside his newspaper and looked at her expectantly. "Have you found a husband?"

She frowned. "No. Something far better—though a husband might be needed in the grand scheme of things." Plunging ahead, she said, "It all began with my agreeing to do a favor for the Duke of Blackmore."

"Blackmore?" Her father's brows arched and then he frowned. "What type of favor?"

"He has hired me to tutor his cousin, Arthur Sutton."

"What? Arabella, you cannot take a position! You are now an earl's daughter."

Already, she could see this was going badly. "Papa, I used the wrong word. He is not paying me. It is not a position of that sort. Young Arthur needs help in his studies."

Quickly, she explained the situation and how the Suttons would be coming to tea today to see if Arthur was agreeable to the idea of a woman tutoring him.

"What this has done is spur within me the need to do more than call upon others in Polite Society. I want to be useful, Papa." Arabella took a deep breath. "What I would like to do is open a school for boys. Boys who are bright and need assistance as they seek a university scholarship. It will cost a great deal of money, though."

She saw by his smile that he had caught her enthusiasm. "What a wonderful idea, my dear. I've felt a bit useless myself, living the life of an idle gentleman. Why, we could look for space. Purchase it. Turn it into what would best suit our needs."

"I don't mean to dampen your enthusiasm, Papa, and I certainly don't want you dead—but if we do this, we must plan for far into the future. Who is the next earl?"

"Malcolm Price looked into for me. It is a cousin twice removed whom I have never met. I see what you are saying. The next Earl of Barrington might not wish to fund such a project in perpetuity."

"That's where I've an idea," she said. "You wish me to wed. If I find a gentleman that I believe suits me, I would first see if he would take over the financial aspects of the school once you have passed, hopefully in the far, far future."

He grew thoughtful. "What if you cannot find such a gentleman, Arabella? The *ton* would not be tolerant of a woman running a school. It is hard to imagine a peer allowing his wife to take on such an enterprise with Polite Society's disapproval."

"Then if no man would consider it, I would like to take on the funding and management myself." She paused. "By using my dowry. If I choose not to wed, I would like to see those funds secured for my personal use. I could live a long time on twenty thousand pounds and see the school thrive. Why, I might even take on some paying pupils and charge fees to help sustain the venture."

He grew thoughtful. "We will compromise.

You must seriously look for a husband during the rest of the Season. Only if one is not forthcoming will I talk to Mr. Price and see about giving you control of your dowry."

She came to her feet and threw her arms about him. "Oh, thank you, Papa! This is exactly what I have needed. A lifelong project that will do some good in the world with the money you've come into." She kissed his brow. "Don't forget tea today. I cannot wait for you to meet Arthur. He is a very nice young man."

"I'll write to Mr. Price for an appointment. I want to discuss this venture with him. He may know of a property that might be suitable for our purpose." He smiled up at her. "This has given me new life, Arabella."

"To both of us, Papa."

JON WAS GLAD when the last of Elizabeth's suitors left. He rang for Thistle.

"Have the carriage brought around and summon my cousin to meet us in the foyer. Lady Elizabeth and I are going to tea at Lord Barrington's."

"Very well, Your Grace."

After the butler left, Elizabeth stared at him. No, glared at him.

"I don't understand you at all, Jon. You mistreated Arabella. Quite badly. Now, you want to run off and have tea with her? I love you. You are my brother—but she is my friend—and far more fragile than she appears."

"What did she say to you?" he asked, wondering how much Arabella had shared.

His sister snorted. "Oh, don't think she went all over town talking about it. I practically had to drag it out of her. I know you kissed her. Then you promptly tossed her aside minutes later." She crossed her arms. "Normally, I would mark that up to your usual rakish behavior and ignore it. But Arabella is not one of your conquests. I thought you were interested in her. That you truly liked her."

"I did. I do," he corrected.

Confusion filled her face. "Then why on earth would you behave toward her as you have?" She hesitated. "Unless you truly do care for her and pushed her away before she could do the same to you. Is that it, Jon? Did you fear she would hear the rumors about you and turn away? Please tell me it's something like that—and that you have come to your senses and changed your mind."

He raked his fingers through his hair. He would censor what he would say and only give Elizabeth part of the truth.

"I have spent almost fourteen years as Duke

of Blackmore. I have felt like a failure and a fraud all of those years," he said frankly. "I like Arabella. She is magnificent in every way. Because of how I feel about myself, though, I thought she deserved better. I fear she believes in love, as you do, and I couldn't give it to her. When I saw Weston propose to Elise in front of hundreds of guests in that ballroom, I saw how they gazed upon one another. How their love was palpable. I didn't feel that way toward Arabella and don't think I ever could. Because of that, I thought I did her a disservice and wanted her to have a chance to find love. To find happiness. With someone else."

"Jon, love can grow," Elizabeth insisted. "It is not always an immediate attraction. I know you felt that toward Arabella."

"I did. I am still attracted to her. I thought about her quite a bit while I was in Suffolk. I decided it would be better to have Arabella in my life that live without her. I will give her every-thing I can. Respect. Friendship. Passion." He shrugged. "It may not be love but I will try to be the best possible husband to her."

She threw her arms about him and squeezed tightly. "I am so relieved to hear this. I feel you *will* fall in love with her, Jon. I think she's already given her heart to you and that's why she has been out of sorts lately. Of course, she hasn't told me this. She has conducted herself beautifully, as always. She has a way about her that causes men to flock to her. It's not just her looks. They see below to her inner beauty." She placed her fists on her waist. "So, what are you going to do to win her back?"

"Selfishly, I am using Arthur as bait," he admitted.

Intrigue filled her face. "How so?"

"I've asked her to be Arthur's tutor," he confessed.

"Oh, that's grand! Arabella is the smartest person I know. Arthur told me of how you were going to find a tutor to help prepare him for his university entrance exams."

"That is why we are going to tea today. So that we might discuss the idea and see if Arthur will go along with it."

"That will put him in Arabella's company quite often," Elizabeth noted. "I'm sure you'll need to see him there or pick him up."

"Something like that. I also want to take him on excursions about town and include Arabella in these. You, too, would need to come along so I don't have to drag her maid about London with us."

She kissed his cheek. "You are forgiven. You saw you were an idiot and will try to win her hand." She paused. "But Jon, about your lack of confidence. You have never shown that. You have never talked of being insecure. I feel you are a fabulous duke."

Little could he tell her that he had killed to become the duke and how guilt was his constant companion. For bits of time, he could shove it aside before it reared its ugly head and tried to swallow him whole.

"I do my best," he said. "Come. Arthur will be waiting for us."

They went to the foyer. Arthur already looked better, thanks to the altering of Jon's clothes which his cousin had worn this morning to the tailor's. He had ordered his cousin a new wardrobe, from nightshirts to waistcoats. They had also visited Jon's bootmaker and, soon, Arthur would be shod as a young man of his class should be. Already, he could see Arthur brimmed with confidence now that he had clothes that fit well.

"Where are we going?" Arthur asked excited-ly as they left the townhouse and entered the carriage.

"To tea at Lord Barrington's. You met his daughter, Lady Arabella, yesterday."

The tips of Arthur's ears pinkened. "Yes, Lady Arabella was very nice."

Jon suspected his young cousin might be infatuated. It shouldn't hurt. If Arthur was, he would be eager to please Arabella and work twice as hard.

Elizabeth cocked her head, her question

unspoken. He shook his, wanting to wait until they were at tea before bringing up the matter at hand.

They arrived and followed the butler to the drawing room. Quick introductions were made and they sat down to tea, Arabella pouring out. Jon noted how graceful her movements were as she passed the saucers to her company. He liked everything about this woman.

Now, to get her to once again favor him, in return.

Jon began. "Arthur, you've been brought to the Barrington household today for a specific reason."

His cousin looked up expectantly. "Yes, Jon?"

"You have been told that Lord Barrington was a former don at Oxford. What you don't know is that Lady Arabella helped her father in many ways during his university days." He glanced at Arabella, who took the reins in hand.

"Arthur, I know of your desire to attend university and that your cousin will provide a tutor for you. I would like to offer to be that tutor."

"You . . . would?" Arthur asked, clearly baffled. "I don't know. I've never heard of a woman tutor before."

"I can assure you I have the necessary background to help prepare you. May I ask you a few questions?"

The young man nodded and Arabella began peppering him with questions, some of which he answered readily and others he wasn't sure of. When he didn't know the answer, she provided it, carefully explaining the how or why. Arthur looked a little frightened and then began to relax.

"If you would like me to help you in your endeavors, we will work on Latin and Greek, philosophy, history, and literature. I am decent with numbers but the duke might have to bring in someone else more well-versed in them than I. What do you say? Would you like to try and work together?"

"I would like that very much, my lady," Arthur said eagerly.

"My father might also step in and discuss various books with you that I ask you to read."

The boy looked to the earl. "I would be grateful, my lord."

"Then it's settled," Jon said. "You can work mornings with Lady Arabella. She has social obligations to meet in the afternoons and evenings."

"I cannot believe my good fortune," Arthur said, shaking his head.

"I am glad you are so willing to work with me," Arabella said. "I think you will be an excellent pupil."

Once the tea had been finished, Elizabeth said they needed to leave and told Arabella she would see her at the ball tonight.

"Let us walk you out," Lord Barrington said to his guests, taking Elizabeth's arm, young Arthur tagging along.

Jon and Arabella followed behind them and he said, "Arthur will be a very willing pupil."

"He is very endearing."

"Might I reserve the supper dance with you tonight, my lady? We could speak of Arthur's needs over our meal."

He felt her stiffen beside him.

"I don't believe that will be necessary, Your Grace. I can learn all I need to from Arthur himself. There is no need to dance and discuss the matter further. I will, however, provide weekly reports to you. Oral or written. Your choice."

"You won't dance with me?"

She boldly looked him in the eyes. "No, I don't believe I will."

"What about us being partners? I am to help you find a worthy, wealthy gentleman to wed. To help you fund your future school."

She swallowed. "I have given that much thought, Your Grace. You yourself told me you keep very few close friends. I know three of them are now wed and thus ineligible to make me an offer. Your fourth friend is away at war. I feel I have already made headway with several gentlemen in the *ton* and can sift through them at my own pace. I also spoke to Papa in regard to opening a school for underprivileged young men. If I don't choose to wed at Season's end and have my new husband fund my school, Papa is willing to do so."

"We spoke of this, Arabella," Jon said, tamping down his frustration. "Your father won't be here forever."

She smiled. "That is why he has agreed to give me access to my dowry. It's incredibly large. Twenty thousand pounds. Since I am of legal age, he said it will be made available to me if I cannot find the right husband."

Damnation.

Jon would have to let the earl in on his scheme to woo and win Arabella. He thought a moment and as they all reached the foyer, he said, "Lord Barrington, we had discussed earlier my having a look at your horseflesh. Why don't we do so now? Tattersall's is open tomorrow. Being educated as a gentleman includes knowing horses as much as Latin and Greek. You and I could attend tomorrow and take young Arthur with us."

"I thought Arthur was to spend mornings with me," Arabella said, clearly put out by his suggestion.

The boy looked torn, glancing between the two of them.

Jon added, "This will give you a day to set your curriculum for Arthur."

Arabella licked her lips, causing desire to flare within Jon. She said, "Then I will keep Arthur with me now. I will thoroughly quiz him in order to evaluate where he stands on various subjects. While he is at Tattersall's tomorrow, I will begin to prepare my lessons."

"But what of the ball tonight?" Elizabeth asked.

Arabella shrugged. "It's only one ball. Papa can send my regrets. He may say I had a headache." She smiled brightly. "Come along, Arthur. I will set a few tasks for you now and ask you about everything under the sun in order to see what gaps need to be filled in." Turning to Jon, she added, "Your Grace, I will see that Arthur gets home safely tonight. I will see you at the garden party tomorrow afternoon, Elizabeth."

With that, she took the boy's arm and led him back up the stairs.

Jon nodded to himself. In their bout, round one had been handily won by Lady Arabella Jennings.

But a match could go many rounds. Jon planned to be the eventual victor and claim Arabella as his prize.

CHAPTER TWENTY-ONE

A MONTH HAD passed. Jon had watched Arabella blossom before him. She was more popular than ever among the gentlemen of the *ton*. Some of the women were still cool toward her though many had changed their opinions and offered her friendship. Her sweet spirit and positive outlook—combined with a modiste who had done wonders with her wardrobe—had allowed Arabella to receive invitations far and wide to various events.

She never danced with him. He hadn't asked her. He knew she would refuse him and while it wouldn't mean anything to him, her action might hurt her reputation. Women in Polite Society didn't go around turning down dukes.

Instead, he tried to be near her at smaller events. She remained coolly polite but showed no real warmth toward him. He was ready to tear his hair out from want and need. He watched men flitting about her, trying to attract her attention, and a slow burn raged within him.

He lived for the weekly reports she presented to him regarding Arthur. Of course, they were never alone when these occurred. She thought it would be helpful for Arthur to hear about his progress at the same time and so the boy was always present. Sometimes, Lord Barrington also sat in on these meetings since he had a hand in the boy's education and discussed books and philosophy with Arthur.

Today, though, everything that Jon had been working toward should come to fruition. He'd whipped Arthur's interest in an exhibit at the British Museum and his cousin was eager to view it once he left Arabella's company today. Jon only hoped the earl would join in the weekly progress report for his plan to work.

He arrived and Stone admitted him. Handing the butler a sealed letter, Jon said, "You are to give this to me when I am leaving with my cousin. Say it just arrived for me and it is important I read it at once."

Being a well-trained butler who would never turn down a request from a duke, Stone nodded. "Yes, Your Grace," and led Jon toward the earl's study, where the weekly meeting took place.

As he entered, he saw Lord Barrington and Arthur engaged in a game of chess. Arabella sat behind her father's desk, chewing on a pencil as she looked at a piece of parchment. She made a mark on it and then glanced up. For a moment, her guard was down and he saw a vulnerability in her before a coolness lit her eyes.

"Good morning, Your Grace. I was just finishing up marking your cousin's latest essay. Won't you have a seat?"

Jon took his usual spot and Arabella sat across from him. The chess game halted and Arthur asked, "How was my essay, my lady?"

"Quite good," she complimented. "You had no fragments and no problems with your subjects and verbs agreeing. I only found one dangling modifier. Your content was strong. Your argument easily persuaded me and the entire paper was organized and cohesive."

Arthur flushed with color, pleased by her praise.

"As for everything else, Arthur has progressed well this week."

Arabella launched into a detailed account of what had been accomplished in their studies over the past several days. Jon only half-listened, thinking his scheme through. He had told the earl of his continued interest in Arabella a month ago when they'd ventured to Tattersall's. The older man had listened and then told Jon that he'd had a chance with his daughter and that others now were showing their interest. It would be up to Arabella to decide whom she wed—or even if she did. The earl's response hadn't pleased Jon but he could certainly see where Arabella got her stubbornness from.

Lord Barrington then reviewed two books Arthur had read at his request and gave a lengthy description of their discussion. Jon tried to not fidget and look interested.

Finally, he said, "I am more than pleased with my cousin's improvement in all areas."

"I still believe you may wish to hire a separate tutor for mathematics," Arabella said. "I am teaching Arthur to the best of my ability but math never was my strong suit."

"I'll consider it," he said thoughtfully. "Arthur, are you ready to attend the exhibit?"

"Yes, Jon," his cousin said enthusiastically. "I shared with Lord Barrington that we were going."

"You did?" He looked to the earl, pleased that Arthur had already laid the groundwork. "Might you have interest in going with us, my lord? The exhibit will end soon. That is, if you do not have plans now."

"I could go," Lord Barrington said. "Young Arthur has piqued my interest in it."

Jon rose. "We should be going."

"Leave the chess pieces where they are, Arthur," the earl said. "We can pick up on our game tomorrow morning."

He deliberately held back so he could walk

with Arabella.

"You are doing excellent work with my cousin," he praised. "How are thoughts of your future school coming along?"

"Papa and I have been looking for a property but haven't settled upon anything yet."

Good.

They reached the foyer and Stone played his role to perfection.

"Your Grace, this just arrived for you. The messenger said it was most urgent."

"Thank you, Stone."

Jon took it and broke the seal. "Hmm."

"Something wrong, Jon?" Arthur asked anxiously.

He frowned and then shook his head. "No, but I won't be able to take you to the British Museum now." He looked at the earl. "Lord Barrington, I hate to disappoint my cousin. Is there any way you might escort him in my stead?"

"I'd be happy to," the earl declared. "Time with Arthur is always time well spent."

"Oh, thank you, my lord," Arthur said.

"Stone, call for the carriage," Lord Barrington ordered. "No, on second thought, let's go to the stables, Arthur. I want to show you a horse I recently purchased. Then we can have the carriage readied."

Jon knew which horse since he had recommended its purchase. The earl had taken up riding again, something he hadn't done since his youth. Jon had tried to talk to Arabella about teaching her to ride but she'd put him off, saying she was much too busy to devote time to learning something new at this point.

The pair left and as he slipped the letter into his coat pocket, she asked, "Is it bad news?"

"Not at all. In fact, it's rather good news." He paused. "I didn't want to get your hopes up but I think I may have found the ideal site for your school."

"What?"

"I had my solicitor look into it and he has found what he believes to be the perfect property. A former bookstore." Jon held up the key which had been placed inside the letter. "Would you care to go see it now? The message reads that the son who inherited the place doesn't wish to follow in his father's footsteps and become a bookseller. He is already a solicitor and is satisfied in his work. My solicitor's note indicates there are several others interested in the property, however, and I should look at it immediately in order not to lose out."

Arabella hesitated a moment and then said, "Stone, please send for Annie so she may accompany us."

The butler left and she asked, "What else do you know about the place?"

He knew everything because he'd not only visited it twice—he had bought it to show her. If Arabella didn't like it, he would merely sell it.

"It stands empty now. According to my man, other bookshop owners have been allowed in to buy up the inventory. Other than that, it is a mystery."

"My lady, you needed me?"

"Yes, Annie. You will accompany His Grace and me on a brief errand."

"Yes, my lady."

They went outside to where his carriage stood. A footman placed the steps down and assisted Arabella into the vehicle.

As he did, Jon turned and quietly told the lady's maid, "If you wish to keep your position after Lady Arabella becomes my duchess, you will stay in this carriage once we reach our destination."

The young woman blinked and then gave an imperceptible nod. She climbed inside, taking a place beside her mistress, and Jon followed, sitting opposite them.

As they rode, Annie placed a hand against her temple and sighed. Arabella, ever in tune to those around her, asked, "Is there something wrong?"

"Just a bit of a headache, my lady. Nothing for you to worry about."

"We should turn the carriage around," Arabella proclaimed.

"No, don't do that, my lady. I merely had a restless night. The headache comes from lack of sleep. I think I'll close my eyes and rest them for a bit."

Annie did so, leaning against the side of the coach. Jon decided she should be on the stage. Her performance was natural and convincing. Arabella placed a finger to her lips to indicate they should be quiet and so the rest of the trip was spent in silence.

When they arrived, Annie was puffing soft breaths at an even rate.

"Don't wake her," he said quietly. "She looks as if she could use the rest."

Arabella nodded as he ventured from the carriage and offered his hand to help her down the steps.

"See that Lady Arabella's maid is not disturbed," he told his footman. "If she awakens, send her inside. We will be viewing the property."

"Yes, Your Grace."

He went and inserted the key and opened the door, ushering Arabella inside. The bottom floor received good light, thanks to the abundant windows. They walked around inspecting things.

"It is nice the bookshelves have been left behind," she said. "They could be used in the school's library."

"I agree. The library could be here." He

walked a ways and added, "This could be a common room for the boys to gather between classes in order to visit or study." Walking further, he added, "This could be reconfigured and a small kitchen added."

Her brows knit together. "Why a kitchen?"

Jon laughed. "I've only been recently reminded how much boys Arthur's age are hungry. They grow faster than weeds. A hungry boy will be thinking about his belly aching and not translating Homer from Greek to English. Especially if you are interested in serving a less fortunate population of pupils, feeding them might be the only time of day they eat well."

Arabella grew thoughtful. "That is a very good point, Your Grace." She pursed her lips as her brow creased as she concentrated.

He wanted to taste those lips. He wanted to hear her call him by his name again. He needed her so badly he ached.

"Shall we look upstairs?"

They moved up the staircase to the first floor. It was entirely open with no divisions or barriers.

"My solicitor told me this is where the bookseller stored his extra stock. You could turn this floor into classrooms. It would be easy to put up several walls. I would also suggest adding several windows to let in more natural light."

"I agree. This would be perfect for that purpose. What is on the third floor?"

"The owner lived above the shop. He also let several rooms out for extra income. There is a rear staircase from the second floor that exits in the alley behind the structure, making it easy for tenants to come and go."

"Perhaps I could turn those into classrooms, as well."

"I think it would be wiser to leave it as it is. Your tutors could live on the top floor. If you hired a cook, room and board could be included, in addition to their salaries, making the position highly attractive."

"That would be convenient," she admitted.

"The owner's rooms could be given to your headmaster since they are much larger."

"Oh." She frowned. "I was thinking I would be in charge of the school."

"You will own it and make sure of its direction. Hire its staff and see which boys are enrolled as pupils. But you would need a headmaster for the day-to-day running of the place."

"I hadn't thought of that."

"Why don't we go see it?"

Jon took her elbow and guided her up the stairs, which narrowed considerably from the first to the second floor. Her subtle, floral fragrance wafted toward him. He knew Annie wouldn't be coming in anytime soon. She knew what he was up to and wouldn't want to interrupt. He allowed Arabella to walk around, viewing all the rooms on that floor, and they finally wound up in what had been the owner's residence. It consisted of a small parlor, kitchen, and a bedroom.

"This is ideal," she said. "Did your solicitor share with you how much the seller wants?"

He named a figure that was half of what he'd paid for the property and her eyes widened.

"Oh, that is far better than what Papa and I have viewed in the last few weeks. This neighborhood is much better, too." She smiled. "I believe we should act quickly to purchase it before someone else makes an offer."

He took her elbows in hand, her eyes widening. "There is another offer that you should consider.

"Mine."

CHAPTER TWENTY-TWO

ARABELLA HAD FOUGHT her feelings for this man long enough. It had been incredibly difficult acting nonchalantly around him since his return from Suffolk. She had encased her heart in stone, tucking it and her foolish dreams away, pretending nothing had taken place between them. She had feigned indifference and avoided speaking to him as much as possible. Their weekly meetings regarding Arthur's progress had been hellacious as she spoke dispassionately and stifled the tremendous attraction she felt for him. She had wasted far too many hours trying to figure out what had gone wrong between them, only knowing something had and it couldn't be cured.

Until now.

The heat is his eyes darkened the blue until his irises were almost black. His grip tightened on her elbows, ensuring she wouldn't be going anywhere until he said whatever he was going to say to her.

"Offer?" she repeated weakly, tamping down the faint hope that had sprung within her when he clasped her.

He didn't speak with words but chose actions instead. Oh, dear Lord, her heart pounded furiously as he slowly lowered his head. She wanted to flee as a scared rabbit might when pursued by hounds but he made sure she stayed in place.

Then his mouth captured hers. The kiss was achingly tender, sweet and soft, rending her heart in two. She thought her heart, though scarred, had healed. That she'd put the shattered pieces back together but they came apart swiftly at his loving touch. His lips caressed hers slowly, causing the blood to rush to her ears, its pounding so fierce that she couldn't hear at all.

Arabella didn't need to hear. She only needed to touch. To taste. To inhale the scent that was Jon. Her fingers found his coat and gripped it tightly. His arms went around her, pulling her to him. She clung to him as if on a ship being battered by a storm at sea. If she let go, she would drown.

He urged her to open to him and she did, feeling like a flower opening to the rising sun. His tongue swept inside her mouth and his kisses were long, deep, passion-filled ones. She heard noises come from both of them, hers more like a mewling kitten, his sounding like the growl of a lion taking possession and declaring he ruled over all.

Her breasts began to ache, the nipples coming to life as Jon crushed her to him. One arm remained secure around her waist as his other hand roamed freely up and down her spine, stroking her like a cat. She arched into him, causing a delicious sound from him. His fingers pushed into her hair, pins spilling everywhere, as he massaged her scalp. Lovely tingles rippled through her and the place between her legs began pounding viciously, wanting . . . something.

He now tugged on her, pulling her head back, the kiss going even deeper, longer, as if he wished to touch her very soul. Arabella found herself melting like butter in a hot pan, beginning to sizzle as sparks of desire ran through her. Her hands slid up his hard chest and entwined around his neck. He broke the kiss and nuzzled her neck, kissing and nipping and licking her, causing waves of shock to run through her.

His lips trailed up her throat and to her ear, his teeth gently tugging on her lobe, sending a flame of fire that heated her throughout. His warm breath tickled as he said, "You are mine, Arabella. Always."

His mouth returned to hers, his kisses hard and demanding. Her legs began to buckle as her bones liquefied. He had her by the waist and lifted her. She found her back against a wall and he pressed his hard body against her soft one. It yielded. She yielded.

She wanted him. Every limb vibrated with need as her core pulsed hard and fast. She whimpered, needing something desperately and not knowing what to ask for.

His hands left her waist and captured her hands, raising them high above her head. Jon pinned her wrists with one large hand, leaving the other free to touch her. He caressed her cheek with the back of his fingers. Stroked her throat. Murmured things she didn't understand, his lips against her skin. His fingers ran along the neckline of her dresses and then plunged inside it. They burned wherever they touched. He found her breast and cupped it, kneading it. She arched her back again, feeling open and exposed with her hands held high, forcing her breasts toward him.

He pushed aside her gown, exposing her breast. Then his mouth was upon it, sucking and laving and driving her to the brink of insanity. His tongue flicked across her nipple, now hard and aching and she whimpered again, her breath coming in uneven spurts. She cried out.

"Say my name," he commanded, his voice low and dangerous.

"Jon," she sputtered.

"Again," he ordered.

"Jon," she said more forcefully.

"Who do you want?" he growled, his eyes hot as their gazes connected.

"You," she whispered, her walls crumbling.

"Yes," he said, satisfaction in his voice. "And by God, I want you, Arabella."

He buried his face against her throat as his hand skimmed along the curve of her hip. Then somehow it was beneath her dress. Her chemise. His fingers slid languidly up her leg, moving to where the drumbeat pounded now out of control.

"Yes," she said, nodding as he came closer. "Yes," she said, her voice breaking.

He touched the nestle of curls and then ran his finger along the seam of her sex, causing her breath to hitch.

"I want to please you," he said hoarsely. "Do you want me to?"

Arabella nodded, beyond speaking now.

Slowly, oh so slowly, he pushed a finger inside her. She gasped.

"Ah. Your heat. Your velvet heat," he muttered.

The finger began stroking her. Another joined it. She writhed against him, crying out.

"There's your sweet nub," he said soothingly, caressing it, driving her wild. "Do you like when I do this, Arabella?"

"Yes," she managed to say.

He continued working some kind of magic and a pressure built within her. She moved against his hand without shame, trying to get closer. Suddenly, it was as if fireworks exploded. She saw light. She felt heat. She inhaled him as waves of pleasure erupted and she babbled like an incoherent fool. Slowly, they subsided.

He released her wrists and her arms fell. She was so limp she would have collapsed if his body hadn't been pressed against hers. She began weeping with emotions so strong, she could not have named them.

"Shh," he said, lifting her in his arms and carrying her to a chair.

Jon cradled her in his arms as she wept, her face buried against his neck. He spoke nonsense to her, calming her, his touch light and sure.

Finally, she quietened and lifted her head. Her gaze met his. In his eyes, she saw a tenderness that almost broke her.

"You are the woman I want, Arabella," he said huskily. "I have never wanted another as I do you."

She blinked. "Then why did you push me away?"

Doubt crept into his eyes. "I thought you were too good for me. Too pure. Too perfect."

She hiccupped. "I am far from perfect."

"You are an angel, my love. I'll always think you perfect."

He kissed her and love swept through her. Yes, love. This is what it had to be. She couldn't live without him. She craved him. She needed him. She wanted him.

She broke the kiss. "What changed your mind?" she asked softly.

"You are the one light in my life. My heart is full of darkness, love. Part of me doesn't want to drag you into the mire I wallow in. I am a selfish man, though. As a duke, I take what I want—and I want you. Desperately. I have from the beginning. Will you marry me? Stay with me forever?"

Arabella looked at the pain in his eyes. She wanted to take it away. "I will accept your offer. I will marry you. I will stay an eternity with you."

She wanted to add that she loved him but something made her hold back. She decided she was right to do so as she saw joy spring to his eyes. He kissed her soundly, over and over.

"You may be making the biggest mistake of your life but you are now mine," he said, glee in his voice. "You are mine, Arabella. Mine, forever and ever."

He kissed her possessively, branding her as his. Then he gentled the kiss and finally broke it.

"We should return to your maid."

"Annie didn't have a headache, did she?"

Jon burst out laughing. "No. She didn't."

"What did you say to her?"

He grinned. "Does it matter?"

She grinned back. "I suppose not. Let me up."

Jon stood and brought her to her feet. She looked around. "My pins. My hair. Oh, no."

"I'll help you."

He got down on hands and knees and collected her hairpins, smoothing her hair and twisting it up before slipping the pins into place. It hurt her a little to see how good he was at this, knowing he had done so for many other women. It didn't matter, though. For some miraculous reason, Jon had chosen her. Her. Arabella Jennings. The other women faded away. They no longer mattered. It was only him. And her. Together. Forever.

As they left the room, he took her hand, his fingers lacing through hers. Warmth filled her.

"I've already bought the property," he said sheepishly.

"You did?"

"It is my wedding present to you."

"Oh, Jon!"

She stopped on the stairs and threw her arms around him, kissing him soundly.

He broke the kiss. "I don't know how much more of that I can take."

"You . . . you don't want me to kiss you."

He laughed. "Oh, but I do. I truly do. Kissing, though, leads to other things. Wicked things.

Those are what I am thinking of now. Stripping every thread from you. Touching and loving every inch of you."

She giggled. "I like the sound of that."

"Good," he said. "I want my duchess enthusiastic about making love with me."

"Your duchess." Suddenly, it hit her. Slammed into her. She would be a duchess. "I don't know how to be a duchess, Jon," she said, her voice rising in hysteria.

"You will be you. The you I know. You will be perfect."

"The *ton* won't think so. They will think you've gone mad wanting to wed someone like me."

He cradled her face between his hands. "Do you think I care what any of them think? We were meant for each other, Arabella. All I need to do now is purchase a special license."

"You wish to marry quickly?"

He laughed. "If I could walk out these doors and wed you now, I would do so, love. All my thoughts are centered upon you. Burying myself in you. Making you scream with pleasure."

Arabella felt her cheeks burn, his words stirring the fire again within her.

Jon kissed her softly. "I'll see if I can get the license this afternoon. If not, tomorrow at the latest. Are you ready to marry me?"

"Yes," she said, never more certain of anything.

"Good. Let us go home and speak to your father then. And I'd like to have our friends know, as well. What is tonight's event?"

"Another ball," she replied.

"We'll skip it. I'll send notes around. I'll hold a dinner party for our friends. We will announce our betrothal at it."

"You are certain this is what you want, Jon?" she asked, doubt suddenly filling her.

"Yes. Why would you ask?"

"Because I feel as if I am dreaming. That I will awaken and find this was all pretend."

He raised her hand to his lips and tenderly kissed her fingers. "This is no dream, Arabella. This is our lives."

She smiled. "You know what will happen tonight?"

"Our friends will congratulate us?" he teased.

"They will begin planning the wedding. The breakfast to follow. They'll want to know where we will go on our honeymoon."

His radiant smile filled her with contentment. "Then it will be a very pleasant evening."

Jon led her down the remaining stairs and he locked the bookstore. Handing the key to her, he said, "It is yours now."

If they hadn't been on a public street, she would have flung her arms about him and kissed him soundly.

As they walked to the carriage, she saw the footman rap against it before he placed the steps down and opened the door. Arabella climbed in and saw Annie still fast asleep—or pretending to be.

Jon sat opposite the servant and pulled her into his lap, kissing her once the door was closed.

"Annie," he said, "I am sure you will sleep until we arrive back at Lord Barrington's."

"Yes, Your Grace," the maid murmured, her eyes remaining closed.

Arabella laughed heartily until her fiancé kissed her—and continued kissing her the entire way home.

CHAPTER TWENTY-THREE

ARABELLA REALIZED WHEN they reached home that her father was still at the British Museum with Arthur.

"Did you also plan for Papa and Arthur to take an excursion?" she asked, not bothering to hide her smile.

"Let's say everything worked out according to my plans," Jon said mysteriously.

"Was Stone in on it?"

He shrugged. "A duke must keep some secrets, you know."

She glanced to the butler, whose face gave nothing away. "My fiancé and I will be in the drawing room, Stone. Please inform Papa where we are when he returns."

Stone's eyes lit up. "Of course, my lady."

She took Jon to her father's study, though. "It would be terrible manners for so many of us to cancel attending tonight's ball at the last minute."

Arabella couldn't help but think despite Jon's assurance, she wouldn't make for a good duchess. She didn't want the *ton* to turn against her or her friends merely for celebrating a betrothal.

"Why don't you write them now and tell them they are invited to an early dinner. Say seven o'clock? We can share our good news and then be only fashionably late to the ball."

He gave her a lingering kiss. "You've already wound me about your finger. I'll do as you ask."

She wandered about the room as he dashed off notes to the Colebournes and Treadwells and then she gave them to a footman.

"See them delivered at once," she said before leading Jon upstairs.

They spent a good hour leisurely kissing. She could have done so forever until she heard a throat clearing and they sprang apart and scrambled to their feet. Her father looked on sternly.

"What is this?" he demanded, glaring daggers at Jon.

"I was merely kissing my fiancée, Lord Barrington."

Her father's countenance relaxed and he beamed at them. Offering his hand, he said, "I will be both proud and pleased to call you my son-in-law, Blackmore."

"I am giving a small dinner party tonight to announce the good news to our friends. Won't you come?" Jon asked.

"No. Celebrate with your friends as you should. You have my blessing and heartiest congratulations."

"There's more, Papa," Arabella said. "Jon has already given me a wedding present."

She explained about the bookstore and how they would turn it into a school.

Looking at her new fiancé, she asked, "Would it be too much to go back and show the property to Papa?"

He laughed. "Not at all. He should see it."

They took the ducal carriage back to the site and walked her father through, noting the changes and improvements to be made. He approved them all and added a few notes of his own to consider. By the time they arrived home, teatime had already passed.

Jon took her hands and raised them to his lips. "I should go. I will see you at seven." He kissed her hands and gazed longingly into her eyes.

"Until then," she said.

He left and her father turned to her. "Are you happy, my dear?"

"Deliriously happy," she proclaimed.

"Do you love him?"

Arabella grew solemn. "I do. I always have. He is everything I could ever imagine wanting in a husband."

"Blackmore is a very powerful man."

"That doesn't matter to me. Thank you for your approval, Papa. And for coming to see the school. You made some excellent suggestions. I will depend upon you as we bring this idea to fruition."

He took her hands. "No, my dear. This is a project for you and your husband. He is the one you should turn to now for advice. While I am always available to you, marriage will change things between us."

She hugged him fiercely, knowing her parents hadn't had what she and Jon did and feeling sorry.

"Go up and get ready for your dinner. I will see you at the ball."

Arabella went to her bedchamber, where Annie awaited her. She shook her head as she looked at the maid.

"You were in on it."

Annie grinned without shame. "That I was, my lady. I knew you were going to be a duchess before you did." She laughed. "I am glad His Grace offered quickly for you because I don't think I could have kept such news to myself."

"You will come with me when I leave this household, won't you, Annie?"

"Where else would I go? To think, I am going to be lady's maid to the Duchess of Blackmore."

"I must dress now. Blackmore is holding a

small dinner party tonight to announce our news to his friends. Then we will go straight to tonight's ball." She paused. "I'll admit that I am very nervous. The news will get out quickly. I want to look my absolute best."

"Never fear, Lady Arabella. You will. Leave everything to me."

Annie removed a ballgown of blush from the wardrobe. "This is what I had in mind for tonight. You haven't worn it before. I pressed it this afternoon. You will make quite a statement in this."

The maid helped Arabella dress. The neckline was low, showing off her bosom, and the color was perfect. Annie brushed Arabella's hair until it shone and dressed it. Her reflection in the mirror almost looked like someone she didn't know. She looked beautiful.

A knock sounded at the door and Annie answered it. She came back with a box and a note.

"It's from His Grace," Annie said excitedly.

Arabella took the note and opened it.

My dearest Arabella –

I know all eyes will be on you tonight and I wanted to give you something from me for others to see. Wear these with pride, as my duchess-to-be.

Jon

She set the note aside and Annie handed her the box. Opening it, she blinked several times, stunned at what she saw. A diamond necklace gleamed with fire, accompanied by a matching bracelet and pair of earrings. She withdrew the necklace and stared at it.

"My stars! Diamonds!" Annie proclaimed. "Oh, that one will spoil you, my lady." She chuckled. "Or I should start calling you *Your Grace*."

Arabella swallowed. "I am not yet Blackmore's duchess." She smiled. "But the set is beautiful, isn't it?"

"It's grand, that's what it is. Let's put it on you."

Annie took the necklace and fastened it about Arabella before slipping the bracelet onto her wrist. Arabella fastened the earrings and then admired her image.

She was going to be the Duchess of Blackmore. She was in love with the most wonderful man in London. In all of England.

Her fingers went to the stones about her neck and she fingered them.

"It's a good thing we chose the gown we did," Annie said. "It will show off His Grace's presents to perfection."

Arabella went downstairs and Stone said, "His Grace sent his carriage for you, my lady."

She saw approval in the butler's eyes for the

thoughtful gesture by her fiancé.

"You must take good care of Papa when I leave the household," she told the butler. "I will visit often but I beg that you keep a watchful eye over him."

"Lord Barrington will be in fine hands, my lady." He smiled. "Just as you will be."

She rode in the ducal carriage to Jon's London townhouse, only blocks away. He greeted her personally, taking her hand and leading her inside. Gathered in the foyer must have been every servant in his employ in London.

"I asked you to gather tonight so that I might present to you my fiancée, Lady Arabella Jennings. She has done me the honor of accepting my proposal and will be your new duchess."

Spontaneous applause broke out and Arabella saw smiles and a few tears at the duke's announcement. Jon had her go down the line and he introduced her to every servant by name. It said a good deal about his character that he would know even the names of his scullery maids.

At the end of the line waited Elizabeth, who threw her arms about Arabella's neck.

"Oh, I am so happy to have you as a sister-in-law, Arabella. No, sister. I always wanted a sister and now Jon has gone out and found me one that I already love dearly."

She blinked back tears and said, "I also wanted a sister. I am most honored to have you as mine, Elizabeth."

The servants began scattering back to their duties and Jon said, "Our dinner guests will arrive soon. Elizabeth, would you serve as hostess and greet them? Go ahead and have everyone seated in the dining room. I need to have a word with Arthur first."

"Should I come with you?" asked Arabella anxiously.

He shook his head. "No, it's best if I see the boy alone. Stay with Elizabeth."

Jon left the pair and made his way to where he knew Arthur was studying. His young cousin needed to hear from Jon himself regarding his plans to wed Arabella. Jon had seen the look in Arthur's eyes and knew he was enamored with her. He thought it best to speak with Arthur now before he announced his intentions to their friends at dinner. The boy had a tender heart and Jon thought Arthur should be prepared at dinner and not taken by surprise by the announcement.

He knocked softly and entered the room when he heard Arthur's voice bid him to come. His cousin closed the book in front of him and set down his quill.

"I was just finishing up an essay that I think Arabella will find interesting. Is it already time for dinner?"

"It is. First, though, I want to share some

news with you."

"News?" Arthur frowned. "Am I . . . do you want me to leave?"

"Of course not." He placed a hand on the boy's shoulder. "You are family, Arthur. That is why I wanted to share something with you. I have just told Elizabeth and wanted you to know before my friends did."

His cousin looked wary. "What is it then?"

"I have asked Arabella to marry me," he said, knowing there was no way to cushion the blow.

"Oh." Arthur licked his lips nervously, his gaze dropping to the floor as he nervously shuffled his feet.

"I know you are quite fond of Arabella. I hope you will help welcome her to our family. And I expect you to be standing by my side when we wed."

Arthur raised his head, meeting Jon's gaze. "You do?"

"I most certainly do. We may have missed out on several years together, Arthur, but we will always be in each other's lives, now and in the future. I value family—as does Arabella—and you are important to both of us. Come, let us go to the dining room and celebrate."

Jon and Arthur went to the dining room, where the Colebournes and Treadwells awaited them. Greetings were exchanged and Jon motioned to Thistle. The butler brought over a tray of champagne flutes and distributed them before stepping aside.

Jon raised his glass. "You are some of my dearest friends and I wanted to be able to share our news with you."

"*Our* news?" asked the Duke of Colebourne, his smile widening.

"What news?" the Duke of Treadwell asked, mischief gleaming in his eyes.

Jon took Arabella's hand and lifted it to his lips for a sweet kiss. "This wonderful woman has agreed to become my duchess."

Samantha and Elise squealed in delight as Elizabeth beamed from ear to ear.

"I will take over the toast, Jon," Colebourne said. He raised his glass. "To a true friend who has found lasting happiness with the woman who is meant for him. To Jon . . . and Arabella!"

As she sipped her champagne, the bubbles tickled her nose. Arabella had never had champagne before and decided she should drink some every day. The light, frothy drink was like drinking liquid happiness and she wanted every day to be a happy one for her and Jon.

"Come, sit, we've dinner to eat and plans to make," Jon urged.

He led her to the seat on his right. Elizabeth took the one on his left as the others also found a place. The first course came out and the buzzing began.

"My first question is where Jon asked you to marry him," Samantha said, "and when?"

Between the two of them, they recounted the plans Arabella had for beginning a school and how Jon had gifted her with a suitable property as a wedding present. Everyone thought the school a terrific idea and begged to see it so plans were made to show it to them tomorrow morning.

"Since I have already seen it multiple times, I will let Arabella show off the property to you. I will be at Doctors' Commons obtaining a special license since it was too late to do so today."

"That is my question," Elise said. "Where—and when—is the wedding?"

"We haven't discussed it," Arabella revealed. "I hate to say I don't care where or when, only that it occurs soon."

"What if Elise and I hosted it?" suggested Treadwell. "George and Sam did so for us. Sam put the wedding and breakfast together quickly, despite feeling so puny."

"Oh, yes," Elise agreed. "Let it be our turn to do so." She smiled at Arabella. "You and Jon can host the next wedding, whenever that occurs."

Everyone turned and looked at Elizabeth. Her cheeks pinkened at the attention. "I don't foresee that happening anytime soon. Besides, Jon seems to chase off any gentleman I show an interest in."

"That's because you seem to attract nothing

but rogues," her brother retorted.

"*You* are a rogue," his sister said. "At least you have been until Arabella tamed you. I am certain now you will be the picture of propriety."

"I will not let him chase off anyone," Arabella proclaimed. "You leave things to me."

"Thank you," Elizabeth said. "I will look to my sister-in-law in the future for advice regarding matters of the heart."

"I still reserve the right to chase away anyone I deem unsuitable," Jon said.

"Unless I truly have feelings for him," Elizabeth interjected. "If Arabella can bring London's biggest rake to heel, she may be able to teach me to do the same. Not that I have any particular rake in mind," she added. "I reserve the right to be interested in whomever I find to be fascinating."

They went through several courses, the women talking of how to decorate the Treadwell townhouse for the occasion and making suggestions on what to serve at the wedding breakfast.

When the meal ended, George said, "We should make for the ball. We'll be fashionably late and have news to share." He looked to Jon. "Will you be making an announcement tonight regarding your betrothal?"

"No. Nothing formal. I may, however, feel the need to mention my fiancée multiple times in various conversations." He grinned. "It's no secret. By this time next week, Arabella and I should be husband and wife."

"Elizabeth, you should ride with us to the ball," Samantha said. "That way your brother and Arabella can be chaperoned by Weston and Elise. Even though we are arriving late, someone might see. It would be best for her reputation to have a chaperone. At least until the happy news gets out tonight."

They made their way to the carriages outside and Jon seated himself beside her, threading his fingers through hers. Contentment filled Arabella. For so long, things hadn't gone her way. Now, though, she had a handsome fiancé and wonderful friends.

What could go wrong?

CHAPTER TWENTY-FOUR

ARABELLA SAW NO receiving line was in place, having ended long before their late arrival. She entered the ballroom on Jon's arm, her loving group of friends surrounding her. Elizabeth was immediately swamped by several handsome young men wishing to claim her attention and spots on her dance card.

"I have no card," she proclaimed. "I will dance with whomever I wish and whenever I wish to do so."

"Hear, hear!" George said. "A Sutton with a mind of her own."

Elizabeth went off with the men, each clamoring for her attention.

"Are you suggesting I have no mind of my own?" Jon asked teasingly.

George chuckled. "Not anymore. To be a well-trained husband, you'll find you'd better be of like mind with your wife on all matters, great and small."

Samantha elbowed him. "You make it sound as if I am a dictator."

He kissed her fingers. "I am merely your slave, Duchess, and eager to do your bidding, especially since you are carrying my child."

"Oh, that reminds me," Elise said. "I received a letter from Phoebe today. The baby is almost six weeks old now and she believes he favors Andrew."

"I cannot wait to meet her," Arabella said. "You all speak of her and Windham so fondly."

"We will visit Andrew and Phoebe after the Season ends," Jon promised. "Once we have gone on a honeymoon."

"Did I hear the word honeymoon?"

She turned and saw none other than Lord Kenyon, the rake who probably would have kissed her if Jon had not interrupted them on the terrace.

Jon possessively slipped his arm around her waist. "Yes. Lady Arabella has promised to marry me."

The viscount's smiled looked genuine to her. "My sincere congratulations, my lady. His Grace is a formidable man. And quite the boxer." He rubbed his nose. "I should know. My nose got in the way of one of his blows." Kenyon turned to Jon. "You have landed an exceptional lady, Blackmore. I wish you much happiness."

Jon thanked him and the viscount moved away. He stopped and said something to a group of people. They all turned and looked at her and Jon.

"And so it begins," her betrothed said. "The music is about to start up and I've heard this is the supper dance. Would you do me the honor of dancing with me, my lady?"

Pure happiness filled her. "Yes, Your Grace. I would be happy to do so."

They danced that number and by the time they left the ballroom floor, well-wishers gathered left and right, congratulating them on their upcoming nuptials. The news must have spread faster than wildfire for as they entered the supper room, applause broke out. The host and hostess for the evening came over, thanking them for attending the ball and allowing their news to be shared during it.

Then the host called for a toast and hundreds of guests raised a glass in their honor. Arabella found herself smiling widely, taking in the moment. She wanted everyone to experience the happiness she now felt.

Jon led her to a seat and leaned over to whisper in her ear. "You may be happy now but I assure you that I can make you even happier later tonight if you wish."

Arabella thought of what he had done to her in the bookstore earlier today and felt her cheeks warming.

"You will kiss me?" she asked, gazing up at him in adoration.

"Oh, I will do more than that. I plan to kiss you everywhere." His blue eyes blazed. "And I do mean *everywhere*, Arabella."

Her face now flamed—but she was intrigued.

"You say you plan to do this tonight?"

"Come home with me now and find out." Jon pulled her to her feet. "My valet knows not to wait up for me," he said quietly. "We will have complete privacy."

"You want . . . me . . . now?" she sputtered.

He framed her face with his large hands. "We will be wed in but a few days. Does it matter if we celebrate a tad early?"

She smiled at him. "What are we waiting for?"

He laughed. "I knew I had chosen right." He tucked her arm through his and said to the table, "The excitement has been a bit much. I am taking Lady Arabella home early."

She saw a knowing look on the faces of their friends as they bid them good evening.

When they reached the foyer, she stopped. "Wait. We don't have a carriage here."

"I told Thistle to have my carriage follow. So that we might leave early." He grinned.

"You knew I would say yes, you scoundrel."

"I had high hopes that you would."

"And if I hadn't?"

"I would have found a way to convince you otherwise."

Jon led her outside and she saw his carriage with its ducal crest waiting. Wordlessly, he opened the door and lifted her inside.

They kissed heatedly until the carriage came to a halt in front of his townhouse. He led her inside, where not one servant appeared, and up the stairs. They reached his bedchamber and he closed the door behind them.

"You will have rooms of your own, where I hope you will store your wardrobe and ready yourself for the day. I hope, though, that you will spend your nights with me. Starting with tonight."

He lowered his lips to hers. The kiss was magical. She pushed her fingers into his thick, dark locks and pulled him closer to her. She knew it was scandalous what they were doing, her in his bedchamber, making love even before they were wed. It didn't matter, though. She wasn't about to waste a moment when she could be with the man she loved.

He broke the kiss, as breathless as she was. "May I undress you?"

She grinned shamelessly. "Your eyes already have, Your Grace. It's your hands that need to catch up."

He kissed her soundly. "Who knew I would

choose such a tigress?"

It took a good half-hour to remove her clothes because he took his time, his hands roaming everywhere as he did, kissing her in-between garments leaving her, kissing her where those garments had just been. Finally, she was down to nothing but her chemise. Even her slippers and stockings were gone. Nerves set in now. What would he think of her when she was laid bare to him?

She looked down, her playfulness gone, feeling inadequate.

Jon's fingers captured her chin, lifting it until their gazes met. "What's wrong?"

Arabella swallowed. She would be truthful. She knew no other way.

"I know you have done this dozens—no, probably hundreds—of times. I am afraid that you will find me . . . lacking."

His hands cupped her face, his thumbs gently stroking her cheeks. "And I have told you that you are different from every other woman I have ever known. The desire I feel is new to me. You have lit that flame within me, Arabella. Yes, there have been others before you. They all fade now into nothingness. And there will be no others but you. I know it is the way of the *ton* to wed and then fall away into affairs once an heir is secured. I am a loyal friend and I intend to be a loyal husband. There is only you, my sweet. Only you."

He kissed her softly and she knew he would be devoted to her. Relief swept through her. He must have sensed it. His mouth left hers and trailed hot, wet kisses down her throat. Then he kissed her breast through her chemise, licking until the thin material grew wet and her nipple hardened. It seemed all the more erotic with the barrier between them and yet she wanted his mouth on her bare skin.

"Take it off," she said breathlessly.

Hot desire flooded his eyes. "With pleasure."

Jon captured the hem of the garment and pulled it over her head, tossing it to the floor. He fastened his mouth on her breast, sucking hard, causing her core to tingle and pulse. He lavished attention on it and then switched to the other, teasing her nipples with his teeth, causing heat to pool in her belly and even lower. His hands drifted everywhere, much as his lips and tongue did, touching, tasting, teasing, filling her.

She broke the kiss. "I want your clothes off. I want to see you."

He laughed and swept her into his arms, carrying her to his massive bed. Their bed. Placing her upon it, she watched as he quickly shed his clothes.

His physique left her gasping. His shoulders were broader than she'd thought. His chest was dusted in a light covering of dark hair which trailed down the flat planes of his belly. His arms and thighs bulged with muscles, making him look like a Greek statue come to life. His manhood jutted, large and proud, from a nestle of dark curls.

Jon joined her on the bed, his hot flesh pressing against hers as his hands again roamed her body and his mouth followed in their wake. Soon, she felt as if she would explode into flames. He kissed his way down her belly and went lower, causing her to tense.

"Where are you going?"

He glanced up. "I said I would kiss you everywhere. I will never break a promise to you."

"Even . . . there?" she squeaked.

"*Especially* there," he said, his grin wicked.

He parted her folds and his tongue plunged inside her, much as his fingers had earlier today. He stroked and suckled and had her writhing on the bed, her breath shallow and fast. Tremendous pressure built. Built. Built. And then exploded. She rocked and bucked and laughed, all the while calling his name.

His mouth joined with hers and she found the taste and scent of her on him oddly erotic. As they kissed, she felt his cock push into her. At first, she shoved against his shoulder, needing him to stop because it hurt. Then something seemed to give and he slid in to the hilt.

"See? A perfect fit," he quipped. "It won't

ever hurt again, love. It's only this first time."

"Good," she said. "I wasn't sure I would like this."

He retreated and then sank into her again. She sighed.

"Did you like that?"

"Oh, yes. In fact, so much I'd like you to do it again, Your Grace. Several times."

"Let it be said that I know how to follow orders."

With that, he eased from her and pushed into her again. Each time, the pleasure seemed greater. Each deep stroke showed her how much he cared for her. He might not love her but he did make her happy. She would take what she could from him. Her love for him would be enough for the both of them.

They settled into a frenetic dance which heated her entire body. She felt herself rising with each thrust, her nails digging into his back, her legs now wrapped about his waist so his strokes penetrated even deeper. Then the same wonderful feeling from before blanketed her again. Something must also be happening with him because he roared with pleasure and then collapsed atop her. She welcomed his weight, clinging to him.

He rolled quickly to his back, bringing her with him. "How was that?"

She smoothed his hair. "I would say you are

rather skilled, Your Grace." She hesitated. "I only hope that I satisfied you."

Jon took her hand and brought it to his lips. He slipped her finger into his mouth and sucked on it, sending a tremor through her. He did it to each finger, lazily sucking on them and kissing them.

"You will always satisfy me, Arabella. Always."

He pulled her head to his chest and her cheek rested against his heart as he stroked her hair. They lay like that for some time and then he said, "I should see you home."

Disappointment filled her. She knew she couldn't stay the night with him but she hated leaving him. The closeness they now shared was the most powerful thing she had ever experienced.

"Must you?" she asked.

"Yes. I won't have you gossiped about. Did you and Elise decide upon a day for our wedding?"

"This is Tuesday. Or it was. I am sure it is Wednesday now. We thought Friday morning would be nice."

"Friday sounds lovely," he told her. "Will you come to me again tonight?"

"I would come to you through the fog. The rain. Sleet. Snow. I would cross a desert or an ocean, Jon. Anything to be with you."

"Good." He kissed her. "Let me help you dress."

He acted as her lady's maid and she returned the favor and played valet. They left his bedchamber and returned downstairs. His carriage still stood in front of the townhouse and they boarded it. Within minutes, they were at her father's.

He walked her to the door and kissed her. "There is a tea party at Lady Winters' residence this afternoon. May I escort you there?"

"Only if you bring the special license," she said smartly. "I'd like to see it."

"Then I will have it in my pocket and show it to you."

He kissed her again.

"I love you," she said and then froze when she saw the look cross his face. "I'm sorry," she said quickly. "I did not mean for that to slip out. I do love you, Jon. I can't help it. But I don't expect you to feel the same. I won't say it again. I promise."

He kissed her brow tenderly. "Goodnight, Arabella," he said wistfully.

She watched him return to his carriage and give her a wave before entering it. As she watched him drive away, she cursed softly for not keeping her feelings to herself. She hoped things wouldn't change between them. She would need to learn to be satisfied with what she did get from him. Jon was attentive and caring. He made love to her in the most marvelous way. They could have a wonderful life together.

As long as she didn't ruin things.

CHAPTER TWENTY-FIVE

JON WAS AT breakfast when Weston burst into the room.

"What are you doing here?" he asked his friend, who took a seat and motioned to the footman, who came and poured coffee for the duke.

Adding a spoonful of sugar and a bit of cream, Weston stirred and then sampled the brew. "Perfect," he proclaimed.

"So, you came to drink my coffee. What else?"

"And to congratulate you again for landing a wonderful woman to be your duchess."

Uneasiness flashed through Jon. "Yes, Arabella will make for an excellent duchess."

"What's wrong?" Weston pressed.

Obviously, he hadn't hid his feelings well enough. That—or Weston knew him far too well.

When Jon didn't speak, Weston asked, "You

do want to marry her, don't you?"

"Of course, I do," he snapped.

Calmly, Weston took another sip of coffee and then placed the cup down. His gaze pierced Jon's and he asked, "Do you love her?"

"What does love have to do with getting married?" he asked, a little too harshly, pushing his plate back and throwing his napkin onto the table.

"Everything," his friend said simply.

"Well, she told me she loved me yesterday," he said, still remembering the hurt in Arabella's eyes as he brushed off her proclamation. "That should be enough."

"Do you love her?" Weston repeated.

He shot to his feet, conscious of the two footmen who now averted their eyes. Jon strode from the room, Weston on his heels. He retreated to his study. His friend entered behind him and closed the door.

"What is it, Jon?"

"I don't want her to love me," he shouted, trying to calm himself. "I don't deserve it."

Weston chuckled. "You sound like me not that long ago." He took a seat and motioned for Jon to do the same.

He did so and sighed. "There are things in my past, Weston. Things I have never told a soul. Things Arabella would hate me for."

"She already knows you are the Duke of

Arrogance and a terrible rake."

"It goes beyond that." He raked his fingers through his hair. "Actually, the arrogance is all an act. It's not who I am at all. My brother, Arch, was the arrogant one. When he . . . died. When I became the duke, I tried . . . to be more like him. To let him live through me. Arch had no respect for rules or people. While he was loveable, he had a distinct disregard for rules and society, in general. I've always felt the need to live for the two of us. Trying to help him be the duke alongside me.

"I abhor breaking rules. I can't stand acting entitled. Yet that's what it was. All an act."

"That is why you are undeserving of Arabella's love?" pressed Weston.

"That . . . and more." His jaw set. He would not reveal the rest, not even to a beloved friend.

"Do you love her?" Weston asked.

"I do," he finally admitted, as much to Weston as himself. "I am being horribly selfish about this, Weston. If she knew who I really am, she wouldn't want me."

"Let me tell you this—Arabella will need the words, Jon. We men are beasts of action. We believe our actions are as good as words. For women, it is a different matter. Yes, we can show them our love but they need to hear that we love them."

Weston sighed. "I didn't believe I deserved

Elise. I went ahead and wed her before I finally told her a truth I've never shared with anyone. I never will."

Jon knew Weston spoke of his broken betrothal. His wedding with Lady Juniper Radwell had been called off and no one ever knew the reason why. Weston, who had been an honorable man to that point, sank into the mire, becoming one of the biggest scoundrels London had ever seen. He never spoke of why the marriage never took place, merely reveling in his Duke of Disrepute moniker.

"When I finally told Elise, I felt a burden lifted from me," Weston continued. "I advise you to do the same with Arabella. Before you wed her. If you truly believe what you've done is so reprehensible, then you need to give her a chance to walk away before she's bound to you for life. If she truly loves you, she will help you conquer your demons. She'll forgive you. And maybe you might forgive yourself."

Weston was right. It wasn't fair to drag Arabella into a marriage without sharing with her that he had murdered his own brother. Either she would turn away—or the light that shone from her would chase away the darkness in his soul.

Forever.

"You're right," he admitted.

"I am always right," Weston said cheerfully. "Unless Elise tells me I am wrong. I may only have been married for six weeks but I know who rules the roost in my own home."

"You're saying it's Elise who runs your life?"

Weston grinned. "We are partners, Jon. You'll see what I mean. It'll all makes sense soon enough."

Doubt flared through him. "What if she won't accept who I truly am?"

"Then she is not the one for you. I sincerely doubt it, though. I've seen the way she looks at you. Her eyes shining with love. Nothing you could tell her would make that vanish."

Jon would see. He owed it to Arabella to be truthful and let her know who he was. If she washed her hands of him in order to protect herself, he would abide by her decision. If, though, she did accept him, flaws and all, he would know she was the woman for him.

Weston stood and brushed his hands along his trousers. "Well, are you coming?"

"Where?"

"Doctors' Commons, you fool. That's why I've come. You need an old married man to lead you through the process of procuring a special license." Weston slapped him on the back.

Jon would go and purchase the license, placing his and Arabella's name on it.

He only hoped that they would use it.

ARABELLA ALLOWED JON to escort her and her father to his carriage, where Elizabeth awaited them. Jon sat beside Arabella. He seemed distant somehow. She blamed herself for his behavior and once again regretted her rash declaration of last night. She swore never to make such a mistake again. She would love him in her heart all she wanted but the words would never leave her lips. Jon was everything she could ever hope for. Driving him away with sentimental drivel would devastate her. She resolved to be calm and unruffled.

Unless they were in bed.

Thoughts of last night's introduction to lovemaking had her blushing throughout the day. He'd told her there was much more to the process and they would have a lifetime to explore it together. Just the thought of his hard, naked body against hers caused her to shiver.

"Are you cold?" he asked.

"No," she said faintly, not wanting him to have a clue what her true thoughts involved.

They arrived at the tea party, which was being held in Lady Winters' garden, and parted ways with her father. Elizabeth excused herself and went to talk with some friends.

"Not that I wanted to get rid of your father,

but we should make plans for tonight," he said quietly.

"You still want to see me?" she asked nervously.

"Of course, I do. I will not attend tonight's event. I have already sent my excuses. You'll go but get a headache an hour into it and leave. My carriage will be waiting for you and bring you directly to me. The door will be open. Come up to my chambers."

"That is very bold." She frowned. "Won't the servants think poorly of me?"

"My servants are giddy with the fact that you are to become their new mistress. Besides, who cares what they think?"

"I care," she said pointedly. "I want them to like me."

He shook his head. "Don't worry. We will have our time together and then I'll see you home before any social events conclude. And if someone does see us together, what will they say? We are to be married the day after tomorrow."

"All right. I'll come."

"Good. Go mingle now. If you don't, I might drag you to some secluded spot and ravish you." He waggled his brows at her and Arabella laughed.

She circulated through the guests, thinking a good fifty people or more must be here. It seemed everyone had heard of her betrothal and wanted to know when the wedding would occur. She told them soon and that it was to be a small, private gathering, with only family and a few friends in attendance. Beyond that, she kept the details to herself.

Lady Winters approached her and congratulated her.

"You have landed a man no one in London thought would wed," her hostess said. "His Grace is considered quite the rogue."

"Oh, I know of what is said about my fiancé," she assured her hostess. "And of his nickname, the Duke of Arrogance. Blackmore is quite different from what the public sees."

"Most men are, my dear," Lady Winters said. "Still, you've snared yourself a duke."

Arabella frowned. "That sounds as if I trapped him. I can assure you, my lady, that is far from the truth."

"I cheer you on for landing him," the woman continued. "Now, if only you can keep him."

She felt her face grow hot. "I am not sure what you mean."

Lady Winters looked at her pointedly. "You do understand that men of Polite Society, once they have their heir, move on to . . . shall we say . . . greener pastures?"

"That won't be the case with us," she said firmly.

Her hostess laughed airily. "Oh, so you fancy yourself in love, do you? I must warn you, Lady Arabella. Be careful. A man like Blackmore will break your heart one day if you believe he will always be faithful to you."

"If you will excuse me," she said firmly and walked away.

Retreating into the house, she asked a maid where the retiring room was and followed the directions. Arabella splashed cold water on her face, trying to cool it. A maid handed her a towel and she dabbed it dry.

She left and had almost made it to the doors leading outside when none other than Lady Walton confronted her.

"You think you are so clever, landing Blackmore so easily."

"I don't think myself clever at all."

"You don't?" the other woman asked. "I have heard the men at balls talk of you and your intellect. How you pretend to know as much as a man with a university education does. How you participated in debates when you were a little no one." Lady Walton sniffed. "You may be called Lady Arabella now but we both know you are as common as any middle class miss. Your father only became Barrington under extreme circumstances. You shouldn't be here. You don't belong."

Arabella knew a bully when she saw one and

stood up to her. "Are you jealous, Lady Walton? Because Blackmore chose to dally with you but he wishes to wed me?'

The older woman slapped Arabella. The sting burned her face but the shock of the action had her shaking. Though she wanted to place her palm against her cheek, she couldn't let this woman see how affected she was.

"You resort to violence? You are no lady yourself, Lady Walton."

"He should be mine!" the woman hissed. "What is Blackmore doing with a little no one such as you? Why, I would guess you have never been kissed before. He must think your innocence can wash away all his many sins."

"Blackmore is the finest man I know," Arabella said, standing her ground. "He knew it was a mistake to be involved with you and dropped you accordingly. I would advise you to hide your jealousy, my lady. Green is not a pretty color on you."

With that, she hurried away, her limbs shaking.

CHAPTER TWENTY-SIX

J ON DIDN'T KNOW how to tell Arabella about his past. He had fought with himself all day on how to present it to her. Finally, he called for Winspeth to draw him a bath an hour before she arrived. He did some of his best thinking in the tub.

"I'll have no need of you the rest of the evening," he told the valet.

Winspeth failed to hide his smile. "Very good, Your Grace."

"There's nothing to smile about, you know."

Winspeth's smile broadened. "There is everything to smile about, Your Grace. You seem happy, which makes all your staff happy. It is wonderful to see you this way. We know it is all due to Lady Arabella."

He didn't know how to tell the loyal servant that, after tonight, there might not be a wedding.

"Go," he commanded and the valet left,

chuckling all the way.

Jon leaned his head back, searching for what to say tonight. Selfishly, he wanted to make love to Arabella before he told her but the price of her giving her body to him before he gave her the truth would be wrong. He clung to the hope that, somehow, she would still want him, despite what he would reveal to her.

He closed his eyes and let his thoughts wander. Suddenly, he jolted. He must have fallen asleep. Quickly, he stood and toweled off. Glancing around, he saw his banyan wasn't in sight. Oftentimes, Winspeth left it across the bed. Jon exited his dressing room and entered his bedchamber. A few candles burned. He saw a shape in the bed and realized Arabella had already arrived. Despite his previous resolve, he padded naked toward the bed, needing the feel of her warm flesh against his. Then he halted in his tracks.

It wasn't Arabella in his bed.

It was Lady Walton. And she was naked.

"What are you doing here?" he asked, his tone deadly.

She sat up, her large breasts drawing his eyes. He forced himself to look at her face.

She stretched lazily, as a cat in the sun, and said, "If you're foolish enough to wed that middle class chit, you're going to need a real woman in your bed to satisfy you. I did that once before,

Blackmore. I am happy to fulfill that role again."

Jon strode to the bed and grabbed her upper arms. "I want you out. Now. Do you understand?"

In reply, her hand shot out and grasped his nape, pulling him down. Her lips touched his. He jerked away.

And heard a gasp.

With trepidation, he glanced up—and saw Arabella standing there, her jaw slack. Quickly, she turned to flee.

"How does green look on you?" Lady Walton called out.

"Arabella! Wait! Wait!" he cried.

Lady Walton laughed low. "Oops. There'll be trouble in paradise now."

He had never struck a woman before and fought the urge to do so now. "Get out!" he roared.

Reaching for his banyan, he slid an arm through it and took off after his fiancée. He raced down the stairs, pulling his other arm in and wrapping the robe about him, belting it as he ran.

She reached the foyer and flung the door open, leaving it that way as she dashed into the night. Jon hesitated a moment, reluctant to go out in public in his current state.

Then he decided it didn't matter. Nothing mattered but Arabella.

Running down the remaining stairs, he followed her outside and saw his carriage pulling away.

"Wait!" he cried loudly, running alongside it and waving his arms, hollering until his driver came to a halt. The coachman recognized him, his eyes wide as he took in his master's state of undress.

"Once I'm inside, drive until I tell you to stop," he ordered.

"Drive where, Your Grace?" the baffled coachman asked, gulping.

"Anywhere!" he roared and then went and opened the carriage door, climbing in.

Arabella shrank inside, fear on her face. She pushed against the far corner. He closed the door and sat on the bench next to her, not touching her. He straightened the banyan with as much dignity as he could muster and said, "It's not what you think."

He was proud as he saw her face her fear. "And what should I think?" she demanded. "I find my fiancé—the man I am to wed come Friday— naked. His mistress, also naked, in his bed. Engaged in a kiss. Explain that," she huffed.

"We had an affair," he admitted. "Briefly. Two years ago. I soon found she is a duplicitous, vengeful woman and dropped her. She has been trying to get me into her bed ever since." He sighed. "How she got into my house tonight, I don't know. I will fire the servant who allowed it."

He swallowed, his throat closing up on him with emotion. "When I tried to remove her from my bed, she kissed me. I pulled away at once. That's the God's truth, Arabella." His head fell, his eyes closed.

Silence filled the coach. Only the clopping of the horses could be heard as they went through the quiet streets.

"I believe you," Arabella said softly.

He opened his eyes and turned his head, meeting her gaze. "You do?"

"Yes. I saw the surprise on her face. She wasn't expecting me to walk in tonight. She was there to seduce you."

"Yes," he said hoarsely. "She wouldn't have succeeded."

"Even though you were naked?"

He gave her a wry smile. "I was waiting for your arrival."

She reached out and stroked his cheek. "Lady Walton confronted me regarding you. The latest was at today's tea party. She is determined to have you. I will not allow that," she said firmly.

Jon captured her wrist and turned her hand, kissing her palm through her glove. Then he released it. "I have something to tell you."

Arabella chuckled. "I don't know how much more excitement I can take."

"No," he said solemnly. "I am serious. There

is something you must know about me. Something so terrible that I don't think you will want to wed me once you've heard it. Weston told me I must tell you my secret in order to be free of it."

"Treadwell knows this?" she asked, her brow knitting in puzzlement.

"No," he said vehemently. "No one knows. Weston had his own secret, which he shared with Elise. He said it liberated him. He encouraged me to do the same, knowing something has weighed heavily upon me for years." He swallowed, trying to force down the lump in his throat. "I have never told a soul. I have lived with it for so long, I feel it has eaten the inside of me and only a hollow husk remains."

Jon took a deep breath and expelled it slowly. "But I cannot allow you to wed me without telling you first. If you choose to walk away, I will understand."

"I would never do that," she insisted quietly. "I love you."

He glanced away, not having the courage to look her in the eyes. After another calming breath, he said, "I am a murderer, Arabella. I killed my own brother."

Arabella stilled. She tried to make sense of the words Jon had just spoken. Yes, he could be arrogant and overbearing—but a murderer?

She didn't believe him.

"Tell me," she said. "Take your time."

Jon let out a loud, guttural wail. He began weeping, his body trembling as if he were chilled. She gently placed a hand on his arm, wanting to show him she was still here and not going anywhere. He wept for some time, heaving sobs that wrenched her heart. She had only seen two men cry before, ones who had been in their cups at Oxford.

This was entirely different. It's as if he tried to purge his soul. She kept her hand in place, knowing once the tidal wave of emotion ran through him that he would finally reveal whatever darkness had threatened his very sanity.

Finally, he calmed. He began speaking, his voice almost monotone. Arabella knew not to interrupt and let him get it all out.

"I was born minutes after my brother, Arch. He was meant to be the duke. We were identical twins, with only a few being able to tell us apart. We were more than brothers. More than being one another's best friend. We had an unbreakable bond between us that nothing could sever.

"Until I killed him."

She kept her hand in place, breathing steadily, trying not to let his words shock her. There had to be more to the story. A hunting accident, perhaps? Something that Jon blamed himself for. Surely, he hadn't actually killed Arch.

Or had he?

She remembered now hearing the name before and wondering if this was a Sutton sibling not currently in London. Now she knew that Arch had died. When and where remained to be revealed.

"Everyone loved Arch," he continued. "He had a sunny nature and was outgoing. Very athletic. I was more reserved. Arch loved to push the boundaries. He thought rules were made to be broken and as a future duke, none applied to him. He would have been in constant trouble if . . ."

Jon's voice faded away and Arabella finished his thought. "If you hadn't taken the blame for him."

Her fiancé nodded. "We looked so much alike. If someone saw Arch committing mischief, it was easy to blame me. Arch was the heir apparent. The golden child. Father lavished praise upon Arch and favored him in all things. I soon earned a reputation as a troublemaker. It was easy to step in and take the punishment."

"You did so willingly?"

"Of course. He was my brother. My twin. I loved him beyond measure. I would have died for him. Killed for him." He choked.

Arabella tightened her grip. "I am here, Jon. Go on."

He sighed. "Arch became ill during our last term at Harrow. Some rash which spread along his body, accompanied by fever. The headmaster sent him home. In a way, I was relieved. We had always competed in everything. For the first time in our lives, we'd been separated. I finished the term with strong marks and raced home, eager to see my twin."

He stared out into the space ahead of him. "When I arrived, I learned Arch had been moved to the dower house. I couldn't understand why Father isolated him and raced to see him. Dr. Broll was there. He told me Arch had syphilis."

Arabella gasped. Unlike most ladies of Polite Society, she knew of the disease. If Arch had been diagnosed with syphilis, it was a death sentence.

"The doctor had used mercury on Arch even though it was dangerous. I learned Arch would likely go blind. He was already half-deaf. Paralysis was a strong possibility, as was his heart being affected. The doctor said dementia, too, would most likely set in and Arch wouldn't know anyone, least of all me."

Tears now streamed down his face. Her heart ached hearing his words.

"When I saw him, I barely recognized him as my brother. He'd lost both hair and weight. His body was covered in the rash and grotesque sores. His vision was fading." Jon paused. "The doctor had been frank with him so Arch knew what lay ahead. He was in great pain. It was terrible seeing him in that state."

She kept her hand on his arm but with her other hand she reached out and covered his fingers with hers.

"He told me I would be Blackmore. Not him. It would be my reward for being punished and ignored for all those years." A strained smile crossed his face. "Arch said I would have to learn to be someone I'd never wanted to be and not to be an arse to my second son, as Father was to me.

"Then he asked me for a final favor. I would have done anything for him. Anything. What he asked . . . what he asked . . . was before his mind and sight went . . . was for me to help kill him. He couldn't stand the pain any longer. The headaches were excruciating. He was living under a death sentence."

Jon fell silent for some minutes, tears glistening his cheeks.

"He pleaded for me to help him. Dr. Broll had been giving Arch laudanum for the pain. I poured all that remained into a cup of water and helped him drink it."

He wiped his face with the back of a hand. "Now you know. I took the life of my beloved brother. I have had to live with that every day."

Jon closed his eyes. Arabella looked at the man she loved, seeing the pain and sorrow that had been his constant companions, knowing he'd never shared this with anyone but her.

"You didn't murder Arch, Jon. You saved

him," she said.

He turned and looked at her. "I took his life, Arabella."

She shook her head. "It was no longer his life. The disease ate away at him. He would never have recovered. He wanted to go out on his terms—and you allowed him to do so. What you did, you did in love, Jon. Love for the one person who meant the most to you. Of the two of you, you were the stronger one. Arch knew that. You had always carried his burdens. This was the final one. But he wouldn't want you to dwell on it. Be consumed by it. He still lives in your heart, Jon. What you do with your life, you do for Arch *and* you."

He began weeping again. His head fell into her lap and she stroked his hair.

"You know I am right," she said after some minutes. "Arch would not want you to feel guilty any longer. You have for over a decade. It's time to put your act of love aside and the guilt and shame it brought and begin living your life to the fullest.

"With me."

He raised his head, his gaze piercing hers. "You still want to marry me?" he asked hoarsely, shock on his face.

"I want to spend every day with the man I love," she replied, deciding more than anything, Jon needed her to speak of her love as well as show him. "I want you to live a full life, doing all the things you want to do, as well as things your twin might have wanted to do and see. I want to bear your children and grow old with you. Without you, my life would be empty. With you, I feel complete."

He cupped her cheeks. "I don't deserve your goodness but maybe Arch sent you to me." He kissed her tenderly. "You are my reason to live, Arabella. You will be my conscience. My guiding light. I will use my wealth and position and power for good." He smiled. "Starting with your school."

"Our school," she corrected.

"Our school," he agreed, a slow smiling spreading across his face.

He leaned up and knocked on the roof of the carriage. "Home!" he shouted, loud enough for the driver to hear. Then he settled back into the cushion and lifted her into his lap. She wound her arms about his neck and rested her cheek against his chest, his skin warm. They remained that way until the carriage pulled up at his townhouse. Then she kissed him, a healing kiss of warmth and forgiveness and sunshine, wanting him to know how much she loved him—and always would.

He leaned over and opened the door and said to her, "It's already early morning. We have been driving most of the night. Go home, my sweetest love."

Taking her hands, his kissed them. "I love you with all my heart, Arabella. I think I did from the moment I saw you. I will love you for all the decades to come. Until the end of time and beyond. Thank you for loving me. For helping me to forgive myself."

Never had Arabella heard sweeter words.

Jon lifted her from his lap and placed her next to him. He pressed a final, soft kiss on her lips.

"I will see you at our wedding."

The ride to his townhouse took but a few minutes with the streets so deserted. He exited the carriage and entered, finding Randall waiting in the foyer for him.

"Your Grace, might I have a word?"

"Come to my study," he suggested.

Neither man spoke until they arrived and the door was closed.

"What is it, Randall?"

"I heard the shouts from before and saw Lady Arabella fleeing, along with you running after her."

"Don't worry. I have set things right between us. She saw something . . . unsavory."

"I know exactly what she bore witness to," Randall said, his face flush with anger. "I took it upon myself to go upstairs after you left and found a naked Lady Walton gathering her clothes. It was apparent what had transpired and how the woman tried to ruin your relationship with Lady Arabella. Believe me, I gave her an earful as she tossed on her garments."

Randall paused. "You should know something, Your Grace. Lady Walton admitted to slapping Lady Arabella."

"She what?" He saw red, rage filling him. "I will ruin her," he said, his voice low and deadly. "She will receive the cut direct from me and all my friends. It will be crystal clear to the *ton* that Lady Walton is not to be invited to any social affair and if she is, the host will feel my wrath."

Jon shook his head. "All I have to do now is discover how she wound up in my bed."

"I know how she gained access, Your Grace. The footman responsible is waiting in the kitchens. Thistle and Winspeth are keeping him company and making certain he does not flee."

He offered Randall his hand. "Thank you. I will see him now."

Jon strode to the kitchens, Randall trailing behind him, where he found his butler and valet standing guard over a footman who sported a black eye.

"What have you to say for yourself, Porter?" he roared. "You did the unthinkable. You betrayed me in the worst possible way."

"I needed the money, Your Grace," the footman whined. "I found myself mired in debt."

"Gambling, Your Grace," Thistle said, disgust

in his voice. "I got that much out of him."

"Lady Walton bribed you?"

Porter nodded. "She did."

"Give me the money," he commanded, his eyes narrowing when the footman hesitated.

Pulling the notes from his pocket, Porter said, "What are you going to do with it? It's mine."

Anger surged through him. "This money is no longer yours, Porter. It is being donated to the school for boys that Lady Arabella is starting. She is to be my duchess—and your foul deed and disrespect of her will not be tolerated. Pack your things. You are to leave at once. Dismissed without references."

The footman's jaw dropped then quickly closed. "Yes, Your Grace," he said, rising to his feet and hurrying from the room.

"I'll make certain he is gone in the next few minutes," Randall said.

"I'll help," Winspeth said and both men followed the footman.

Left with Thistle, Jon said, "Thank you for making certain Porter didn't slip away."

"It was the least I could do, Your Grace.

"And the black eye?" he asked.

Thistle smiled. "That would be my doing, Your Grace."

Jon grinned. "Well done, Thistle. Well done."

CHAPTER TWENTY-SEVEN

J ON ESCORTED ELIZABETH to the carriage. His sister looked lovely in a soft peach gown, her blue eyes shining with love for him. Arthur opened the door and helped his cousin up and then climbed in after Jon entered the carriage.

As they settled themselves in the vehicle, she teasingly asked, "Are you ready to give up being a bachelor and a rake?"

In truth, he had never been comfortable with the role of rake. He did it more because he thought it was what Arch would have been. His carefree twin would have worked his way through the willing women of the *ton*, reveling in every encounter. Arch's zest for life and breaking the rules were what guided Jon all the years since his brother's death.

Now, he could finally become himself— thanks to Arabella.

"Who would want to be a bachelor and a

rake when they could be wed to the most amazing woman in all of London?" he asked.

"You do love her, don't you, Jon?" Elizabeth asked anxiously.

"I do."

"And you've told her so?"

He smiled. "I have."

He finally had told her of his love in the carriage, after the cathartic experience of baring his soul to the woman he loved. She hadn't judged. Hadn't fled. Arabella merely listened and, in all her wisdom, helped him forgive himself. He planned to tell her every day—every waking hour—that he loved her. Why, he might just wake her in the night and not only tell her so but show her just how much he loved her. She had saved him. She would continue to do so. They would be a couple who always listened to one another and met the challenges of life head on.

"Have you settled where to go on your honeymoon?" Arthur asked.

"We're going to one of my estates in Kent," he shared. "We can reach it in half a day."

"Kent is beautiful this time of year," Elizabeth said. "And don't worry about us. I will take good care of Arthur and he of me."

"Lord Barrington is going to take me in hand while you are gone," Arthur revealed. "He doesn't wish for me to get behind in my studies. He's also promised that we will start selecting books for the school's library."

"That will keep the two of you busy while we are gone," Jon said. Though he loved his sister and had grown quite fond of Cousin Arthur, he was looking forward to having time with Arabella with no others around.

After the brief trip of a few blocks, the carriage pulled up at the Treadwell townhouse and Jon helped Elizabeth out and escorted her inside, Arthur behind them. Weston greeted Jon, enveloping him in a bear hug.

His friend pulled away and said, "You told her, didn't you?"

"I did. She understood. She has embraced me for who I am, flaws and all."

"Good. Come outside into the garden. Elise has everything set."

"A garden wedding?" Elizabeth asked. "Oh, I didn't know the ceremony was to be held outdoors. How very romantic."

They went to the rear of the house and through the open French doors. George came and greeted them.

"You are already looking like a reformed rake, Jon. It's said reformed rakes make the best husbands."

"I would agree with that," Elise said, coming and kissing his cheek. "Weston and George had terribly black reputations and Samantha and I are the happiest of wives. I am certain Arabella will feel the same. Come along and meet Reverend Saunders."

The clergyman had a ready smile. "I hear this is a love match, Your Grace."

"Very much," he agreed. "I not only love Arabella but I respect and admire her."

"Have you the special license?" Reverend Saunders asked.

Jon produced it and the clergyman looked it over.

"All in order. Very good, Your Grace. It is almost time. If you would, come and stand here."

"Of course. Arthur, you're to come stand with me." The young man nodded with a huge grin plastered on his face.

The clergyman indicated an archway leading into the garden. The sweet smell of roses blooming filled the air. His friends and family gathered in a semi-circle. Jon only wished Andrew and Phoebe could have made the trip from Devon. With a small babe, though, and the speed at which he and Arabella had decided to wed, that had been impossible. He would join his friends in visiting the Windhams once the Season ended, so that they could meet Arabella.

The love of his life.

He also longed for Sebastian to return to England. He'd missed his friend from university days. They corresponded regularly but he had yet to write him regarding Arabella. Jon would like to see Sebastian's face when he opened the missive that revealed Jon had wed. Hopefully, Sebastian would return to England soon since it looked as if Bonaparte's days were numbered.

Elise nodded and music began. He turned and saw a harpist and violinist some feet behind them. The sweet strains of music filled the spring air.

Then he caught sight of Arabella on her father's arm. Lord Barrington beamed with pride as he escorted his only child toward Jon. But his attention was focused on Arabella.

Her gown was of the palest blue, trimmed in a darker blue. The diamonds he'd gifted her glittered in the sun. What warmed him, though, was her radiant smile. She reached him and they only had eyes for each other. Lord Barrington took his daughter's hand and kissed it before placing it on Jon's arm and stepping aside.

His heart pounded with a mixture of nerves and excitement as they spoke their vows. Jon knew the best decision of his life was asking this woman to become his wife. Life would be good and rich and sweet with her by his side.

Reverend Saunders indicated he could now kiss his bride. Unlike most grooms, who gave their new wives a quick peck, Jon allowed himself to drink in Arabella. He could kiss this woman all day and never tire of her.

"Should we begin the breakfast without you

two?" he heard Weston call out playfully, causing Jon to break the kiss.

He stared into the sky blue eyes of his duchess, seeing them filled with love.

"Shall we allow breakfast to start without us?" he asked.

"The sooner we go into our own wedding breakfast, the sooner we may depart," she said, mischief causing the corners of her mouth to turn up.

Jon kissed her hard and swift and then laughed. "Then to the breakfast we go."

An hour later, all the toasts had been given and he and Arabella had changed into traveling clothes. They waved goodbye to their friends and boarded his carriage, bound for Kent.

As they drove away, Arabella said, "You have made every dream of mine come true, Jon. I do love you so."

He captured her face in his hands. "Keep dreaming big, my love. Something tells me there are many more things we will accomplish together."

Jon kissed his duchess, knowing life with Arabella, Duchess of Blackmore, would be a magnificent adventure.

EPILOGUE

Blackstone Manor, Dorset—May 1820

JON VENTURED INTO the parlor and saw that Arabella and their two daughters were having a tea party. A pretend one since neither a two-year-old child nor a four-year-old girl could be trusted with fine china. He stood in the doorway and watched as they held up imaginary cups, sipping from them daintily.

"How are my three angels?" he called out, immediately causing the girls to discard the idea of tea and run to him, shouting, "Papa! Papa!"

Arabella looked on with a smile. "You missed our tea party, Papa."

"Then you will have to hold another one tomorrow."

He ruffled the hair of both girls as they hugged his legs. They favored their mother, with Arabella's golden curls and sky blue eyes.

"Nanny," his wife said to the nursery governess sitting in the corner. "Would you take the girls to the nursery?"

"Of course, Your Grace. Come along, my little ladies. It's your nap time."

The girls squeezed his legs once more for good measure and he bent and kissed them before the servant escorted them from the room.

Jon went to his wife, who now wore a pained expression. She'd placed one hand to her back and winced.

"Is it time?" he asked.

Arabella nodded. "I think so. I should go to my bedchamber."

He took her hands and pulled her from the settee. Her huge, rounded belly brushed against his.

She rubbed her hands over it. "I do think it's a boy this time," she said. "I have carried this babe differently."

Leaning down, he brushed his lips against hers. "You know I don't care. We could have a dozen girls. Arthur can always be my heir. As it is, he's already learning about how to manage an estate. In fact, I am ready to give him one to run on his own."

"You had said you would gift him one after university. Have you decided which one?"

He told her and she nodded in agreement. "It will be good for him to have his own place but I will miss having him here with us. The girls adore him." She paused. "Oh!"

Her hands went to her belly again and he heard a slight noise. Being an experienced father, he knew exactly what had occurred.

"Your water has broken. We need to get you to bed and call in the midwife," he said, sounding calm but worry already filling him.

It did so each time Arabella went into labor. He knew so many things could go wrong. The thought of losing his wife almost paralyzed him.

Scooping her up, Jon carried her from the room. She knew not to protest and merely looped her arms about his neck. They passed their butler and he told Roy to send for the midwife and to find Annie and send her up.

"At once, Your Grace." Roy took off.

They reached Arabella's bedchamber. The only other two times she had occupied its bed were to deliver their girls. Jon set her on her feet.

"What do I need to do?" he asked.

"Kiss me," she responded.

He did so, tasting her sweetness and giving thanks for having such a wonderful family.

"I'll take it from here, Your Grace," Annie said as she breezed into the room. "This one will probably come as quickly as the last."

Jon had learned that first babies took an eternity but that subsequent children could come very quickly.

Just then, Arabella gasped and then groaned.

"Outside, Your Grace," Annie ordered. "I will take care of Her Grace for you."

Reluctantly, he kissed Arabella once more and then left. He retreated to his study, where he paced for an hour. Arthur came in and advised him to go spend some time with the girls so Jon made his way to the nursery. They were having their supper and he kept quiet about the baby coming. If there were complications, he didn't want them to know.

"Help put us to bed, Papa," his oldest demanded. She was quite stubborn and both he and Arabella accused each other of having passed that along to her.

The nursery governess got them into their nightclothes and he tucked them in, kissing them both goodnight. He returned downstairs and went to stand outside Arabella's bedchamber. He could hear her cries. They tore at his heart.

Then they stopped. His heart went to his throat. He stared at the door, a silent prayer on his lips, begging God to let her and the babe be all right.

A few minutes later, the door opened and Annie came out.

"Your Grace! You startled me."

"Is she . . . is everything . . ."

The maid smiled. "Her Grace is doing wonderfully. So is your son."

"My son?" His voice broke.

He had a son.

"I was just coming to get you. She's ready for you."

Jon hugged the servant. "Thank you, Annie. You always take such good care of my wife."

He released her and entered the room. Another servant bustled about, wadding up bedsheets to be washed. The midwife was placing a bundle in Arabella's arms. His wife caught sight of him and broke out in a brilliant smile.

Crossing to her, he sat on the bed beside her. Pillows were propped behind her and as always, Arabella looked radiant. He glanced down at the child in her arms and blinked back tears.

"It's a boy," she said. "The future Duke of Blackmore."

Jon placed his hand on the baby's head. "Our son."

"Do you want to hold him?" she asked softly.

"Yes. Very much so."

He accepted the babe and held him to his chest. Gazing down, he saw black hair.

"You know what we will name him," his wife reminded, as if Jon didn't know. "Archibald Jonathan Sutton. Do you want to call him Arch, after your brother?"

"He will be his own man," Jon said. "Perhaps we can call him Archie for now. Later, if he wishes to shorten it, he can." He pressed a soft kiss to his son's brow. "You, my boy, will be my heir. One day, Archibald Sutton will become the Duke of Blackmore. As was always meant to be."

"For now, I'll be happy that he is the Marquess of Grafton," Arabella said. "I want the present duke to live for a very long time."

Jon kissed her tenderly. "Thank you. For three wonderful, beautiful children."

Arabella smiled at him. "I hope there will be many more, my love."

Archie opened his eyes and stared up at his father. In that instant, Jon believed Arch looked down upon them and gave his blessing.

About the Author

Award-winning and internationally bestselling author Alexa Aston's historical romances use history as a backdrop to place her characters in extraordinary circumstances, where their intense desire for one another grows into the treasured gift of love.

She is the author of Regency and Medieval romance, including: Dukes of Distinction; Soldiers & Soulmates; The St. Clairs; The King's Cousins; and The Knights of Honor.

A native Texan, Alexa lives with her husband in a Dallas suburb, where she eats her fair share of dark chocolate and plots out stories while she walks every morning. She enjoys a good Netflix binge; travel; seafood; and can't get enough of *Survivor* or *The Crown*.

www.ingramcontent.com/pod-product-compliance
Lightning Source LLC
Chambersburg PA
CBHW070746190726
48292CB00002B/438